careless

Deborah Robertson

SCEPTRE

Copyright © 2006 Deborah Robertson

First published in Australia in 2006 by Picador
A division of Pan Macmillan Australia

First published in Great Britain in 2007 by Hodder & Stoughton
A division of Hodder Headline

The right of Deborah Robertson to be identified as the Author
of the Work has been asserted by her in accordance with the
Copyright, Designs and Patents Act 1988.

Photograph of *Fallingwater* © Richard A. Cooke/Corbis

A Sceptre paperback

I

A CIP catalogue record for this title is available from the British Library

ISBN 978 0 340 93824 9

Typeset in Granjon by
Hewer Text UK Ltd, Edinburgh

Printed and bound by
Mackays of Chatham Ltd, Chatham, Kent

Hodder Headline's policy is to use papers that are natural,
renewable and recyclable products and made from wood grown in
sustainable forests. The logging and manufacturing processes are expected
to conform to the environmental regulations of the country of origin.

Hodder & Stoughton Ltd
A division of Hodder Headline
338 Euston Road
London NW1 3BH

For my brothers, Scott and Tony

Childcare

THE CHILDREN COME OUT of the blue.

They have walked a long way, but they're used to it. They're familiar with the patterns in the footpaths and the bitumen's glitter, and the wind on the bridges, and the law of the traffic lights.

Sometimes they take their time on the green light, but if there are cars stopped there, rumbling like lions, Pearl pulls on Riley's hand to hurry him across, her shoulder bag banging her hip in time with her heart. She knows that other people feel as she does, she has looked into their faces and seen the effort not to care, their heads lowered as if they are just thinking and strolling, as if for them no-one else exists. But they all wish they could be like Riley, who is too young yet to know that anyone watches him as he crosses the road, who dawdles and looks around, and even stares back at the cars if they interest him.

Their feet slip in their sandals but they are used to the heat. Pearl carries a small bottle of water in her shoulder bag, and sometimes they stop to drink. They're not far away now from where they want to be.

A woman wearing a baseball cap and yellow zinc on her nose looks across the sports oval as the two children walk towards her. They look very small against the straight white goalposts and the tall spreading gums. All around, brown houses slumber.

Every morning of the school holidays, Trish drives her white Barina to the council offices and swaps it for the orange Kombi with the face painted on the front, and then she drives the Kombi to the train station where the work-experience girl is waiting, eating the pastry she has bought for her breakfast.

They set up on the edge of the oval in the shade of the Moreton Bay, close to the toilets. One by one, the children's bright backpacks collect around the tree's massive roots. The door of the Kombi sticks but with a sharp tug it slides open. The red plastic chairs and tables come out first, and the boxes of paints and pens. There are cricket balls and footballs and a huge silver ball that inflates with a pump. For dress-ups and face-painting, a skinny mirror leans against the side of the bus. On top of the Esky that will soon fill with the children's fruit and juices there is a giant bottle of sunscreen. Trish and Bree buy ice on the way.

Trish waves to the two children. It's always like this, Pearl and Riley turning up alone. The playleader and the playleader-in-training once discussed the problem, puttering along in the Kombi, its face grinning out at the traffic.

Technically they weren't social workers, and they couldn't intervene. Pearl and Riley had always declined their offer of a lift home, which was right, which was what children were taught to do. They couldn't kidnap them or manhandle them for information about where they lived and how they got there and who looked after them. All they really knew was that Pearl was eight and Riley was five.

'Pearl always knows what he's doing,' said Trish.

'And he seems to know she knows,' said Bree.

'She's anxious and he isn't.'

'Riley has Pearl. I wonder who looks out for her?'

'Someone must, mustn't they?'

'I wish I knew.'

'Those teeny-weeny shoulders.'

'Oh, I know.'

'Someone helps her look after that long hair.'

'She'd do it herself. You've seen how she draws.'

'It's a lovely colour, isn't it?'

'Her hair?'

'Mousy-brown, but sort of lilac in it?'

'When she's in the sun.'

'I wouldn't mind betting they've got different fathers. Riley's so olivey and yummy.'

'And she's so pale.'

'Grey eyes?'

'Sort of plain.'

'Sort of pretty too.'

'She could go either way.'

'Have you seen her dance?'

'Oh, awful.'

'Frozen. Just frozen.'

'Compared to the other kids.'

'She doesn't put herself forward, does she?'

'No, she doesn't.'

'It's a worry.'

'It sure is.'

Now that Pearl and Riley have arrived, there are seven children. The playleaders try to keep the games from spreading too far over the playing field, they try to keep everyone close to the bus. They want them near shade and liquids, and their watchful eye.

Bree is painting the faces of two small girls. Once again, Pearl is the oldest child there. But Pearl will draw, so Trish helps her set up a table and chair, her back to the Kombi so that she can look out on Riley's game. Trish sets down a large sheet of paper.

Pearl smooths the white paper with her hand. It smells like Panadol. What does she want to draw?

She lifts the lid on the box of coloured pencils. First there is the familiar woody perfume and then, one by one, the different colours reach out to her, like notes of music. But today there is noise. Orange Chrome has been placed next to Mineral Green. Blue Violet Lake is too close to Vandyke Brown. She can't begin with things this way. The orange pencil must go into its correct place between Deep Cadmium and Scarlet Lake, and the browns have to be arranged into a line of descending bass notes.

It's peaceful work, this restoration of order, and it helps her leave the upset of the morning behind.

When Pearl and Riley woke that morning the little TV was gone. The TV belonged to their mother's new boyfriend, and all through the holidays Pearl and Riley had spent each morning watching the cartoons, sitting close to the screen so the sound didn't wake Lily and Ed.

There would be no point asking their mother where the television was. Even if Lily had an answer, it didn't always make sense.

One morning when Pearl woke, the ladder that she climbed down from the top bunk had gone. When she asked her mother about it, Lily said she was sure the ladder would come back soon, as if it was a pet that had simply wandered away from home.

Pearl had watched other people's faces as they listened to Lily's explanations of puzzling events, and she'd felt sorry for her mother, she had wished she would stop.

Sometimes the other people were policemen. It had started one winter night when Lily brought home a cardboard box full of cream and brown puppies.

'Someone owed me some money,' Lily said, dragging her wet hair from her face, 'but I took these instead.'

Pearl looked at the slick of hair that divided her mother's cheek. She wondered how Lily could go on excitedly telling them about her plans, the turquoise vein in her throat flashing, not noticing that she had hair in her mouth, not blowing it aside or emptying one hand of dogs to hook it clear. Soon Pearl would have to reach up and do it for her and Lily would be annoyed, she would turn her head crossly, like a baby who didn't like its face being wiped.

Weeks later, when the puppies had pissed and chewed their way through her patience and still none had been sold, Lily gathered them from all the corners of the flat and returned them to the cardboard box. It was another wet night and although they were already in their pyjamas, Lily said she needed their help.

They had to catch a bus and walk down a dark road to reach the dog pound.

When the headlights of the police van picked them out in the rain, Pearl was reaching up to hand a puppy to her mother, standing on tiptoes on a rubbish bin pulled up to the fence. Riley was crouched by the box, cuddling the others, keeping them quiet.

'Why are you throwing dogs over the fence?' asked the policeman, holding out an umbrella.

'Because they wouldn't fit *under* it,' Lily said.

There had been a TV on the shelf when they went to bed but now there was only a space. They sat on the edge of the pink couch in their pyjamas. They could see that the sun was shining outside but it couldn't reach them there in the dark room with the small window five floors in the air.

'What can we do?' asked Riley.

'Have some breakfast?'

'Mmm,' Riley said, turning his attention to dragging his pyjama top over his knees and patting at the bumps.

'Don't stretch your jarmies,' said Pearl.

'Don't stretch your jarmies,' said Riley.

'Don't say what I say.'

'Don't say what I say.'

'Don't be annoying.'

'Don't be annoying.'

The only thing she could do was to tickle him. She went for his stomach first, not hard because he was only small, the tips of her fingers paddling his skin, reaching behind his ears when his hands beat her away. He scrunched his neck and folded at the waist and they fell back on the couch giggling.

They knew they would have to stop soon because they were being too loud.

Pearl's page is still blank, she can't decide what to draw. She looks up and searches for Riley amongst the group of boys out on the oval, wrestling around a ball. The red stripe across his jumper makes him easy to find. Trish had tried many times to persuade him that it was too hot to play in this jumper, but Pearl knew that nothing would change his mind.

It was winter when she lost him at the shopping centre, the day the thing with the jumper began. They had decided to go into the newsagency. She helped Riley find the comics and then she wandered the aisles searching for the magazines about people's homes. A magazine with a white room on its cover caught her eye, but before she opened it she looked around and found Riley's forehead and dark fringe above the pages of *The Phantom*.

'What do I do?' she had asked Lily when her new brother was held out to her for the first time. She was frightened of his rockmelon head and tiny Chinese eyes. 'Just kiss his forehead,' Lily said.

Inside, the magazine was full of white rooms. She turned the pages and stopped to study one that had white walls and a white painted floor. Across a white bedspread fell a long, clear shaft of light. It made her think about the light above her own bed. All winter, late in the afternoon, while Riley played on the floor below, she had pushed a chair up to the wonky chest of drawers in her bedroom and clambered over it in her socks onto her bed. She settled her head on the pillow, and waited. It wasn't long before a brilliant circle of light as big as a fifty cent piece appeared on the ceiling above her. As she lay there watching, the light travelled across the ceiling until slowly, carefully, it stretched across the sharp angle between the ceiling and the wall and began its journey downward, just as perfect as before; just as round, just as bright. All the time, the soundtrack to her happiness, Riley crashed his cars on the carpet below.

When Pearl looked up from the magazine she couldn't see him. She closed the pages and returned the magazine to its pile. She expected to find Riley on the floor as she turned the corner into the next aisle but *The Phantom* lay on top of the car magazines and he wasn't there. She put the comic back in its place and checked the other aisles. He was not there either.

Outside the newsagency, people crossed busily to and fro, and a baby with food on its face travelled past in a pram and stared out at her, communicating the superior contentment of its safe, rugged-up and fluffy, strung-with-ducks world.

Pearl knew she should wait where she was. There were three levels of shopping centre and she might become lost herself. She stood guarding the entrance to the newsagency, not asking for help, trying to think where Riley was and why he had gone away from her.

Her legs ached, and everything that caught her eye was just something that wasn't him. She didn't know how much time had passed since she had seen him across the magazines but it felt like a long time, as long as lunchtime at school perhaps, but even at lunchtime she could see him eating his sandwiches on a bench with the other boys, or running around.

Suddenly she heard her name. *Pearl! Pearl!* People turned to frown in the direction the voice came from.

Finally Riley was walking towards her. She could see in his wide eyes and turned-in toes that he'd been afraid. But he wasn't alone, he was holding on to a man's hand as if he belonged to him.

The man crouched beside her and delivered Riley's hand into hers. She noticed that the man's fingernails were creamy and pink against his dark skin. She noticed, too, that the adults passing by were looking at them now; now that everything was all right.

'I thought I saw Mum,' said Riley. 'I went out of the shop and got lost. Matt found me.'

'It wouldn't have been Mum,' said Pearl.

Matt was wearing a blue sweat top with the hood pulled over his dark hair and he smelled of perfume. She could see that Riley didn't want to let him go. Riley kept a photo of his father in a plastic wallet under his mattress. It wasn't a normal photo but the cover of a CD, and Riley's father was with a group of other men, standing at the back, where Lily had said drummers usually go.

'So you reckon you'll be OK now?' Matt asked, looking closely at both of them.

Riley nodded his head.

'Thanks,' said Pearl.

Matt stood up and it was just the two of them again.

It was only a short time later that Pearl and Riley were watching television at Lily's friend's house. Lily and her friend had put on their coats and gone out for a while. Everything on TV was boring until they found a game of football to watch, and then they settled back on the couch, their hands deep in a packet of chips.

Suddenly Riley jumped up and pointed to the TV screen.

'There's Matt!' he cried.

Pearl saw men running and the ball moving between them. 'Where?' she said.

Riley dropped to his knees in front of the television. 'There,' he said, his finger on the screen. 'There!'

Pearl saw him then: a player in a black jumper with a red stripe across the front. He was tall and he was Aboriginal, but he wasn't Matt. The ball seemed to cling to his fingers.

'That's not Matt,' she said gently.

'It is! It is!' insisted Riley, his eyes scanning the screen wildly.

'It just looks like him,' said Pearl. 'Don't get too close to the heater.'

'Look!' Riley demanded. He was on the edge of tears.

'Have some more chips,' she said, holding the bag out to him.

One day soon after, Pearl and Riley wandered into the Good Samaritans. They liked to look. Pearl was going through the girls' tops when she heard Riley cry out: 'There's Matt's jumper!'

It hadn't been him on television but Riley was right – there was a football jumper, black with a red stripe.

She had never done it before, and her heart pounded, but she did what she'd seen Lily do; she took the jumper from the boys' rack and slipped it off the hanger and rolled it tight and stuffed it right to the bottom of her shoulder bag. It was Matt's jumper, she had to.

Pearl watches Riley out on the oval, tumbling with another boy. What will she draw? It's so hot her hands are sticking to the paper. She had done a drawing earlier that morning. After they ate some toast she washed their dishes and took the rubbish down the five flights of stairs. The bins smelt bad and the light flared painfully off the parked cars.

At the kitchen table she drew a shell, and on a piece of paper she gave him Riley drew a monster. She wanted her shell to be like the one that was on the shelf at school. A tiny creature had lived inside it, so the shell was like a house. She wanted to show the smooth spiral inside. To get the curves and lines right she used her ruler and a small empty glass and when the pencil marks went wrong she rubbed them out and just tried again, thinking about the creature and its shell, and how they'd been made for each other.

Riley's fist zigzagged back and forth with a stump of green crayon, his monster half on the page and half on the table. Lily was still asleep, and they were being good. When she woke, if she was alone, she might call them into her bed where they would snuggle down, one on each side, until Lily's eyes closed and she drifted off to sleep again. Then they would lift their heads and whisper to each other over her body, intoxicated by the nearness and warmth of her, her heartbeat, her hair lemony bright.

Bree calls out to her: 'Pearl, you wanna help with this?'

Bree has set up a table nearby, and the girls and a couple of boys who have broken away from the game are cutting up coloured rags and tying them to the tail of a kite. Pearl shakes her head. If she can't think of what to draw, she will just colour in.

She takes off the plastic bangle she wears on her wrist and with a black pencil draws inside it until the page is covered with overlapping circles. There are four shades of green but she chooses Grasshopper. She starts close to the edge of the page where the circles have made a half-moon and she colours for a while at its centre, warming up, before her hand takes the pencil out to the edge of the crescent and she begins the careful work of colouring inside the lines.

She leans close to the page. She moves the pencil parallel to the black line, right up to the edge, touching but never going over, until just when her hand is starting to hurt she finds that she is back at the beginning and she has created a solid border of brilliant green. She has secured the half-moon and now nothing can go wrong. Now all she has to do is fill the white space, pour in the green. She can breathe again.

Trish lifts the lid of the Esky and grasps a handful of the oranges that are bobbing around in the melted ice. As she walks towards Pearl carrying a plate of the quartered fruit, she studies the girl's head bent over her drawing, its neat, pale parting, and her fierce grip on the pencil. Pearl looks up as she senses Trish draw close, but when Trish's hand reaches out to brush hair from her hot cheek, unmistakably Pearl flinches.

Trish is sorry, so sorry she has done this. She has not yet been able to answer for herself the question of how she must care for other people's children but not *care*, and how she must never forget herself, and how she must not, ever, reach out.

Pearl stares at the colours on her page. She wishes she could go back and do it again. This time she wouldn't jump, she would just feel how her cheek was suddenly cool. This time she would just smile as if it was the most normal thing in the world, to be touched like this. And then she would take some orange.

Lily didn't call them into her bed that morning. When their mother's bedroom door opened, Pearl was still drawing at the table but Riley had already grown restless and found something to do on the floor, every now and then his fingers scrabbling at the soles of Pearl's feet. When they heard her, Riley's head shot up and he scrambled onto his chair.

'Jesus, it's hot,' said Lily, stretching over the sink to push open the window. On the back of her black silky dressing gown a gold dragon breathed fire. 'Has anyone rung?'

'No,' said Pearl.

Lily filled the kettle and took down a jar of coffee. The children's breakfast dishes were neat and dry on the sink.

'My good babies,' Lily said, spooning sugar into a mug. 'What've you been drawing?'

Behind them the kettle creaked. Lily stood between them and spread the pages on the table in front of her. Riley's green monster bulged out at them and Lily laughed and ran her fingers through his hair.

'What's yours meant to be?' she asked Pearl, as she reached for a chair.

'A shell,' said Pearl. ' But I haven't got the spiral right.'

The kettle started to scream.

Lily sighed.

'Get that for me, will you?' said Lily, pushing the pages aside.

Trish wanders with the plate, collecting orange peel. Riley and some of the boys have pressed the peel against their teeth and are running amongst the other children, boggling their eyes and making muffled ape sounds.

Pearl dries her fingers on her skirt. When she looks at her page again she notices that when two of her circles intersect they make a shape that is the same as the orange peels. This is strange, but not unfamiliar; the world makes patterns.

She can see that the kite won't fly today, even as the children lift it from the table. The sky is still and there's no movement in the trees. It feels like they're the only people awake on this hot afternoon. Her mother will be lying down, wearing her sarong, the fan blowing. They have done as Lily told them to, and they have stayed away long enough for things to be different when they return.

She chooses the next colour.

Trish decides she wants all the children in from the sun. She shades her eyes and calls to those tangling with the kite out on the grass. Bree seizes the boys' ball and shepherds them closer to the Kombi as a dark blue Nissan Patrol pulls into the shade at the edge of the oval.

'It's the twins' dad,' Trish says to her. 'What's he doing here?'

There is only an hour to go now and the kids need to quieten down. Trish and Bree can set up potato shapes, and most of the boys will be happy on the grass with a pack of cards. There's Monopoly money because they love to gamble. Pearl will have to move her table along soon because she's losing her shade.

Trish watches the twins' father walk towards her.

'Had a haircut, Mal?' she says, smiling.

Pearl looks up from her drawing as the man runs a hand over his bald head.

'I had the kids on the weekend,' he says. 'They'd let me give them a haircut if I got one too, but we were mucking around too much and they made a real botch of it, had to shave it all off.'

'It makes you look like one of those swimmers,' says Bree, joining them.

Pearl understands why everyone laughs then because the twins' dad is smaller than both Trish and Bree, and skinny.

His boys run up and jump at him, surprised to see him too.

'I noticed they'd had haircuts,' said Bree. 'You did a good job.'

'So how come you're here in the middle of the day, Mal?' asks Trish.

Pearl can see that the man's yellow T-shirt is wet under the arms and sticking to his back. She notices that although he is talking and laughing the arms hanging by his sides end in fists. But she has reached the edge of a circle now, she has to concentrate, and she drops her eyes to the page.

'There was a pretty bad accident at work,' she hears the man say, 'and I just cleared out.'

Pearl turns her hand and the red pencil sideways.

'I was thinking I'd pick up the kids and spend a bit of time with them,' the man says.

Pearl feels the sudden tension in the air but she can't look up, she has to stay inside the line.

'I'm sorry about the accident,' says Trish. 'But when Jeanie dropped the boys off this morning she said her mother would pick them up. You know that I'm not supposed to let them go off with anyone else.'

Pearl looks up to find Riley. He's sitting cross-legged with a group of boys under a tree, trying to shuffle a pack of cards with his small hands.

'You kids go and play,' the man says to the twins, who have fallen silent between their father and the playleaders. 'I want to talk to Trish.'

'I'll get the potato shapes started,' says Bree, turning away.

Pearl looks closely at the man and Trish.

'I'm their father,' he says.

Trish folds her arms and looks at the ground for a moment. When she looks up she is frowning.

'I know you've been having a bad time with all of this, Mal.

And I'm sorry. But Jeanie stays away when you have them, like she's supposed to.'

'She kicked up this big stink about me cutting the kids' hair – like I didn't have a say anymore.'

'Mal –'

'It's just this one time.'

'But what happens when their grandmother arrives?'

'I don't give a shit what happens. You should've seen this bloke at work, half his arm gone and . . .'

Pearl looks over at Riley. He's faster than the other boys. *SNAP!* The card is hardly out of someone's hand and he has slapped his own down.

If she colours over the red again it will make it darker.

'Why don't you spend some time with the boys here?' she hears Trish ask.

'I don't want to run into her mother. They're with their mates here. I need some time alone with my kids.'

'I'm sorry,' says Trish.

Pearl's chest tightens. The red pencil is harder to control this time around, slippery.

She looks up and sees the man is shaking. Suddenly he folds at the waist as if he has been hooked from behind with a rope.

When he lifts his head again, his eyes are small and hard.

'How did it get to this?' he hisses. 'How does a fucken dyke get to tell me when I can or can't be with my kids?'

Pearl knows the place that Trish and the man have reached.

'*SNAP!*' Riley's voice rings out.

'Mal – ' Trish reaches out to touch the man's arm but he knocks her hand away and turns and strides off.

'Dad!' the twins call, as he heads towards his car.

Bree looks up from the potato shapes.

'It's OK, boys,' Trish says, moving to hold them back. 'Your dad's just a bit upset. Let's give him time to calm down.'

Pearl watches as the man wrenches open his car door and slumps behind the wheel. Riley is looking up at the twins. Everything is quiet.

In the kitchen, Pearl and Riley listened to the sounds of their mother in the shower.

'Do you think we'll go out?' Riley asked.

'Maybe,' said Pearl.

'We might go to Centrelink?'

'Maybe.'

Lily came into the kitchen with a towel wrapped around her, her hair tied up and damp around her face.

'Pass me the telephone, Pearlie,' she said.

From the kitchen table they watched her walk down the corridor. Sometimes if they watched closely, they learned how the day would go. But this time there were only her pink heels to see, and a few drops of water along her shoulders, the bedroom door closing.

'Can we ask?' said Riley, standing on the lino.

'Not yet,' replied Pearl.

'When?'

'Maybe when she's more awake.'

Riley lined up the magnets on the fridge for a while, and Pearl studied her drawing, but soon they heard Lily shouting on the phone. There was a long silence, then the sound of the phone ringing and their mother shouting again, and they understood why the television had gone.

Riley opened the fridge and stood there, gazing inside.

'I'm hungry,' he said.

Lily's bedroom door flew open, and Riley quickly closed the fridge.

Their mother was holding the telephone between her ear and her shoulder.

Riley stepped out of her path.

'You're pathetic!' she said into the phone, opening a drawer and rummaging around for her tobacco and lighter.

Pearl watched as her mother sat down at the table. She wanted to tell Lily there was some moisturiser on her neck that she hadn't rubbed in properly, but Lily was busy rolling a cigarette and listening. The faint sound of a guitar came from the other end of the phone.

Riley had edged close to Pearl. 'I'm thirsty,' he whispered.

Lily tore the phone away from her ear and hung up.

'Have some water,' Pearl said quietly.

Lily picked up her little pink lighter.

Riley dragged a chair over to the sink. If he kneeled carefully on a chair, he could reach a glass and the tap, and turn it on.

A hissing sound came from Lily's lighter.

Riley filled a glass and lifted it slowly to his mouth; it always looked like he closed his eyes when he drank. The glass was almost empty when something upset his balance. As he lurched forward, the glass fell from his hand and smashed in the sink.

Lily slapped the lighter down on the table. Riley turned to her with his eyes wide.

'Why can't you be more careful?' Lily yelled, tearing at the scrunchie on top of her head.

She turned sharply to Pearl. 'Why didn't you get it for him?'

Lily looked slowly from Pearl to Riley as if she had asked them real questions and was waiting for answers. The day had begun.

'Get out of my hair,' she said tiredly.

They looked at the scrunchie wound around her fingers, and all her hair sticking out.

'*Get out!*' she screamed, the cords in her neck stretching.

'I have to get my bag,' said Pearl.

'*Well, get it!*'

Pearl hurried to her room and when she returned to the kitchen she reached for Riley's hand and they moved towards the door. Behind them the lighter hissed again. As she put her hand to the door, Pearl looked around and saw her mother's head bowed and her hands pulling furiously at her hair, as if she could still feel them both there, as if to loosen them, to be rid of them once and for all.

Riley has called the twins back to the game and Trish and Bree sit on small chairs with the girls making potato shapes. The kite is out on the oval, becalmed.

Pearl's page is nearly filled. She can feel the man in his car, still parked at the edge of the oval. She will choose one more colour. If she chooses the right one, everything will be all right.

Suddenly, light falls across her page. Cubes of light waver – blue, pink, mauve, lemon – like a chopped-up rainbow. When she puts her hand on the colours her hand becomes coloured too. She looks up at the sky, thinking of the light that comes into her bedroom, knowing that the sun must be doing this, but the sun gives no clue.

'Trish,' she calls, 'there's coloured lights on my paper. Where are they coming from?'

Trish looks up. And then she smiles, pointing to the Kombi behind Pearl's chair. 'It's my crystal,' she says, 'hanging from the rear-vision mirror.'

'Can I have a look?' Pearl asks.

'Sure.'

Pearl opens the door to the cabin of the Kombi and pulls herself up.

'*SNAP!*' she hears, and she's sure it's Riley. Inside the Kombi is messy. The crystal hangs like a huge teardrop on a length of ribbon, rainbows trembling across the dashboard and floor. Through the side window she can see the twins' father in his car and from the circle of his arms upon the steering wheel and the movement of his yellow back she thinks he must be crying.

Suddenly he sits up very straight in his seat, and she hears the engine turn over. She lifts the ribbon over the mirror and holds the crystal in her palm.

The engine revs once, twice. He must be going, she thinks. He must have calmed down.

Pearl and Riley closed the door behind them. From inside they could hear their mother crying. They were five storeys in the air and it was a hot day. Riley's lips quivered.

'What will we do?' he said.

She looked down. And then she smiled for him the madonna of smiles: serene and consoling, a smile so at odds with her own true feelings that only a grown woman should have been capable of it.

The Children of Lir

THE NIGHT IS COOL at last, and Sonia decides she will read a book. She's rinsed her plate and wine glass, wiped the bench and swept the kitchen floor. She will pick up a book and be, simply, a woman alone, filling the hours before bed with a story that is not her own.

She takes down from the shelves in the lounge room David Marr's biography of Patrick White, and studies the familiar Whiteley portrait on its cover. The writer as an old man with *Village of the Damned* eyes and womanly, unstill hands. How long had it been since she watched her two sons pass this gift to their father at Christmas? She'd been proud of them for making this choice, for showing how well they knew him.

She searches the first few pages. Nineteen ninety-one. It's a long time ago but, of course, it does not feel like it. She can still see Pieter in his Hawaiian shirt, stretched out on the lounge those January evenings, taking up all the space, the heavy book resting easily in his hands. This was when she always wanted him the most: when he went away from her, when he was avid for something else.

Pieter's Hawaiian shirts. He had worn his first one nearly thirty years earlier. They hadn't been in Australia long when she asked him: 'Why do the men here wear those noisy shirts?'

In order to answer her, he had gone and bought one. 'Do you see now?' he asked, muscling out from the bedroom in the green, blue and yellow shirt with the palm trees and waves and surfboards.

'No,' she said, 'you look horrible.'

He smiled at her. 'But you don't get the joke. *Me? Surf?* Do I *look* like I surf? It's funny.'

'No,' she said. 'I don't see it. It must be an Australian thing.'

'That's because we are *in* Australia,' he said.

'But why would you wear something that made you look funny?'

'It's not about looking funny, it's about *being* funny.'

'No,' she said finally. 'I don't see it.'

She sits down on the lounge and turns the book's pages. He had always removed the dust jacket from the book he was reading, and now there is no sense of him having held it, there's no trace.

Pieter had made a chair for Patrick White in 1972. She's sure of the date, because it was the year that Karl started school. Pieter's workshop had just been built in the backyard, and she remembers hanging her son's small grey uniform on the washing line, and having her husband near. The writer had wanted a reading chair. Something comfortable, he said, but not so comfortable that he would fall asleep. At the washing line she could feel Pieter in the workshop, thinking, making. She remembers there was so much polyester in Karl's school uniform that by the time she had pegged the last piece of washing on the line, the uniform was nearly dry.

She switches on a lamp and lies on the lounge and arranges cushions beneath her head. Around her the house drifts in darkness. She rests the book against her knees. Patrick had approved of the chair. He told Pieter that he had found the readingness of a reading chair, and Pieter had been pleased. It looked right at home, Pieter told her, in the house on Martin Road.

She doesn't like the beginning of biographies, the pages she thinks of as sepia-toned, the ones about the subject's parents and grandparents and all the others that went before. But ever since she began reading books in English, she has obeyed all their rules. She starts at the beginning and reads carefully to the end, and always has a dictionary on hand. She hardly ever speaks Danish anymore, and she thinks mostly in English, but she continues to believe that she must be well-behaved in a language that is not her own.

She finishes the first page and is halfway through the second when a loose thread in the hem of her skirt catches her eye. After she has pulled at the thread and returned to the page she realises she has not taken in all that she has read, and so she begins again. But soon the words on the page begin to clot; she has to read a sentence several times before she can under-stand it, before she can move on. In her head, she can hear the whooshing of her own blood.

She puts the pressed-flower bookmark that Gabriel made for her between the pages, and closes the book. This inability to read is another of grief's surprises. She has been alone all day and now all she wants is to part company with herself.

There's the remote. She watches a medical drama and then she changes channels and watches a police one. The same actor, a young Puerto Rican, features in both. His Puerto Ricanness is important to the stories, neither of which are happy ones. She is still a lucky woman, she thinks, and she must not forget it. To forget one's luck is to place oneself in peril.

She rises from the lounge with a hand on her lower back. The wood is warm and smooth under her feet. She still has this, she thinks, as she makes her way to the kitchen. But she must be allowed one small thing. Her doctor has told her that there is a risk of becoming addicted to the pretty aqua capsules she moves towards, but she has assessed the situation. She is sixty-one years old; what does it matter if she depends upon a pill? It can't ruin her life, she's already had most of it. Only one rule for living remains: she must not lie awake, thinking. She manages the long hours of her day; she simply asks to be relieved of the responsibility of putting herself to sleep each night.

A long time ago, when their sons were small and Pieter was working hard and it seemed they were both always tired, sometimes it was better to lie beside one another in bed at night, to kiss tenderly and whisper a few words, and then each attend to their own orgasm. Her body had been pressed by the children all day; now she liked this distance and cool selfishness. They were like two archers standing side by side, bows drawn, targets ahead, sights set tight. And it was simple to come together. It took only a few more murmurings, an alignment of rhythms, a holding back or bringing on. Then the wiping-up, the light kissing, the quick heavy curtain of sleep.

Now she sleeps alone in their bed. Narrow zones of her body can still liven to her own fingers and a simple sexual fantasy, especially one tinged with cruelty, but too often now, as her body climbs the ladder of orgasm, one of the rungs will prove to be infirm, weakened by memory or sadness or loss, and she will fall down crying.

She looks through the kitchen window onto the patio and the jasmine shimmering palely in the dark. These are the wet nights of summer when its scent should fill the air, but she can smell only her night cream and something unpleasant in the drain.

There is no point in crying; she must take a tablet instead.

Forty years before, on the first night she and Pieter spent in the house, she woke in the middle of the night with a headache. She had carried heavy boxes all day, and her neck and shoulders hurt. The bedroom smelled sharply of polish, the night was still warm. She made her way across the unfamiliar floor and pushed the window open as far as it would go. Below her the backyard stretched away into darkness but for the pale trunks of gum trees lit by the fat cut of moon. She had always yearned, when she looked at the moon. As if the moon were an emissary from another place, and its message to her was always: *life is better elsewhere*. But now that she was elsewhere, she would not allow herself to yearn, or the moon to speak to her in the old way.

She turned and studied Pieter as he lay sleeping in their new bed. He slept close to the edge, not yet stretching out into its great width, as though he were still lying on their old narrow mattress. The bed was his wedding gift to her, even though they had been married now for two years. He had made a bed that promised her everything she wanted from their marriage.

The headboard was tall, and four elegant wings of dark wood unfolded from the bed's sides. On the kitchen table in their old flat he showed her the drawings he had made, and then – as if he had just thought of it – he pulled his Swiss army knife from the pocket of his trousers and drew out its blade, returned the blade to its recess in the body of the knife, and drew it out again.

'Basically the same principle,' he said, 'with folding supports beneath. One wing on each side of the bed, like a table, one for your things, and one for mine.'

Sonia took the knife from him and with her fingernails she pulled out the blade again, and from below the blade she pulled another, finer blade, this one with a saw-tooth edge. She arranged the two blades carefully in relation to each other and to the rest of the knife.

'What if you had two wings on each side, like a butterfly?' she said.

Pieter looked at the knife. 'Yes, it's possible. Do you want two on each side?' he asked.

'Yes,' she smiled.

'What would you do with two?'

'One for my water and one for my wine,' she laughed.

He put his arms around her. 'You greedy girl,' he said.

She didn't want to wake him. She didn't want to put on a light, even if she could find one, even though she was clumsy and a new house invited accidents. Her hand felt its way along the wall until she reached the open door. She stepped slowly across the long landing and then held firmly on to the stair-rail until she reached the ground floor.

She had never before lived in a house where more than eight steps were not stopped by a wall. Or lived in a street where nine steps did not take a curved path. But here she had counted twenty-five steps across the landing, and twelve down the stairs, and she calculated that if there were a formula for the happiness to be found in a home, twenty-five and twelve might be it. There were no walls on either side of the staircase, no attic stairs, no cellar stairs, no alleyways, no thin and winding. Just long and straight, just stepping freely out.

In the kitchen she made her way by moonlight. The kitchen felt like the wheelhouse of a large ship, floating on a dark sea. She reached inside an open tea chest on the floor, careful not to cut her hand again on its sharp metal lip, and unwrapped a glass from its newspaper. The headache tablets were on the windowsill where Pieter had left them. All day he had played his hangover for laughs, rolling his eyes as he hefted heavy boxes and furniture, but she could see now by the number of tablets he'd taken that his pain had been real.

The dinner the night before had been important to him. He'd told her that she would like his clients, that he was honoured to share their first meal at the table he had made for them.

She bought a small bottle of colour to touch up her high heels. She wrapped her dark hair in a French roll, untangled her long silver earrings and clipped them to her ears. It was a hot night and she wanted to wear the one dress she had bought since arriving in Australia. It was a bare, lovely dress but she had her period and she couldn't take the risk of leaking onto the pale blue silk and the dress was too tight for the line of the elastic belt that held her sanitary napkin. In such a dress if her pad slipped during the evening, nudging its way upwards between her buttocks, she would look as if she had a small tail, like a lamb or a rabbit. It had to be the black dress she had brought from home. Its crepe and beading were heavy, and the sleeves a little too long.

Pieter turned from fastening his tie-pin in the mirror as she was snaking into it. 'Why aren't you wearing the other dress on a night like this?' he asked.

'Because I have put on this little amount of weight,' she fibbed to him, making a half-inch between her thumb and forefinger.

She moved towards him and reached to straighten the knot of his tie. He lifted his chin slightly. This was when she loved him the most, she thought, smelling of soap and the oil in his hair. She stroked his long, smooth cheek with the back of her finger.

Pieter's clients led them down a corridor hung with paintings into a deep-cushioned living room lit warmly by lamps. Godfrey and Yvonne might have been brother and sister, Sonia thought. She could see in them the gentleness that Pieter had talked about, but she sensed tiredness too, a feeling of strain. A hot blush stood out on Yvonne's chest and neck. Their son, whom Pieter had never mentioned, was standing behind a wood-panelled bar at the far end of the room, agitating a cocktail shaker and whistling to jazz. When Godfrey introduced him, Reggie made an elaborate play of positioning his cigarette on the edge of the bar and striding towards his parents' guests.

'I wasn't planning to be in for dinner tonight,' he said to Pieter as he offered his hand. 'But when I saw the marvellous new table I felt a *simpatico* between me and its maker.'

He took Sonia's hand and looked into her eyes.

'The table is so *confident*,' he continued. 'The legs at bold angles. The long, dark, sensuous grain. It gives one a rush that can only be thought of as *modern*.'

His face was as round as a plate and his mouth turned down, like a sulking child's. A streak of greased black hair bisected his forehead.

'Come on,' said Yvonne, placing a hand on Sonia's arm, 'I'll show you around.'

Sonia was becoming accustomed to this ritual: the departure from the men and the tour of the house by its senior female. It hadn't been like this at home. There, visitors were contained in one or two lit rooms while the rest of the dwelling crouched darkly around them, mindful of its many privacies.

She was thinking about Reggie as she followed Yvonne's gold heels out of the living room and into the kitchen. Usually she felt a moment of anxiety as she turned away from the men's crisp shirts and aftershave to be led by an unfamiliar woman into her intimate realm. Away from the men, the woman's full-blooded attention would be upon her: the terrible divining sensibility of a woman reaching out. But this time she was happy to leave. She looked at the hand that a moment ago had held Reggie's.

'Your husband is very talented,' said Yvonne, stopping in the middle of the kitchen. The redness on her chest had gone.

'Yes, he is,' said Sonia, 'and he works very hard.'

'No good having one without the other,' Yvonne said, moving towards the refrigerator. 'Would you like a drink? The men will be getting under way.'

Fluorescent tubes cast a cool light on the black and white checked floor.

'Yes, thank you,' she said, 'I'd like a drink.'

Yvonne opened the fridge door. Sonia had never seen so much food.

'Do you drink beer?' Yvonne asked, extracting a brown bottle from a row inside the door.

'I do.' Pieter would be pleased with her, she thought.

'I have to say, I think you're both very brave coming all this way from Copenhagen. How long have you been here now?' Yvonne closed the fridge door with her hip.

'Two years. We have been here two years. And tomorrow we move into our first house.'

'Tomorrow! How wonderful! I look forward to seeing it.'

Sonia tried to imagine standing with Yvonne in the bedroom of her new home, fingering the curtains, or chatting in the bathroom about the colour of the tiles.

'And we look forward to having you,' she said.

Pieter had been drunk before the steaks arrived, and now Reggie had persuaded him to take off his shirt and tie and continue their conversation outside in the night air.

'I'll help you with the dishes,' said Sonia, rising from the table with a plate in each hand.

'No, they can wait,' said Yvonne. 'Let's just sit for a while.'

She pulled a cigarette from its packet and brought a candle close to light it.

Yes, thought Sonia.

The two women looked out through the French doors. In the darkness they could see the white vests of the two younger men.

Pieter had been nervous. Godfrey and Yvonne meant a lot to him; their custom certainly, but their kindness too. He missed his own parents a great deal.

But he was not a complex drunk. He laughed loudly and became a little sentimental, lit one cigarette from another and urged people to dance. But all this was simply an exaggeration of things that already existed in him. Yvonne and Godfrey, however, had attempted to restrain their son's drinking, and had struggled to protect Pieter from the aggressive joking by which Reggie encouraged him to drink further. They were engaged, Sonia was sure, in familiar exertions to hold their son back from a point that must not, at all costs, be reached.

Yvonne had served dessert and sat down. Reggie pushed the food aside and leaned back in his chair. With one eye squinted, he ran his hand slowly over the dark, polished surface of the new table.

'You know what, Pieter?' he said. 'This table is as smooth as the inside of a black woman's thigh.'

Sonia stared down at the white peaks of meringue on her plate and felt an emptiness open inside her. I will never go home again, she thought.

'What do you think, Sonia?' she heard Reggie say. 'About this man of yours making a table like a black woman's thigh?'

Godfrey spoke Reggie's name softly but Reggie repeated his question. Sonia lifted her head because finally she had found some words for Reggie, but Godfrey's words came first.

'Reg. Please.'

Reggie sighed deeply, and then he picked up the crumpled serviette that lay beneath his hand, and flung it at his father. The serviette opened in the air and fell, momentarily, like a small white sheet of death, across Godfrey's face.

Sonia felt the scald of Godfrey's shame. But he folded the serviette quietly and placed it on the table.

'Pieter,' he said, 'Yvonne and I were hoping you would make us a new set of bookshelves for the study.'

Pieter looked eagerly at Godfrey and then at Yvonne. Sonia saw how young he was.

'Yes, yes,' he said. 'I would be very happy to do that. Thank you for asking me.'

On the way home in the car, Sonia wanted to talk. She had been saving it all evening, waiting for the moment when she could put words to what she had felt.

'Yvonne showed me the house,' she said, watching the black road disappear beneath them.

'Did you like it?' Pieter slurred. He cast a look in her direction. 'Can you come here and do the gears for me?'

Sonia slid across the seat until their thighs were touching. 'Straight down when I say, right?'

'Right,' she said nervously, putting her hand on the stick at the wheel. 'She showed me their bedroom. It was green. Why does she show me the bedroom?'

'Now,' he said. 'Straight down, now.'

She pushed the gearstick down. She looked at the side of his face, covered in shadow.

'Why?' she repeated.

'Why not?' he said, moving both hands to the centre of the wheel.

At times like this she feared she was losing him. He was becoming Australian. She had asked him a question to which she needed a reply, and instead he had asked her another question. Her desire to understand remained unmet, and she felt somehow diminished.

The houses lining the road were in darkness.

'Reggie is your age,' she said. 'But he has a bedroom like a little boy.'

'Reggie is OK, he was just drunk,' Pieter said, slowing to take a corner. 'Now!'

'Now what?' she said, her hand hovering over the gearstick.

'*Now in and up!*'

Sonia tried to do as he said but there was the sound of crunching metal and the car swerved over the road.

'Here, let me do it,' he said.

She slid back to her side of the car.

There had been a smell. This was what she really wanted to say. Yvonne had led her down the corridor.

'This is Reggie's room,' she said, and they both stopped in the doorway.

Yvonne lifted the bottle of beer. 'Top-up?' she said, and Sonia understood the gesture, if not the meaning of the words.

There was a single bed, and a desk with two drawers. A shelf on the wall held small silver trophies. Yvonne noticed Sonia looking at them.

'Reggie is very good with words,' she said. 'He won those in debating.'

Magazine photographs of a man playing a saxophone and a girl in a spotted bikini running out of the surf were sticky-taped to the wall. The smell was warm and physical, and tinged with despair. The room had recently been tidied, Sonia thought. She could see Yvonne plumping the pillows, smoothing the brown bedspread.

And she could see Reggie, lying naked on his boy's bed, a hand on his man's genitals.

This was what happened when people opened their private places for your viewing, this was the problem. You saw what you saw. You could not help what you saw and once you had seen it, it could not be forgotten.

When they reached home, Pieter fell onto the bed fully dressed. Sonia untied his shoes and slipped them off his feet and loosened his tie and pulled it free of his collar.

In the bathroom she discovered that she had bled onto her underpants. She unhooked the warm, wet sanitary napkin from the metal teeth that held it between her legs and wrapped it in several sheets of the newspaper she kept by the toilet.

As she secured a fresh napkin, she remembered the tiny bathroom in the apartment in Norrebro and the dirty yellow light and her mother's used sanitary napkins lying dried and brown on the pale green tiles. She remembered her disgust and shame, and how she had picked them up and wrapped them and disposed of them herself, in order to protect her father.

She had always believed that her father had left them because their home was never clean, and their food not good enough. But the events of the evening made her wonder now if these blood-soaked pads were more than just dirtiness; she wondered if, like Reggie's serviette, they were deliberate acts of aggression. There had been no more soiled napkins after her father had gone. And certainly her mother's fury had found different expression then, when it was just the two of them.

Sonia pulled on clean underpants and a short cotton night-gown. She slipped under the sheet and wrapped her arm around Pieter's warm body.

God give me sons, she thought: *put an end to this*.

Sonia swallowed a headache tablet and turned the glass upside down on the sink. She had woken Pieter after all. He came naked down the stairs and together, in darkness, they walked slowly through the empty rooms of the house. In the lounge room they stretched out, one at each end of the long sofa. Pieter smoked a cigarette and stroked the inside of her foot with his toes. They spoke quietly in Danish, except when they talked of how to place the coffee table, rug, lamp and chair; for these new things they used English.

Three long rectangles of moonlight fell over them, and over the space in between.

'What will come to fill this?' she asked, patting the empty patch of light.

'Good things,' he replied. 'Children, love, happiness.'

'Is that all?' she said, laughing.

'And beauty, work, completeness,' he offered.

'Promise?' she said.

With his cigarette held loosely between his long fingers, he made the sign of a cross over his heart.

She curled her legs and slunk like a cat towards him. Out of her light, across the light that awaited them, into his.

'I promise,' he said, opening his arms to her.

Sonia swallows her sleeping tablet and puts the glass in the dishwasher. Forty years ago, and everything promised had come to be. Only Pieter had been dead for just over a year now; she had neglected to ask for time. Time had been the last thing on her mind.

She has twenty minutes before the pill will take effect. She reaches into the cupboard below the sink and takes out a little packet and tears it open and drops the detergent tablet into its place in the door of the dishwasher.

And not everything had come to be, she remembers. Pieter had never made the bookshelves for Yvonne and Godfrey, but she does not want to think of that.

The sound of the dishwasher soothes her. Television light flickers in the lounge room. Sonia picks up the remote from the coffee table and moves to switch it off, but she sees something on the screen that stops her.

There are police cars and ambulances, and people's unchoreographed movements tell her that this is real life.

For the first time that day she is outside herself, searching amongst the vehicles and flashing lights and the people with grave, withholding faces. It's some kind of open space that is revealed to her, a place with grass – a sports oval, perhaps. There are bodies on stretchers under white sheets and suddenly she notices how small these white shapes are and she lowers herself onto the lounge with both hands to her face. '*Oh*,' she exhales, the first word she has spoken out loud that day, realising that the bodies are those of children.

'*Don't show this*,' she says sharply, four words now, spoken to the pitiless camera as it records its tally, but she cannot look away. By the time she finds the volume the vision has moved to a suburban street, an untended garden, a roller-door, the glimpse of a blue four-wheel drive.

And then there's an advertisement.

She switches off the TV. And then one lamp, and another. She has always liked these dark, silent rounds, this time of walking slowly from room to room, checking windows for air and security, bringing together the heavy doors onto the patio. She was always the last to check on the children, the last one to bed. But it's different now, and not just because the house is empty, and she is alone. In fifteen minutes the sleeping pill will take it all away. It won't be like falling asleep, when the mind slowly loses its hold on thoughts and closes on itself. The sleeping pill is a black cancellation of everything. She is there, and then she is not.

As she climbs the stairs she wonders if this is what death

is like. Perhaps, if death is merciful. She thinks of what she has just seen on TV and how she doesn't fully understand it yet, and can't yet believe it, but that if it is true some children have gone, how she hopes they have gone like this.

In the bathroom she turns on the tap and squeezes out toothpaste and thinks of the summer she was pregnant with Karl, pregnant for the first time, heavily pregnant, and the three Beaumont children went missing.

She and Pieter had been in Australia for three years but she was living still in her own small land, within the walls of her house, under the protectorate of her marriage. But Pieter was changing. He was going to be an Australian, he said, he was home. She had tried but she hadn't yet found this home that Pieter talked about.

Jane and Arnna and Grant Beaumont vanished from a beach in Adelaide on Australia Day, 1966. They were nine and seven and four. It was a hot day, the children caught a bus, they had money, people saw them at play. How could children just vanish?

Pieter was away all day. All day the baby kicked at her, and still the children didn't appear. She listened to the radio and she began to watch the news on TV. In order to read about the children, she walked slowly to the shops each morning to buy a newspaper. As she handed her money to the woman behind the counter she found she wanted to speak, although she hadn't spoken to the woman before.

'Isn't it terrible about the children?' she said.

'Shocking,' said the woman, shaking her head. 'Imagine if you were the parents.'

'Imagine,' she said, holding out her hand for the change. Soon there would be a new currency.

'When's your littlie due?' asked the woman.

'In six weeks.'

'Is it your first?'

Sonia nodded.

'Thought so. You're carrying high, it's usually like that.'

'Oh?'

'You take care of yourself now. It's going to be a hot one.'

She walked home using the newspaper to shield her eyes from the sun. Still the children had not been found. On the roads that she walked there were dense bush blocks with 'For Sale' signs. Other blocks had already been cleared, and on some, building had begun. This was where her child would grow up, where she would try to keep him safe.

Imagine if you were the parents. The words came back to her like an instruction. She could do nothing about the missing children, she was helpless, like the children's parents, but she could be on the parents' side, she could try to imagine what they were living through. She might not imagine well – there were her own fears and the limits of her own mind – but she could try. She couldn't pray because she didn't believe; imagining was all she could do.

Outside her house she stopped to check the letterbox. She saw a woman further down the street getting out of her car and she lingered, slowly opening her mail, until the call came.

'Another hot day?'

'Yes,' said Sonia, walking to the edge of her driveway. Between the two women was an area of bush. Banksia flowers stood on trees like strange, fat candles.

'I wondered who lived in this house,' the woman said, shading her eyes with her hand. 'They've nearly finished ours. We'll be moving in pretty soon.'

The woman and Sonia exchanged names and the names of their husbands. The woman told her that she had two children.

'Isn't it awful about the Beaumont children?' said Sonia, realising that this was why she had waited.

'Awful. Makes you wonder,' said Susan.

'Imagine if you were the parents.'

'I can't bear to think about it,' said Susan, shaking her head.

Sonia looked at her white eye shadow and the freckles above her top lip. *But you must*, she wanted to implore, *you must not leave them alone*.

'I'm getting burnt,' she said. 'I should go inside.'

She turned and walked slowly down the drive, managing the steep slope and her huge belly. *How will the baby survive you?* Pieter had laughed, watching her crash into the glass screen as she tried to step out of the shower.

As she climbed the stairs to her bedroom a variation on the words came into her head. *Imagine if you were the children.* On her side of the bed only the top wing was out. She lay down and switched on the fan, and placed her hands on her stomach. She should do this too, she thought, imagine the children, try to be with them, wherever they were, whatever they might be suffering. But imagining for the children was harder still because she couldn't remember, not really, what it was like to be a four or seven or nine year old, to live inside a small body. And she wondered if taking her imagination to a place where harm was done to the children was, in a sense, to harm them also. It was as if only a clear imagination, or no imagination at all, might hold the children aloft.

She thought of the boy – for it was a boy, she was sure of that – who kicked inside her. So many times she had imagined lifting and holding and comforting him. She understood the vigilance and labour that this would require, but she saw now that there would be more than this; that in order to make the world safe for him she would also have to make her own mind safe, that she could no longer stray into its darkness, for fear of leading him there too.

The fan poured warm air along her body. Her feet throbbed. As she thought about the Beaumont children she remembered a story from her childhood and how that story had made her feel. A child's sadness, and yet not all that different from what she was feeling now.

She had been about ten years old when their teacher told the class the story of the children of Lir. The class knew about the old women at Odense Hospital who had cared for Hans Christian Andersen, and how he had listened to their folktales and how from these tales he had imagined his own stories, as the children should imagine theirs. The long face of Hans Christian Andersen gazed down on them from the portrait on the wall and sometimes it seemed he was crying.

'Did you know that in Ireland if someone kills a swan the punishment is death?' the teacher asked.

The children shook their heads slowly.

Sonia looked out the bedroom window at the hot blue sky. The baby kicked again. She didn't know how much of the story she could remember.

In Ireland, there was a king whose name was Lir.

Lir had a daughter, Fionnuala, and three small sons. When the king's wife died he married her sister, so that life could go on.

The king's new wife was jealous of his love for the children, and one day she invited them to ride in her chariot. They rode all day through the forest until the horses stopped beside a lake. Their stepmother told the children they must bathe after their long journey, but as the children swam she struck the water with a magic rod. The children screamed in fear but soon they saw that it was not with hands and arms that they thrashed against the water, but with white-feathered wings, and then they saw that they were not children anymore, but swans.

The children wept.

'You will be swans for nine hundred years,' their aunt called out to them. 'Only when the first bells of Christianity are heard throughout the land will you be free.'

Fionnuala folded her wings over her brothers as night came down on the Lake of Oaks.

After three hundred years had passed, the swans flew to the sea that lay between Scotland and Ireland and they made a home there upon the Rock of Seals. The winter rose up black and cruel; ice tore their feathers and salt ate their wounds, and in their pain they almost forgot they were children, the children of Lir, with children's hope.

But they were cursed to endure. After another three hundred years, they were exiled to the Inish Glora, where storms parted them and only by singing did they find each other again.

One day, nine hundred years after they had been led to the lake's edge, the children rose up from the Atlantic waters and flew to the land of their father. But there was no kingdom there anymore, and their hearts were so heavy they could no longer fly. They came down to land in a calm bay – and it was there that they first heard the ringing of a bell. It was such a lovely sound, a sound made by the movement of a human hand, that they sang out in reply. High up in his church on the land, the bell-ringer heard the voices of children and followed the sound to the bay.

'Are you the children of Lir?' he said to the four white swans.

'We are,' said the children, dipping their long necks. 'We are the children of Lir.'

The bell-ringer slipped a silver chain around their necks and led them onto the land. Soon, the children believed, they would be free.

One day a young king arrived at the church and ordered the bell-ringer to give him the birds with the voices of children. He had promised his wife he would bring her this prize.

'They are under my protection,' the bell-ringer said. 'You cannot have them for your sport.'

The king flew into a rage and rushed towards them, but no sooner had he grasped the chain around their necks than the coats of the swans fell to the ground and in place of them shivered a pale, withered old woman, and three withered old men.

The children of Lir cried out one last time, and died.

It had all been inside her, Sonia thought. The whole story, folded up tight, like origami. She wondered about the other children who had listened to the story in the schoolroom that day, whether it had become part of them. Did she care so much for the fate of the Beaumont children because this story already existed within her?

She would heave her belly off the bed and go downstairs and feed herself and her baby. She wanted to eat forever. Soon the news would be on the radio and she would hear about the search for the children. She didn't think they'd be found. She realised this as her feet touched the floor. Perhaps she had known it all along, and this was what the children of Lir had taught her.

Stories about children did not always have a happy end. And the years might pass and the world might move on, but the loss would never be recovered.

Sonia rubs Nivea into her elbows. It is only minutes now before the sleeping pill will work.

She had her baby, and he was a boy, as she knew. And four years later there was another. It was as she had wanted: the female line stopped at her.

She had kept her children safe; she had tried not to enter the dark in her mind. But Karl had been an anxious child, his blue eyes watching her, as if she might merely be pretending to be his mother. And Gabriel, the easy child? She is not sure that Gabriel is easy now. But they are far away, sometimes she hardly feels like their mother anymore.

In the bedroom she can see by the moon. She will need only a sheet, and she pulls the blanket to the end of the bed.

The Beaumont children had never been found. *Imagine if you were the parents*.

But Sonia had found something. She had cared about the fate of three children, children of Australia, and on the radio and television, and in newspapers and talk, she had found home.

She pushes the window open and thinks of Pieter. The distance between her and nothing is closing. It's the peaceful part of the day. But she has seen dead children, under white sheets. She will set the alarm so that she can hear the news when she wakes.

Death Studies

THE ARTIST OFFERS THE journalist another peppermint tea. Or perhaps this time she'd prefer fennel?

Neither of these choices really appeals to her. The interview has gone on for much longer than she expected – he has been so willing to talk – and now that it's twilight she wants white wine or even a proper coffee.

'I'll just have what you're having,' she says.

He holds up the Peanuts mug from which she has been drinking all afternoon. 'Hot water and lemon?' he asks.

'Yes, thanks.'

Adam Logan turns his back and reaches for the kettle. Nina studies his white Bonds T-shirt and his slim hips and the ripped pocket of his jeans. This is only her second story for *Q and A*, and she has researched carefully.

'I believe he's charming,' her editor had said. But his photograph hadn't appealed to her. She hadn't liked his rock star hair-in-the-eyes and the topiary sideburns that pointed to his delicate, self-conscious mouth, but when he opened the door of his flat earlier that afternoon, a door painted shiny red, the full force of his glamour hit her.

The interview has been demanding. He had a way of leaning back in his chair and listening carefully to a question with a look on his face that suggested criticism, or faint ridicule. When she finished speaking he gathered the silence tensely around him before responding with such surprising sympathy or encouragement that she felt weak with relief.

'That is such . . .' he would say, pausing to drink deeply from his Turkish tea-glass, '. . . an important question.'

She has drunk so much tea her bladder is full to bursting, but she is afraid a request for the toilet will break the spell.

It's going well, he thinks, slicing a lemon at the kitchen bench. The disturbance of the morning is receding. Only occasionally now, while listening to the young reporter or when moving about the small kitchen preparing their drinks, do the events come back to him.

When he opened his computer at the start of the day, her name appeared on his screen. He and Marlo hadn't used this form of communication when they were seeing each other, they had sent text messages and talked late at night on the phone. But there she was among his emails suddenly, and he knew that he was supposed to feel guilty. Her subject was one designed to get his attention: *abortion*.

Marlo had lizard-lidded, blue bedroom eyes, and a deep, musical laugh, and her name suggested to him the new America, even though he suspected that the new America was already old. It had been smooth between them for two or three months, and there had even been times when he'd imagined a future with her, in New York, the home town she wore like a gloss. But the moment had come, and he had known it was over between them. He respected these moments; he believed in them. These days there was not even regret, as there had been in the past, for all the possibilities lost.

They were sitting on her balcony, and the dusk sky was unusually agitated and bright. Marlo remembered that a volcano had erupted somewhere. Close to the horizon there were long streaks of dark red cloud that reminded him of striated muscle, and then layers of yellow, like fat, and above it all, the pale skin of the sky.

'It's an interesting sky,' he said. 'It looks like a cross-section of the human body.'

'You and your body stuff,' she said, pressing her bare feet against the pretty iron railing. She had made martinis, and she was speaking around the olive.

'I always wanted to be a surgeon,' he said. He didn't know if this were exactly true, but she should have listened to him then. She should have had the right question. He wanted to explore something; he wasn't sure what it was but it was something he wanted both of them to learn about him.

'God, no,' she said, tossing her toothpick over the railing. 'I could never do anything like that.'

He said nothing. He drank from his glass, holding it tightly by the stem. She examined her toenail polish.

After a while she placed her warm hand on his thigh and pressed her nails gently into his flesh. 'Do you feel like fucking?' she said quietly, her eyes searching the side of his face.

'Not right now,' he said, without turning. 'I'm still interested in the sky.'

When it grew dark they went inside and she turned on the lights. He looked through her CD collection again. She passed him a bottle of wine and a corkscrew.

It was while she was salting the eggplant that he came up behind her and lifted her dress. Nick Cave was playing.

She turned around to welcome him. Her spine met the edge of the table and he pushed her slowly backwards and lifted her legs around him. She opened his jeans. He stared lengthily into her eyes, recording their colour for the last time.

Afterwards, he thought about his obligations to her; it hadn't been long, it hadn't been a relationship. If he sat her down and told her, would she cry or would she just laugh at him?

He hadn't phoned or texted her for days, as he tried to work out what to do, but late one night as he was going to bed he had a sudden, warm thought of her and he reached for his phone and sent *sweet dreams* before he had thought it through. The next morning when he saw that she had replied with a long, rhythmic, syntactically complex sentence, achingly capitalised and punctuated, he took fright and erased the message and her number from his phone.

Her phone calls stopped after a week. Good for her, he thought. It almost made him want her again.

If he were to be truthful, the timing had been perfect. So much had happened for him since the showing of his new work, and it was better not to be with one woman. There was something inside him, he thought, something as precise and knowing as a timepiece, something that delivered him to new possibilities, as the big hand delivers the hour.

And then, today, Marlo's email appeared in front of him.

Adam, it read, *since you won't return my calls, I have to tell you this way. I'm having an abortion, Wednesday.*

He stretched out his arm and turned on the fan by his desk and clamped some loose papers down with a book.

He looked at the screen again. His feelings reminded him strangely of those he experienced when he read about a sexual assault in the newspaper – an unpleasant mixture of aversion, vexation and sympathy, and below all of these, in a part of himself that was out of his control but not his censure, a tingling, diffuse arousal that was undeniably sexual.

He would have to call her, he knew that. He shut down his laptop and walked into the kitchen. He drank three glasses of iced water and stared at the dull red laminex of the benchtop. She would be waiting. It seemed that all along she had been waiting.

There were his car keys. His Ray-Bans. He would call, but he would go to the gym first.

Nina sips her hot water and lemon. Through the dirty kitchen window she can see a line of blue ocean underneath the darkening sky. Adam Logan's flat had surprised her. He is thirty-two years old and everybody is talking about him. Even people who have not seen his new work have an opinion about what he has done. There have been queues all the way down the steps of the gallery and onto the street.

When she learned she was being sent to write about the sculptor, she imagined him living in a large white space with austere furniture and difficult art, like the residence of the artist in a film she liked, *New York Stories*. But the flat she found Adam in was nothing like that. From the outside, his building looked like a home for men who had lost their way in life: a peeling, despairing old yellow with faded curtains at each window.

Inside, the flat was filled with a light that suggested the distant ocean, but the bricks-and-board shelves and the shabby furniture-with-personality reminded her of student dwellings in her past. Balls of fluff drifted in the soft breeze over the rough, grey floorboards. A collection of road signs was displayed – Stop! Wrong Way Go Back! – something she had also seen before but usually in the rooms of younger men given to drunken, late-night thieving. Half a dozen orange witches' hats were triangled like circus performers against a wall.

But Nina is impressed by the way the artist speaks.

'Death has been torn from us,' he says. 'We are no longer able to look upon the dead in order to learn the lessons of our lives.'

She had approached Adam Logan's new work, *Katy's Gone*, with trepidation, but she had left the gallery feeling somehow uplifted. And although she lined up now with those who supported the work because it made them *feel* something, still she had mistrusted its maker.

She had gone to see Adam's work late in the day, in the middle of the week, when it seemed to her she wouldn't be jostled by crowds. She was aware of carrying, up the gallery steps and into the hushed lobby, a flinty feeling of disdain towards the work of art she was about to confront. She carried, too, a nervous excitement that she judged was somehow illicit, and she tried to push it away.

She was about to view the body of a dead girl.

But she found the toilet first. After peeing she washed her hands with opalescent soap from a stainless-steel dispenser that looked like a Fabergé egg. The overhead lighting was flattering and she looked closely at her skin in the mirror. The antibiotics were beginning to work. She reapplied her bisque lipstick, searched in her bag for her notebook, and neatened her disdain and excitement ready for the job ahead.

The room was velvety dark, and she was almost alone. A woman was reading some information lit dimly on the wall, and another was headed for the exit. Nina looked at this woman for a clue, but she could find none.

In the centre of the room a cone of light illuminated Adam Logan's death-cast of Katy, who had died of a heroin overdose at lunchtime on a rainy Tuesday, three days after her sixteenth birthday. The light reminded Nina of the one in which she had just examined her complexion; spilling warmly from the ceiling in order to show a girl at her best.

Or at least, half a girl. Only Katy's head and torso had been cast, and were now completely gold, while carved white stone suggested draped fabric and the lower part of her body. The entire arrangement lay horizontally, in the manner of an eighteenth century funerary sculpture, atop a high bier that was woven with porcelain vines and roses. Nina felt a kind of vertigo as she drew near.

She would have reached out and touched the lovely face if the sign forbidding it was not hovering at the edge of her vision. It was the compulsion one had to touch another person when they could not deter you, like touching the cheek of a sleeping child. But it was also, Nina thought, the compulsion one had to touch art; to feel its materials, its textures, the thing it is.

Sleeping Beauty. Goldfinger's girl.

Nina knew the story behind the work, she had done her research. She imagined the story on the wall was the same one.

The sculptor Adam Logan had known his subject, Katy, casually for a period of six months. Adam had a studio in a warehouse where Katy sometimes stayed with friends, having lived on the streets as a heroin addict since the age of fourteen.

When Adam met Katy he learned of her interest in art.

'Her life was raw and desperate,' he said. 'I encouraged her to draw what she saw.' He gave her some paper and pens.

One day Katy told the sculptor about a dream that was troubling her. In the dream, she said, she was dragging a stick down a street full of shadows. Adam told Katy that her dream reminded him of a famous painting by Giorgio de Chirico, called *Melancholy and Mystery of a Street*. He suggested that she look for this painting in a book in the library. Katy told Adam that she didn't really know what to do in libraries, and he said he would go with her.

It was a half-hour walk. While they were walking they talked about Adam's art. Katy had seen the wax hands and feet on the shelves in his studio, and the wax faces too, some of which were the faces of Katy's friends in the warehouse. She asked about these things, and about the strange pictures on his walls; anatomical drawings, and the death masks of famous people, and misshapen bodies that looked beautiful and bodies that were so beautiful they almost looked misshapen too.

'I told her that I knew some people found it a bit weird but I didn't care,' Adam said. 'I told her I thought it was important to be unflinching in one's art.'

In the library, Adam found a book of de Chirico's paintings and he showed Katy the painting he had talked about.

'It's just like my dream,' Katy said.

'That's what an artist is for,' said Adam.

A few months later, at lunchtime on a Tuesday, one of Katy's friends banged on Adam's studio door.

'Katy's gone,' he said to the sculptor.

'Gone where?' asked Adam.

He told Adam that he and Katy had been shooting up drugs and the gear was good, by which he meant strong, and he nodded off and when he came round, Katy was dead.

'He was hysterical,' said Adam. 'He was full of guilt and fear and so I said I would go downstairs and help him.'

Adam found Katy lying on her back on a mattress on the floor. He asked Katy's friend to make some tea and when it was ready he took one of the mugs for himself and told the junkie to sit against the wall and try to focus on his breathing.

Adam found a towel to wipe away the vomit around Katy's mouth.

'I looked at her and was suddenly struck by the mystery and melancholy of her face,' he said. 'Suddenly the beautiful girl she was became clear to me. All her torment had left her. I sat with her quietly for a while. I thought about how in other cultures people spent time with the dead, saying their goodbyes and helping the dead to cross over.

'I don't know when the thought of making a cast of Katy came to me but I never had any doubt. Strangers would take her away and we wouldn't see her again. She'd been on the street for years, and she'd never spoken about family. She wanted to be an artist, and in this way, finally, perhaps she could be.

'I had everything in my studio. All I needed was some more Vaseline, and I could send Katy's friend out for this. He was calm now, slumped against the wall.

'If there were consequences, I thought, I would deal with them later.'

So there in front of Nina now was Adam Logan's Katy: gold leaf, resin, porcelain, marble. Please do not touch. Nina tried to imagine the real Katy. She knew that the sculptor didn't answer questions about her, beyond what had already been told: 'The work of art is before them,' he said. 'That's how they should know her, and judge me.'

Nina knew that what Adam Logan had done raised many questions – there was even talk that the police had become involved and had decided not to press charges – but the fact was, another Katy existed now; in disregard of the sign she could reach out and touch her, her thin gold arm surprisingly warm, an effect of the day's concentrated light.

Once something was in the world one was forced to apprehend it with all of one's senses, not just with one's mind. The disdain she had carried up the steps – she hadn't liked the idea of Adam Logan handling a dead girl and putting stuff all over her and plastering her up – had been replaced by the urge to touch, to look, to bend lower over the body in order to know her.

Nina walked slowly around the bier, studying its ornamentation and the pose of the body closely. She didn't know a lot about the world of art but her editor said it was a celebrity profile she was being assigned, and her knowledge, or lack of it, didn't matter. After all, wasn't this exactly what was being said about Adam Logan? That he had brought into an art gallery people who had never before been into one? That people not normally concerned with the politics of aesthetics were concerning themselves now?

She had visited Westminster Abbey once, on a schoolgirl tour, and the marble tombs and funerary sculptures that she'd seen there came to mind as she looked down on Katy. The same antiquity could be seen in Adam Logan's work but this time the body upon the slab belonged not to a time long past, a time beyond her imagining, but to the very moment; to the time into which she'd been born, and which she must try to understand.

She remembered that the hands of the Tudor women had been folded in prayer, but Katy's hands lay lightly over her ribs, one below the other, as if nursing a pain. Nina was astonished by the fine detail the casting had accomplished. She could see clearly the torn cuticles on Katy's long, tapering fingers and the moons of scar tissue on the back of one hand. There was a slight deformity of her left thumb which Nina recognised, because it was like her own sister's: the mark of a thumb-sucker. Katy had died wearing a little singlet with shoestring straps. It seemed an odd way to have been dressed on a rainy day, Nina thought, but she didn't know much about junkies, maybe they didn't feel the cold.

There was something familiar in what Nina was doing: moving slowly around the body, scrutinising its detail. She became aware that she was, in fact, copying something she had seen. Not knowing how else to look at a dead girl, she had been impersonating the forensics experts in the crime shows she watched on TV. Every body has a story, those experts had taught her.

She was ready to talk to Adam Logan, Nina thought, as she went down the gallery steps. All around her, the city was going home. She asked herself what she felt.

She felt she had seen something it was important to see. Poor girl, she thought, looking up the street for a cab.

She will have to ask for the toilet soon, Nina thinks, draining the warm water in her mug. But just a few more questions.

'Your work has been described in many ways,' she says.

'Some people have called it a tender and haunting revision of funerary sculpture. Others have called it –'

'Grave-robbing?' he offers, frowning.

'Yes,' she says. It's so much easier now that he's said it for her. 'How would you describe this work?'

He is silent for a time, staring down at his hands. Nina notes the diver's watch he wears on one wrist and the plaited crimson thread around the other.

He looks her directly in the eye. 'I would describe the work as a form of self-portrait,' he says. 'Katy is both the subject and the artist. It's a portrait of despair and dark beauty. I am simply its copyist.'

Nina Fredericks is finding Adam Logan increasingly plausible. He has a way, she thinks, of giving meaning to things; when seen through his eyes, even suffering becomes aristocratic. If Katy is more than just a dead drug addict, then perhaps, in some small part of herself, Nina might make way for a nobler version of herself too. Inside her, dark stewy clumps of bad feeling recompose themselves as tight-closed flowers.

'It all started when I killed a cat,' Adam says.

Nina draws herself to attention.

'It was when I was at art school,' he continues. 'I'd been for a surf and I was driving home. It was the time of day the French call *entre le chien et le loup*. Meaning between the dog and the wolf. When the certainties of the day give way to the fears of the night. Dusk, in other words. A cat ran out onto the road. It was a black cat. It's almost as if the cat was meant to fall under my wheels.

'It was dead. I pulled the body to the side of the road and wrapped it in the towel I'd been using down the beach. I figured the cat had run out of a block of flats opposite and it seemed like the right thing to try to find its owner. I carried the dead cat up and down the stairs of those flats, knocking on every door, but I couldn't find its home. Back down on the ground I looked around me. It was almost dark. I –'

'I'm sorry, Adam,' says Nina suddenly, leaning over the table as if she has a cramp, 'I want to be able to concentrate on your story but first – can you tell me where the toilet is?'

The artist feels a sharp retraction within him. She should have waited a bit longer. He was telling her something important about himself.

'Down the corridor.' He gestures. 'Second door on the right.'

While Nina is gone, Adam looks out the window at the darkness and waits for the kettle to boil. He's not able to prevent his thoughts from wandering to the girl reporter. An image has formed in his mind of her buttocks over his toilet seat. He tries to breathe deeply.

He thinks perhaps this will have to be the last day of his cleansing diet. He wants to be pure and strong but perhaps this is not the day to make things hard for himself, what with the demands of the interview and everything that has happened with Marlo.

Marlo had answered the phone immediately. Abortion, he thought; he had wanted to be free of her and there he was, back in the cradle of her body.

'Hi,' he said.

'Who is this?' she asked.

He knew that she had been waiting. 'Pizza Express,' he wanted to say, 'did you want thin crust or regular?'

'Hello, Adam,' she said.

There were words he didn't want to use – baby, blood, conclusion, us – so he spoke in generalities, all the time sketching on paper, with an AW Faber-Castell Goldfaber 1221 H, a grid of tightly interlocking lines. He was relieved to hear that his voice carried its coffin of a subject ceremoniously forward even as his mind performed clownish, defensive back-flips away from it.

'Would you like me to come with you?' he asked. 'Do you need any money?'

'I'll be all right,' she said.

'Are you sure?'

He noted the hesitation before her answer. He listened care-fully.

'Yes,' she said.

It was then that he knew he could use any word he wanted, because Right was packing up its belongings and marching straight over that big old line between them, to take up camp on *his* side.

'Marlo,' he said, 'are you telling me the truth about this abortion?'

He heard her breath catch on the other end of the line. There was a long pause.

'No,' she whispered at last, in a guilty child's voice.

He remembered the way she dipped her long finger deli-cately into his anus, the tiny scratch of her fingernail as it withdrew. He felt exultant. His mind stopped its somersaulting and the pencil paused on the page. She had all his attention.

'Why would you lie to me about something like that?' he asked.

'I just wanted you to react,' she said. And then she began a quiet, shamed weeping.

Now that he was finding this out, he was surer than ever about letting her go.

'It was an ugly thing to do,' she whispered. 'I know that. I'm sorry.'

It was not hard to give a little, now that the scales had tipped so heavily in his favour. 'Perhaps I handled things badly,' he said.

Her crying deepened. 'What happened?' she asked. 'It was going so well. And then all of a sudden you were gone. What was I supposed to do with all my . . . *feelings*?'

'Look,' he said, 'we'll probably just do more damage if we get into that stuff. It seems we're both sorry, let's leave it at that.'

'Are you sorry?' her voice trembled.

'I just said I was, didn't I?'

He regretted the note of impatience, but what could he do?

The kettle has boiled but he can't face another water and lemon. He doubts now that he can get through the evening without something to eat. The reporter is taking her time. He is still nursing the bruise he suffered when she interrupted his story.

He opens the fridge and looks for food. As he slices cheese on the bench, he wonders about the hurt Marlo felt when he cancelled their intimacy. The two bruises hang side by side in his mind, like two stained shirts on a line. He recalls her awful crying on the phone. He hadn't wanted that. It was just that he'd only ever really known her within the terms that he knew himself, and he didn't think he'd been unkind. For as long as he could remember, this had been a great puzzle to him, this getting inside another's skin. He feels what he feels. She feels whatever it is she feels. All they can do is hang alongside each other on the line.

Nina emerges from the hallway wiping her hands on her skirt. The relief of having an empty bladder and of seeing him now, bent over the bench in an act of food preparation, makes her forget herself.

'Food!' she exclaims. 'Great idea!'

Actually, he had been preparing a snack for himself, but he sees no harm in taking down another plate and putting together something for her too. There are green apples, and a last bit of vodka, and from inside some white deli paper at the back of the fridge, a few slices of ham.

Adam and Nina sit at the kitchen table and eat with their fingers, in hungry, concentrated silence, small pieces of food from little flowered plates, like children at a nursery tea. Fatty smudges cloud their vodka glasses. When finally their plates are empty and the liquor gone, they look up to see that, in line with their own inner feeling of warmth and well-being, the other is glowing too. There's fresh energy in the room.

'So,' says Nina. 'It was getting dark and you'd tried all the flats without luck. You were on the ground holding the dead cat in your beach towel. Then what happened?'

He smiles at her. 'I didn't know what to do,' he says, crossing his legs, settling. 'You can imagine. But then I saw a row of rubbish bins belonging to the flats. Most of them were full but one wasn't, so I put the cat in. I put the towel in too. I knew it wasn't the best ending for the cat but –' His hands open outward into the air.

'That night I couldn't forget about it. I lay in bed and imagined the cat curled up cold in the garbage. I felt I should do something – rescue the cat, but rescue *us* too – claim something back from this throwaway society.'

Nina is not sure that she's keeping up, but her tape-recorder is on.

'Before sunrise I drove back to the flats and found the right bin and pulled the cat out. I took it home, and bagged it, and popped it in the freezer. The next day, or maybe the day after that, I hunted down my sculpture lecturer at college and learnt from him all I could about the techniques of casting.'

I could never be an artist, thinks Nina, feeling this as a lack within herself; a failure of imagination, and courage. I could never keep a cat in the fridge.

'I've got one of the early wax casts here,' says Adam, pushing back his chair. 'I'll show you.'

For the purposes of the interview Nina is not sure she needs to see an old wax cat, but she expresses interest anyway, and while he is in another part of the flat making banging and scraping sounds, she clears the plates and glasses from the table and carries them over to the sink. She doesn't much like cats, she finds them sharp and creepy; she wonders sometimes if she might not unconsciously be suppressing a bad experience she once had with one.

Adam sets a cardboard box down on the kitchen table. Nina leans against the sink and watches him lift from it a yellowy, cat-sized shape. Even at a distance she feels the same tug of attraction that she felt in the presence of Katy's replica body.

Adam places the box on the ground and centres the cat on the pink laminex, turning it this way and that until he's satisfied that Nina is viewing the work at its best.

Nina is surprised by what she feels. The cast has captured the very essence of the cat: the triangular head sunk onto blind paws; the elegant curve of its body and the coiled spring within; its old Egyptian soul. Once more she marvels at the detail

Adam has preserved. There is so much life in this death, and the dull yellow wax only adds to its poignancy; an impermanent substance, as the cat had been, and therefore she is herself.

Adam watches her study the cat and thinks about how much better he feels. It's been good to get the old moggy out, and to witness again its power. It gives him a sense of continuity to see this early work; it helps him to assemble, if only for a short time, a more coherent sense of himself from the anxious fragments of which he feels largely composed. It is good to have company, to tell his stories, to find himself credible after all.

He feels a rush of good feeling for the girl reporter. If only she would stay a bit longer; she is telling him that he has changed her mind about cats. She is becoming pretty.

In the kitchen's naked light he can see that she has trouble with her skin. She has a rosy stippling along her girl's firm jawline and a pockmark as perfect as a sequin on her cheek. His mind moves to imagine her gone and the flat in silence, the dust lying thickly on the skirting boards, the thoughts of Marlo that will come crowding in. It is hours yet before he can get the paper. Tonight, loneliness is a hurdle he might not clear.

Nina watches him return the box to the table and carefully pack the cat away. Now that everything has relaxed a bit she wonders if he might be open to a more personal line of questioning, because she wants to know how an artist lives. He's already told her that he spent all of a small inheritance on making Katy, and that he is worried about when it will sell. A museum in Boston had seriously considered it but the deal fell through. She knows herself, as a freelancer, how hard it is to pay bills and have something left over for a few of the nice things in life, and she imagines – she can see the scraping-together all around her in this flat – that it is even harder for someone in his line of work. He had come from obscurity, had been in a few group shows previously, won some minor prizes and a grant, but nothing like the success that Katy had brought.

She waits until he has taken his chair and then she sits down again. Once more they face each other across the empty table. Nina is thinking about how she might word it.

'Did you have a happy childhood?' he asks suddenly.

Nina looks at him, and adjusts to the shifting of ground.

'No, it wasn't very happy,' she says, feeling the catch in her throat.

It was the right question, thinks Adam.

'What was your father like?'

For a moment Adam thinks that she is not going to answer but then she shifts her gaze to a point on the wall behind him, and speaks.

'Big man, little man,' she says.

Her words have the dull shine of wear, and he wonders if she's used them before.

Her father is a businessman, she tells him. He wears good suits and expensive aftershave. She has a weak mother and two sisters, and he bullies them all.

'How has it affected you?' asks Adam.

'Oh, you know, trust issues, power issues, body issues, fear.'

He listens. He turns his attention on her.

Parts of Nina Fredericks' body are moving unbidden towards him. First one shoulder, and then the other, tilts forward. A clip slides down her hair. Her thin fingers in their rings of low order gemstones trace ever widening circles over his tabletop.

It's the most natural thing in the world now to reach out and touch her.

'It's been a long day,' he says quietly. 'Why don't we lie down for a while?'

In the bedroom, Adam turns on the small TV that rests on the Coke crate at the foot of his bed. When they are lying side by side on his futon, he puts his arm around her, and she wishes he hadn't. It's too old-fashioned, it makes her feel too girly. She lifts herself on one elbow and looks at him. He has pores now, and capillaries.

'I have a tiny bit of thrush,' she says, 'so it's probably best if you don't go down on me.'

'Fine,' he replies, pushing briefly at her hair before returning his eyes to the television.

She lies on her back again. With his free arm he lifts the remote and changes the channel.

'Hey, it's *The Dead Zone*,' he says. 'I love this film. Stephen King, Christopher Walken.'

The net curtain at the window lifts in the breeze.

'Is that the ocean I can hear?' Nina asks.

'Traffic,' he says.

She has put her head on his arm in such a way that his hand can only fumble at her fringe. An ad comes on.

'What about the other?' he says.

'Other what?'

'Fucking,' he says.

'Oh, that's OK,' she says. 'It's only an itch.'

'Well, then,' he says, moving over her, 'perhaps I should scratch it.'

The joke is feeble, and she's heard it before. Where have his elegant words gone? All the lights in her body go out. She wishes, for a moment, that she wasn't there. But perhaps it's her fault for saying it? Perhaps she expects too much?

Adam's mouth finds hers.

'*What was it like?*' she imagines Amy asking at lunch.

Adam is on top of her, inside her, and her attention wanders to the curtain and the conversation she will have with her friend the next day. She will start by telling Amy what Adam looks like.

'What was it like?' she thinks. 'What was it like?'

'Well,' she imagines herself saying, 'it was a bit like the transaction that takes place between an iron and an ironing board.'

Amy will laugh. And then she won't. 'Never mind,' Amy will say. 'Maybe it will be better next time, you know how first times are. You can't expect too much.'

Adam comes quietly. He breathes on her neck for a while and then lifts himself. *The Dead Zone* is back on and he twists at the waist so that he can see the screen.

He is still inside her. In the flickering light Nina studies his chest and shoulders. She is still wanting. She tightens the muscles of her vagina around him. He smiles weakly in the direction of the television and with the hand that's not fumbling for the remote, dabs at her navel. She is waiting. He watches Christopher Walken suffer one of his premonitions and then he turns around and pulls out of her, his hand clamped around the condom.

'I'm going to have a shower,' he says.

Nina cannot calculate in exactly how many ways she has been insulted. She feels open, unclosed. She should leave; when he gets out of the shower she should be gone. But perhaps it's not really as bad as it seems?

She stretches across the bed and switches off the TV. Perhaps when he comes back it will be different. Or in the morning, when they are not so tired. It is, after all, the end of a long, hot day.

He comes into the bedroom with a thin towel around his waist and sits down on the edge of the bed.

'Can you lie straight, please?' he says, glancing at her foot.

She shifts and draws the sheet over her.

'How will you get home?' he asks, extracting his underpants from the jeans he has picked up from the floor.

She has been stupid, she thinks, really stupid. In the light of day, how will she reckon with her professionalism?

'I'll get a taxi,' she replies.

'There's a cab rank on the corner,' he says. 'I need to buy a paper. I'll walk down with you.'

The street is quiet and dark. They walk for a time in silence, the width of the pavement between them, but when they turn the corner the lights of the 24 Hour are bright and there are people moving listlessly after the heat of the day. There is fresh rubbish everywhere and a streetsweeper moving slowly down the road.

Adam is wearing a blue T-shirt and his hair is wet from the shower and he seems to Nina like the artist again, the one she had known across the kitchen table, but could not find in bed. She walks closer to him now, and leaves her hand by her side whereby he might take it, or touch her with emphasis.

'Did you know that people have been leaving things at the gallery?' he says, as they cross the road. 'Things for Katy?'

'What kind of things?' she asks.

'Flowers, cards with stuff written on them, soft toys, once a cross on a gold chain. The people at the gallery have collected a box full of it. But they don't want it talked about. They say it could become cultish.'

Nina thinks of Katy; Vaselined and plastered and resined and gold-leafed into eternity.

'But I don't see the problem if it's known that some people find the work moving,' continues Adam, looking at her.

'I suppose there's no problem with a moment of genuine expression,' says Nina. 'But these things can get kind of whipped up, hysterical. You don't want it to turn into a circus.'

Adam stops in the street and turns to her. 'It's nothing like a circus,' he says, digging his hands into his pockets.

'I'm not saying it is. But what do you think Katy would want?'

He bristles. She had forgotten not to speak of Katy.

'I think she'd like to know that people cared,' he says.

'I guess it's complicated,' says Nina.

'What's so complicated about it? Don't you think it's something your readers would want to know about?'

She is suddenly tired; dog-tired. She will have to sleep in.

They come to a stop outside the 24 Hour.

'This is where I get the paper,' says Adam, and then gestures down the road. 'The cab rank's just there.'

Nina thanks Adam Logan for the interview. He tells her that it's been a pleasure, and he leans so heavily on the word, his gaze is so direct, that once more she is open to him. She will send him the article, she thinks. He will like it, and they will talk about her writing and about her feelings this night, and they will try again.

She hands him her card, and he kisses her lightly on the cheek.

She still smells sweet, he thinks, turning away. How do girls do it?

Inside the hard light of the 24 Hour, everyone looks like a convict.

The paper is there. Christ, it's there. He has been waiting for this article for weeks now. He'd met Wes Allen on a Thursday at the Crown of Thorns. They'd eaten steaks, shared a joke about those that didn't, and drunk red wine and beer.

Wes Allen had been overweight and a little too sure of himself. But he'd leaned back in his chair and listened in silence while Adam spoke about his work, moving only to refresh their glasses.

Adam takes the paper outside and searches through its pages until he finds the arts section. He puts his back to the wall and squats. He sees the photograph of himself, unsmiling, as is appropriate.

The article is headed 'New Kid on the Block'. Alarm bells ring but just small ones; wind chimes, really. Katy lies on a block, it's simply an unfortunate pun, no need to panic. He reads:

In all the dinner party talk, in all the words around the water cooler, the question is surely not whether any artist should manipulate a dead body in order to make their art (and, admittedly, Adam Logan achieves some superb effects in Katy's Gone) *but whether it's OK, whether it is ever OK, decent even, in these indecent times, to render another's damage and waste as beautiful? When confronted by Adam Logan's sensationalism, one can't help but think of the sobriety and the quietude of Henry Moore . . .*

Adam feels like he's been kicked in the stomach. He feels like throwing up, in the gutter, like the old wino he sees out of the corner of his eye.

What did Wes Allen know? Didn't he know how to stand in front of a work of art and feel something; feel it viscerally, spiritually? What does he believe in, this fat man with his desperate hold on truth and power? The fat man in history, the fat man who thinks he *owns* history.

The streetsweeper labours futilely on. Tomorrow there will be more shit on the street. Here and now is an old wino. Here and now are two women, kissing in the half-light. Is Wes Allen here? Does *he* see this? It's two a.m. and where is he now? In his safe bed troubling his menopausal wife with his snoring? Fat in the throat, that's what causes it. Fat outside, and fat inside too. Those that can, do; those that can't, *review*.

Adam tears out the page that contains the article and shoves it into the pocket of his jeans. He will have to reply, but how does he reply?

He walks over to the bin outside the 24 Hour and dumps the rest of the newspaper there. He wishes he wasn't alone, that Nina hadn't gone. Maybe she would have comforted him, reminded him of old men and their envy.

The fat man is *ancient* history.

He crosses the road on the red light, the wino watching him from the shadows. When Adam is gone, the man shuffles his way to the rubbish bin. He pulls out what Adam has put in. There's a whole newspaper to read. Today's news, fresh, all of it.

His hands shake over the pages. He unfolds the paper and holds the front page close to his face where he can read it.

There are children dead, on the front page. Six children dead, and two women, and one child escaped.

He has his own children, somewhere.

A man takes his car and runs them all down, his twin sons too. Can that be? How can that be? There's a photograph: a roller-door, a car in a garage – where the man died, where the man killed himself – and he knows those cars, they fill up the road as if they own it.

His wife took his babies away, a long time ago. Where were his own babies tonight?

The Seventh Child

THE MORNINGS ARE COLD, but there's no shock now when Pearl wakes. She knows where she is and what has happened and that nothing will change it.

She pulls a blanket from her bed and drags it into the lounge room. There's a television there, a new one, and in the kitchen there's a microwave. The microwave heats her Chocmilk so quickly her feet hardly have time to get cold on the floor. New things appear in the flat now and Pearl knows that, in one way or another, they are all because Riley is dead. The television was a gift from the TV people who came to the flat to ask her questions.

'I feel sad for the children,' she said. 'And for Trish and Bree.'

She was urged to say more, and Lily was disappointed in her, but no other words came.

The television was so big it had to stand on the floor. From her place on the couch, Pearl learned from the TV exactly what happened as she lay curled on the floor of the Kombi and the man went insane in his car outside. She watched all day and into the night, while Lily slept. She saw again the faces of the dead children and the two playleaders she had liked. The mother of one of the little girls said that Kahlia had just learnt to whistle. The twins' teacher called Harrison and Denzil true gentlemen. People were trying to understand, she saw that.

She saw herself. She hadn't known that her hair was so long in comparison with her face. Some people thought that the deaths were the car's fault. She saw the Prime Minister and the counsellor with the moles on his face who talked to her at the hospital. They were not pronouncing the name of the Eric Cahill Oval correctly. It was Carl, not Kay-hill, she knew that. Some people thought it was the fault of divorce.

On every channel a man wearing a blue bow-tie talked about the murderer, and why he had shaved his head. She thought that what he was saying was wrong, but she didn't know in exactly what way it was wrong, and she didn't know how important it was, or even if it was important at all.

And then it all stopped. The pictures, the talking. It all disappeared.

There had never been Chocmilk in the fridge before, or chicken nuggets or Vienetta Roll. Now there were all these things, and perfumed tissues in the bathroom and soft, patterned toilet paper and soap from a bottle.

'People have been kind,' was all Lily said.

The people who opened the Kombi door were kind.

Everything was quiet outside. The sounds of the car and

the children had stopped. She'd heard the man driving away fast, across the oval. Her eyes stared at the child's sock and the ice-cream wrapper on the floor. There were small stones and grass on the rubber mat on which her cheek lay. *Drumstick*, she read, *peppermint*. She didn't think of moving; the little space fitted her so well.

When the door opened she smelled petrol and grass and heard a man and a woman speaking. The man's arms lifted her. He leaned into the cabin of the Kombi and she heard him bang his head on the door. He was carrying her and his hand was over her eyes but it didn't matter, she knew.

The man laid her on the backseat of a car. The car smelled of fish and chips, and her head was lifted and placed in the woman's lap. The woman's hand stroked her hair. She heard a key turning, and humming, and all the windows went up. Cool air moved over her face. She looked up and saw the man outside. He had a phone held up to his ear and red all over the sleeve of his shirt. Underneath her cheek the woman's skirt was wet.

Where was the crystal? The crystal was still in her hand, where it couldn't make colours.

She had dropped to the floor of the Kombi and curled up tight. The twins' father didn't know she was there; she had seen it in the mask of his face as he raced the screaming machine towards Trish and Bree and the children. She knew the huge, crushing will of adults, their tears and their rage. She knew that Riley's jumper made him easy to see.

She was carried from the Kombi, and the ambulance carried her too. Wheels carried her down corridors beneath long tubes of light. She was lifted onto a hospital bed and a nurse laid a cotton blanket over her. The blanket was white.

A woman wearing a police uniform came into the room but Pearl knew from the look on her face that she wasn't really a policewoman. She thought the nurse knew this too. Then there was orange juice in her hand, it was the brightest thing in the room. She had coloured orange on her paper and then the children ate it. The woman in the police uniform leaned close and asked for her name and address.

The nurse mopped at the orange juice on the blanket. 'I'll get you a straw,' she said. 'I won't be a second.'

There wasn't a window. There was only one chair. She couldn't think what colour it was and then she knew, it was mouse.

The room and the world outside were without Riley. She hadn't wanted this to happen but now that it had it wouldn't be long. She would have to go with him, as she had always done.

She heard her name. Her eyes opened.

Her mother was standing by the bed. A nurse held Lily's arm and a policeman stood behind her, as if she was going to fall. Lily was wearing a shirt over her bikini top, and her face was red and ruined.

Pearl felt Lily's sadness slowly filling up her chest. One by one, she felt the doors to Riley closing within her. She reached out to hold her mother's shaking hands.

'We've lost him, Pearlie,' Lily wept.

The days begin the same way now. Pearl drinks hot Chocmilk under the blanket on the couch and watches Judge Judy. No-one talks about school anymore. When the program is finished she turns the TV off and goes to the kitchen and makes coffee and takes it to Lily in bed. Sometimes she will watch TV again or she'll go to her room and lie down on the unmade bed and practise what Dr Sanderson has taught her. Feel your toes. Feel your toes growing warm and relaxed. Let your toes go loose. And then your feet. Feel your feet.

But today is Tuesday, the day they have a visitor. Pearl waits until Lily is sitting up in bed with the mug of coffee in her hands and then she goes to get ready. The blue plastic step that Riley stood on to clean his teeth is still in the bathroom. She washes her hair in the shower. Since he died they have a different shampoo and conditioner and she doesn't have a problem with tangles anymore. In her bedroom she combs her wet hair and fixes it with a mauve headband, and puts on her denim mini and a skinny pink jumper.

Her mother gets up slowly and pulls on her grey track pants. Pearl can't understand why Lily doesn't dress properly for Anna Zanetti's visit; she doesn't even clean her teeth or brush her hair. When Anna arrives and kisses Lily at the door, Pearl wonders if her mother smells all right. Anna kisses Lily on the cheek and sometimes her mother sits through the whole visit with Anna's lipstick on her face.

Anna bends at the knees to kiss Pearl, she doesn't swoop from above. Up close, her lipstick is dark red and there are lines above her top lip. When Anna straightens there's a cracking sound in her knees. 'My old bones,' she says.

Anna Zanetti has been visiting Lily and Pearl since Riley died. Lily has told Pearl that Anna is from a Support Group, and that when she and Anna are talking, Pearl must find something to do.

From the couch Pearl can see the two women sitting at the kitchen table, the small heater glowing at their feet. She has one hand keeping warm under the blanket and the other controlling the volume on the TV so that she can hear what Anna and Lily are saying. From the moment Anna first walked into their kitchen, Pearl has heard every word that's been said. She knows Anna's story.

Anna Zanetti had only one child, a daughter who was twenty-two years old. Tania worked in a florist's shop, and she was saving to have a shop of her own. Anna and Tania spoke on the phone every day, but there came a time when Tania didn't call and Tania's boyfriend told Anna that she had gone away with another man. Your daughter isn't who you think she is, he said. But Anna knew that something was wrong. Her bank account and credit card were still being used. The police said they would look into it but Anna feared that the police would believe Tania's boyfriend because he was a good cricketer, and he had a nice boat.

Anna wasn't sure what she knew, but she had a feeling.

For a week the world went on as if nothing had happened but Anna didn't sleep anymore. She wandered around the house in the dark. She couldn't lie awake beside her husband while he slept; how could he sleep when their child was gone?

One night while Anna was watering the herbs she decided that it was wrong that Tania's boyfriend should be resting when she could not. She waited. At three in the morning, Anna called Tania's number and when she heard the boyfriend's sleepy voice on the line she stayed quiet. It felt good. It was the first time she'd felt good since Tania disappeared. So when he hung up, she called again. And again. She called until finally he took the phone off the hook, and then she lay down and slept.

The next morning Tania's boyfriend rang her, as she hoped he would.

'I know it was you,' he said.

Deborah Robertson

'What are you talking about?' asked Anna Zanetti. Her cat was on her knees for comfort.

'The phone calls. In the middle of the night. Someone there but not saying anything,' he said.

'Maybe it was Tania,' said Anna, stroking the cat. 'Maybe she's sorry but can't find the words to say it.'

She listened carefully then. She listened to Tania's boyfriend slowly strangling himself with words of his own.

That night, while her husband slept, Anna rested in the recliner in the lounge room and listened to Pavarotti. But the next night she made the calls to Tania's boyfriend again. On the third night his phone was off the hook so she sat at the dining room table with a pen and a pad of paper, and made a list of all the ways in which she might drive him out of his mind. The next day she asked her old schoolfriend Diana Kimble for help, and Diana's son, Jamie, drove to Anna's house in his lunch hour later the same day.

Yes, it was possible to send untraceable emails, Jamie told her. In fact, he would do it for her himself. If Anna wrote down the things she wanted to say, he would go to an Internet cafe and send an email to Tania's boyfriend straight away.

'Aunty,' said Jamie as he was leaving, 'I know Tansie wouldn't just go off like that. Let's see what this creep's up to.'

Every day in his lunch hour Jamie went to the Internet cafe and called Anna on his mobile phone. Anna had composed the words the night before, sitting alone in the lounge room after her husband had gone to bed.

She pretended to be Tania. She was sorry she had run away. She wanted to come back. She wanted him to forgive her. Anna and her daughter had been best friends. They had talked about everything. Tania's boyfriend had said that there were things Anna didn't know about her daughter, but there were things that Tania's boyfriend didn't know Anna knew about him. He didn't like Tania taking a shower alone. He liked his clothes laid out for him every morning on a well-made bed. Babydoll, he called her, in moments of love. Anna put all these things she knew into the emails that were sent to Tania's boyfriend. Jamie printed his replies and every afternoon after work he took them to Anna. They knew they were under his skin when he started to use capitals: I KNOW YOUR NOT MY TANIA GO AWAY.

Sometimes Jamie stayed for dinner. One night, two weeks after the emailing had begun, he was fixing her a brandy and dry, when Anna kissed him on the cheek.

'You've been a big help to me, Jamie,' she said.

Jamie put down the dry ginger ale and wrapped his arms around her.

'You know me, Aunty,' he said. 'Any excuse to give someone the shits.'

That night Anna and Jamie ate chicken cacciatore on the verandah under the crimson bougainvillea. Anna's husband was at his backgammon club.

'The chicken's delicious,' said Jamie.

'It's Tania's recipe,' said Anna. 'Hers is better than mine.'

'We should take some to Bozo,' said Jamie, and he laughed.

After a moment, Anna put down her knife and fork.

'Why not?' she said. 'I'm sure he's missing her cooking.'

Anna put a serving of chicken and a small garden salad on a picnic plate and covered it with aluminium foil.

The plate was warm in her lap as they drove to Tania's house. Her boyfriend's car wasn't there but the porch light was on. It hurt Anna to see the long weeds in the garden and the roses dead. Tania always had flowers in the house. Jamie took the plate from Anna and sprinted across the unmown lawn and up the front steps.

On the drive home, Anna and Jamie agreed that Tania's boyfriend would expect another home delivery, and that he would be on the lookout.

But later that night, Anna still couldn't sleep. Where is all this taking me? she thought. She lay next to her sleeping husband and felt herself falling. In the dark she remembered how her daughter smelled of flowers and earth and J'adore. She remembered her fierce embrace. How would this pursuit of Tania's boyfriend lead her to the truth? Perhaps it was she who would lose her mind.

She struggled to control her tears, for fear of waking her husband. But then she felt Leo move, she felt him roll onto his back. They were side by side in the dark.

'Take my hand, Anna,' he said suddenly, and she smelled his stale breath in the air.

The heat of his hands always surprised her.

'I'm sorry I woke you,' she said.

'I wasn't asleep,' he said. 'I never sleep.'

'Oh,' said Anna.

She would stop, she decided. It would be over.

The next day Anna drove to another suburb for an aroma-therapy massage that Diana Kimble had booked for her. She couldn't stop the tears that flowed when a stranger touched her in the little room with the tea lights and burning oil and music of rain. Her tears ran from the corners of her eyes into her ears. The woman stroked the sides of Anna's neck with her thumbs.

'Just try to be here,' the woman said.

Later, as Anna pulled into her driveway, she saw that there was someone at her front door.

'I was just leaving my card, Mrs Zanetti,' the young man said.

Anna had seen him before. He was a detective she had spoken to when Tania first disappeared.

'I'd like to talk to you,' he said, offering to take her groceries.

She fitted her key into the door lock. He had dark hair and eyes and he was wearing a smart suit. He was a man she'd have liked for Tania.

They sat on the lounge.

'This is good coffee,' he said.

'It's from East Timor,' said Anna.

'That's good. Good for East Timor, I mean.'

'Yes,' said Anna.

'Mrs Zanetti,' said the detective, 'your daughter's fiancé alleges that you've been harassing him.'

'He's not her fiancé. It would never have lasted.'

'Mrs Zanetti?'

Why not tell the truth? thought Anna. She wasn't afraid of trouble; trouble had already come.

'I've made some phone calls,' she said. 'At night. And sent some emails.'

'And left a meal on his doorstep?'

'Is that such a terrible thing to do?'

'Chicken cacciatore?'

'Yes.'

'Why did you do these things, Mrs Zanetti?'

'Because my daughter has gone and no-one will help me.'

'But why harass Mr Johnston?'

'Because I think he's hiding something.'

'What makes you think that?'

'A mother's intuition.'

The detective put his cup and saucer on the coffee table next to the family of brass elephants.

'I have a lot of respect for a mother's intuition, Mrs Zanetti,' he said.

When Pearl first heard Anna tell Lily her story, the two women were sitting at either end of the couch with their legs crossed because they didn't know each other well yet. Pearl was at the kitchen table drawing, and stealing long looks at them.

At this point Anna's voice had wavered: 'That's what he said to me, Lily. I have a lot of respect for a mother's intuition. That's all it took, one good person.'

Lily sucked on her bottom lip and nodded.

Tania's body had never been found, because after her boyfriend stabbed her he dumped her at sea. The good-looking detective told Anna that once they had the DNA from the bathroom and boat, it hadn't been difficult to break him. 'When I found her in the shower that night, I knew she must've been washing off another man,' her killer confessed.

'Prison's too good for him,' said Anna. 'You're lucky, Lily, that your monster did the right thing and killed himself.'

Pearl watched as her mother uncrossed her legs and hugged them to her chest.

'You're lucky to still have your little girl,' Anna added.

Pearl dropped her eyes to the page because she didn't want to see the look on her mother's face.

At the end of her visit that day, Anna was standing in the kitchen saying goodbye to Lily, when she looked at Pearl sitting at the table and a soft look came into her eyes.

'Would you like some Tic Tacs, Pearl?' she said, rummaging around in her bag.

It was Riley who liked Tic Tacs – Pearl didn't really see what could be so good about something as small as a Tic Tac – but she said thank you anyway and now every week, at the end of her visit, Anna pretends that she is searching for her keys and sunglasses in her red handbag and then she says: 'What's this? I don't know how this got here.'

It might be a roll of chocolates or soaps from a hotel or a piece of wedding cake in a satiny bag.

'I suppose I'll just have to give it to Pearl,' Anna says.

When Anna is preparing to leave, Pearl tries hard to be busy and to keep her face very still. She doesn't want to be seen to be expecting anything. Because this could end at any moment: Anna might decide not to bring her little things anymore, or she might simply forget that she ever had.

It's not just Anna and Lily, there are other eyes too. It feels as if the whole world is watching; as if the whole world would turn away in disgust if she was to show one single sign of disappointment.

Lily is sitting too close to the heater. Pearl watches her from the couch. She will get a headache or worse – it's happened before – when she stands up, she'll faint. On the TV screen two men are cooking. Anna is taking photographs out of her bag. Pearl knows that they are photographs of what Anna has called the Memorial Day.

Anna has been talking about this day for weeks.

'When you don't have a body to bury there's just this emptiness,' Anna said.

When Pearl heard Anna say this she thought of Riley's ashes under her mother's bed. They would do something nice with them one day, Lily promised.

Anna had told Lily that she needed a marker to say that Tania had once been alive. 'I just wanted a reminder on the earth, somewhere I could go and talk to her,' she said.

Tania's boss at the florist's shop had given Anna a white rosebush in Tania's memory. Anna and her husband planted it, and Diana and Syd Kimble helped with a small ceremony. Anna tried hard to make the rosebush a special place. Every morning she poured coffee into her favourite cup and carried it on its saucer across the verandah and down the steps to the backyard. Leo had bought a stone bench and placed it beside the rosebush. Anna sat down and sipped her coffee, and waited patiently to find Tania there.

Her cup emptied. Sometimes she tried to speak but the words were not like the words that had passed between mother and daughter as they strolled together through shopping centres or attended to small domestic tasks, each in her own home, the telephone held between bent head and shoulder, doing their necks no good but unwilling to let go, for the words to end. *Are you still there, Mum?* Yes, darling, I am still here.

The stone bench hurt her back.

'I saw a dress that you would love,' Anna said once, to the air around the rosebush. The air said nothing but in the nothingness came an awful realisation. She had forgotten – if Tania had been alive, she might have disagreed. 'You're kidding,' she might have said. 'You wouldn't catch me dead in that.'

Tania had been twenty-two years old. She'd been in the

business of proving to the world that it was not safe to make assumptions about her. Now that she was gone, Anna would never again be surprised by wonderful, undeniable evidence of her daughter's difference from her.

No matter how hard she wished it to be otherwise, Anna was talking to herself.

Anna began to think about the white crosses people placed at the sites of fatal road accidents. Sometimes there were plastic flowers, and if the death were recent, real ones. Each one of the crosses said: I was here; and here is where I lost my life.

But Anna couldn't place a white cross on the shore where Tania's boyfriend had told the police he launched his boat and headed out to sea with her body. A single white cross against the vastness of water and stretching white sand would only echo the loneliness of her death.

One morning when Anna was out walking she came to a park where Tania had played as a child. The trees were bigger but not much else had changed. Children were still playing on the swings. Anna looked carefully at the park. She looked at the weeping willow at the edge of the lake and imagined a little seat beneath it. A wooden seat, something simple, with a plaque bearing Tania's name and a few words about her life. It would be somewhere cool and shady for people to sit, or for someone to read a book. Anna could sit on this seat herself – it was not very far from home – and she wouldn't try to talk to Tania anymore, she would just watch the children and the movement of time through the trees.

Anna wrote to her local council and six weeks later she received a reply. Her request had been considered, the letter said, but unfortunately it was denied. Anna thought she might not have made herself clear. She wanted to *provide* the seat for the patrons of the park; the cost of the seat and any upkeep would, most certainly, be met by her. She wrote another letter and six weeks later she received another reply.

'Your first letter was clear, Mrs Zanetti,' it read. 'Unfortunately, yours is not the only request we have received of this kind. We cannot meet one, without having to meet them all.'

Anna thought of all the letters written; all the beloved gone.

Every now and then the young detective came by for coffee. Anna noticed changes in him: a new definition in his features, softening around his waist, and finally a gold wedding band. The world had moved on. Somewhere, in a place she didn't know, a lovely young woman took this man in her arms. The thought made her unbearably sad.

Anna and the detective spoke only of Tania's case. Each time the same things were said, but it didn't feel like repetition or that there was nothing else to say, only that the detective was helping her to believe something which could not yet be believed. But on one visit, shortly after the council's rejection of the memorial seat, Anna began a new conversation.

'If only she had a grave,' Anna said. 'There's nowhere for her to rest.'

'And nowhere for you?' asked the detective.

'And nowhere for me,' said Anna.

One afternoon, a little while later, the detective rang Anna. She was lying under a blanket on her bed. It was one of the bad days.

'I've been thinking since I saw you, Anna,' he said. 'About what you said about Tania having no place to rest and nowhere for you to visit her?'

'Yes?' said Anna, drawing herself up on the pillows.

'It's something us detectives talk about too – the lack of a body. We can see what that does to people, and it doesn't do us much good either.'

The detective went on to say that in his years on the force he had seen it more times than he'd have liked, the certainty of a crime having been committed and of the victim never coming back, but the absence of the deceased's body. Some of the men who had been longer on the job said they were the cases you couldn't forget.

'I've been thinking,' he said, 'that a memorial might help.'

'A memorial?' said Anna.

'Yes. A memorial for victims of crime whose bodies have never been recovered.'

Anna felt a wave of panic rise within her. She didn't want Tania to be placed in the company of others; she mourned her, and her alone. There would be many different types of people commemorated by a memorial such as this – people who may even have contributed to their own demise.

'I'm not sure, Danny,' Anna said. 'What if it was a memorial just for the young women?'

There was a long pause on the line.

'That leaves out a lot of people, Anna,' he said finally. 'Young men, kids, parents like yourself, even a few old people. I think we'd be accused of discrimination.'

She didn't want to be accused of that. But Danny had surprised her; somehow she had always felt that he paid her close attention because he understood how special Tania was, had maybe been just a little bit in love with her, not in an unsavoury way, just that he felt fully how much had been lost. Now he was suggesting that she was just one of many, and that she should be remembered that way.

'Look, Anna,' he said, 'you don't have to like the idea right away. Plenty of others didn't.'

'You've spoken to others?'

'Well, yes.'

There were others, she thought. Tania was not special, and neither was she.

'Anna?'

'Yes,' she said quietly.

'I'll send you details of a meeting. Just a few people, to talk. Tell Leo about it, see what he thinks.'

'I will, Danny. Thanks for the call.'

'Take care, Anna.'

'You too.'

Anna took drinks out onto the verandah. Her husband dragged off his work boots as he read the detective's letter on the table beside him.

'We should go,' he said, taking the can of beer from her.

Anna looked at his pink, tender feet. To find the humanity in one's enemy, she remembered, one need only look at their feet.

She had already told him she didn't like the idea of the memorial.

'You have backgammon on Wednesday nights,' she said, pulling his hardened socks out of his boots.

'She was happy in a crowd,' said Leo, 'she loved being with people.'

He cannot say her name, thought Anna, and I cannot stop saying it.

'Tania?' she said.

'She never liked being left out of anything. Do you think she'd like being left out?'

A sharp, living sense of her daughter came over Anna. It was true. She sat down heavily on a chair.

He remembers her better than me, she thought bitterly.

Anna sweeps the table free of cake crumbs before laying out the photos for Lily to see.

'That's the Police Commissioner, making his speech,' says Anna, pointing to one. As she glances up, she catches Pearl looking at her from the couch.

'You want to look at these photos too?' she says.

Pearl stands next to Anna and the heater warms the backs of her legs. In front of her are pictures of strangers, and the way they're dressed reminds her of Riley's funeral. She had heard Anna tell Lily that the Memorial for the Unrecovered was in a park in the city, and she can see grass and tall trees, many with red leaves.

'That's the memorial there,' says Anna.

Pearl looks closely at the group of photos that Anna indicates. She sees a huge metal standing-up wheel thing, in a kind of pond.

'The water trickles in here,' says Anna, pointing, 'and then the pressure builds up here, and these fill up and then tip over and the wheel goes around.'

Pearl can see water pouring from the wheel and the wet metal glistening in the sun.

'It's bronze,' says Anna.

'So does the wheel just go round and round?' asks Pearl.

'It never stops,' says Anna, looking at her. 'As long as there is water, it never stops.'

'What does it mean?' asks Pearl. She is aware that Lily is staring off into space.

'It means lots of different things. But for me, I guess, it means as long as I live, my love for Tania will never end.'

'Who thought of it?'

'Well, it was the detective's idea to have a memorial,' says Anna.

'No, I mean – who thought of the wheel and the water?'

'Oh, that was an architect and an engineer.'

'What are their names?'

'David and Felicity.'

'Did they lose their people's bodies too?'

'No, but we told them about our experiences.'

'But how did they know to make the water like love?'

'Well, I guess . . . they just used their imaginations.'

Lily scrapes back her chair and stands up.

'Has it helped?' Lily says.

'What?' says Anna, looking up at her.

Lily is filling the kettle. 'The memorial,' she says.

'Yes,' says Anna, looking down at the photos again. 'It's helped a lot.'

'You're lucky,' says Lily, rubbing her hands over her face. 'To have something that helps.'

In the taxi on the way to the Community Health Centre, Pearl looks at the people going about in the world. Small children walk along the streets with their mothers and people go in and out of shops and there are cars, cars, cars. She thinks of the children at school, who know nothing of this. She sits in the backseat behind the driver as she has been told to do. Lily is supposed to go with her when she sees Dr Sanderson, in case he wants to speak to her after he has talked to Pearl, but Lily was upset after Anna's visit that morning and she asked Pearl to go alone. The cab vouchers they use for these visits are kept in the top drawer in the kitchen. Pearl only had to tear two vouchers from the book, and call the taxi company – she didn't have to speak, they knew where she was – and go down the five flights of stairs and sit on the low brick wall at the front of the flats, and wait.

The Community Health Centre is made of bricks the colour of Milk Arrowroot biscuits. She gives one of the vouchers to the taxi driver and says thank you. She doesn't use her old shoulder bag anymore, the one she carried when Riley was alive. She just carries the cab vouchers and her door key in her hand.

She takes the lift to the third floor, where all the psychiatrists are. In the waiting room there is a large photograph of a snow-covered mountain, and toys on the floor. In one corner a revolving stand holds pamphlets about smoking, grief, insomnia, alcohol, depression, anxiety and drugs. Sometimes, Lily takes a few of these pamphlets home with her and puts them in the drawer with the cab vouchers.

There are only two old ladies in the waiting room today, reading magazines.

'Hiya, Pearl,' says the young woman behind the desk.

'Hello, Caitlin,' says Pearl.

'Where's your mum?' asks Caitlin.

'She's sick today.'

'Again? That's no good. Hey, I've got a mini-skirt on too.' She stands up so that Pearl can see her red tartan skirt.

'Those are nice boots,' says Pearl.

'I just got them,' says Caitlin.

'Is it nearly time to see Gus?' asks Pearl.

'He's been delayed at the hospital,' says Caitlin, 'but he won't be too long. Do you want to do some drawing or – oh, look, here he is now.'

Pearl looks behind her and sees Dr Sanderson walking through the door. Gus is a bit overweight. He wears T-shirts sometimes; Riley would have liked the one he wears with the farting dog. Today Gus is wearing jeans and a purple shirt that has white singlet showing at the buttons.

'Ah, the Pearly Queen,' Gus says, swinging his briefcase.

She doesn't really understand what this means but he has said it before and it makes her stomach flip with pleasure.

'No mama today?' he says.

'She's sick.'

'That's too bad,' says Gus. 'I'm going to ask Caitlin to rustle up a coffee. You want a hot chocolate?'

'Yes, please.'

'Do you mind?' he says to Caitlin. 'You two look like sisters in those skirts. Don't your legs get cold?'

'Nope,' they both say.

It's better when Lily isn't there, she knows everyone is thinking that. She will make it up to her, somehow, tonight.

Gus takes some books off a chair in his office so that she can sit down, then he sits in his chair opposite. On one of Pearl's first visits to Gus he had been leaning back in his chair, chewing his pen and talking, when the back of his chair suddenly collapsed, his feet shot up in the air and the back of his head banged on the desk behind him.

Pearl screamed. She jumped to her feet and the scream was like a thin, evil snake leaving her mouth. It was awful but she couldn't stop. Caitlin knocked on the door as Gus clambered to his feet.

'Just hold her, Cate, hold her tight,' Gus said, over the noise.

As soon as she felt Caitlin's arms around her, the screaming stopped. The doctor and his receptionist looked at her carefully.

'I just got a fright,' said Pearl.

'Me too,' Gus said, rubbing the back of his head. 'I feel like a good cry myself.'

'I wasn't crying,' said Pearl.

'A scream then, Miss Particular,' he said.

Pearl sat through the rest of her session with Gus that day with a sick feeling in her stomach. She knew what particular meant, but not exactly, and she suspected the name Miss Particular was a reprimand to her personality.

A few days later she went with her mother to the shopping centre. In the drawer with the cab vouchers there were other vouchers too, and Lily took one for a manicure. While her mother was at the beauty shop, Pearl went to the newsagents to look for a dictionary. She found the *Collins Dictionary*, the same as the one they had at school, and she took it off the shelf and knelt on the floor. The dictionary was heavy, so she placed it on the floor while she turned its pages in search of *particular*. When she eventually found the word she saw that there were many different meanings, but it was only the fourth definition that was the one she thought she was looking for: 'exacting or difficult to please, esp. in details; fussy'.

She sat back on her heels. Gus thought she was fussy, and difficult to please. She didn't think she was, she just liked things to be right, but Gus had said it and he was an expert about people. Lily thought it too, she could see that now. Lily said Pearl was always picking on her. She felt like crying.

She looked around her at the rows of magazines and remembered that this was where she had first lost Riley, a long time ago. She remembered him walking towards her, holding Matt's hand, and it seemed to her that she hadn't known anything then, that it was almost as if she was a baby.

Caitlin brings Gus his coffee and Pearl her hot chocolate. It's not really hot chocolate, it's Milo, but she would not say to anyone that there's a difference because that is an unattractive part of her; knowing the difference.

'I have to make a quick phone call,' Gus says.

Pearl sips from her mug. She has been coming here every week for three months now, since the day at the oval. Her mother has told her that the government is paying, because she has been traumatised. When she first came here the light through the window behind Gus was so strong she couldn't see him properly, but now she can see the greenish colour of his eyes and the odd silver hair twisting in his black curls.

There are thank you cards lined up along the top of a cupboard and posters of people she doesn't know on the walls. On a noticeboard above Gus's desk is a large photograph of a house.

Sometimes when she is in Gus's office Pearl doesn't know what to say, and so they just sit for a while. Gus sometimes draws on the notebook he rests on his knee, but Pearl always looks at the photograph.

The house stands in a forest of tall, straight trees, and it is built on top of a waterfall. Below the house the water pours over a ledge of rock and pools on another ledge until it spills once more, and joins a fast flowing stream. The rock looks ancient to her and the house seems to rise out of it, so that although the rock and the water belong to nature and the house to people, they appear to be one.

The house is built on different levels, like the rock. There are vertical stone sections, and shooting out from them – they are not really shooting because they do not move, but they have a force that makes her think of it – are balconies that are like huge trays, but also like the ledges of rock.

The house is made of right angles – it is a poem about right angles – and she needs to count them all, if she is to get her drawing right.

Gus says goodbye to the person on the telephone and sits down.

'How are you?' he says.

'Good,' says Pearl.

'Good,' he says.

His notebook comes out.

'Had any more nightmares?' asks Gus.

Pearl nods her head.

'Did you try what I suggested?'

Gus had told Pearl that she should try to draw what she sees in her nightmares. She doesn't want to tell him that this seems silly to her, because he will think that she is being difficult. The only thing she draws now is the beautiful house.

Pearl shrugs. A shrug is not a lie but it is not the truth either. She knows enough of Gus now to know that he will not question the meaning of a shrug.

She tells him about the present Anna gave her that morning – a small frame in the shape of a heart.

'Anna probably thinks I can put a picture of Riley in it,' she says. 'But I don't have one.'

Her mother had never owned a camera, she tells him, and the only photo of Riley was one that was taken at school and a newspaper still had it. Their grandmother might have the photos that Lily sent her, taken at a shopping centre when Pearl and Riley were small – they stood on some plastic grass in front of a picture of a horse so that it looked like a farm – but Lily wasn't sure, because her parents had stopped speaking to her when she ran away to do modelling.

'How do you feel about that?' asks Gus.

'What do you mean?' says Pearl.

'How do you feel about the fact that you have grandparents that you don't see?'

'It's all right.'

Gus writes something in his notebook. There is more that Pearl could say about her grandparents; sometimes she imagines visiting them and what their faces might look like, but she knows that Gus will want to talk about Lily then and when she gets home Lily will know, just from the look on her face.

'Who is Travis Bickle?' she asks. She hadn't intended to ask this, she had not even made up her mind if she ever would, but this happens sometimes in the silences in Gus's room, this sudden speaking of a secret. Her Milo is gone and she puts the empty mug on top of some books on the table in front of her.

'Travis Bickle?' says Gus, lifting his shaggy eyebrows. 'Sounds familiar. Who is he?'

'That's what I asked you,' says Pearl.

'Yes, but what I mean is – is this a person you've heard Lily, or maybe Anna, talk about? Someone you learnt about at school?'

'I just heard someone say something,' says Pearl.

'What were they saying about him?'

She doesn't want to tell Gus the whole story; she just wants to know about Travis so she can work the rest out for herself.

'It doesn't matter,' she says.

Gus looks at her carefully. 'Travis Bickle?' he says. 'Travis Bickle. It *is* a bit familiar. Not a common name.'

He puts his notebook on the table. It sits awkwardly against her empty mug so she leans forward to adjust it. She creates a neat right-angled triangle between the cover of the top book and the sides of the notebook and the mug, a triangle filled with the blue of Gus's jeans.

But suddenly Gus is on his feet. 'Let's Google him,' he says, 'and see what we get.'

Gus sits at his desk under the picture of the house. He mutters Trav-is Bick-le, Trav-is Bick-le, and hits the keys.

They wait.

'Of course!' says Gus excitedly, rolling back in his chair.

'What?' she asks.

He looks at her quickly.

'Travis Bickle is the name of someone in a film,' he says.

She is surprised, she hadn't imagined it to be anything like this.

'What film?' she asks.

'A film called *Taxi Driver*.' Gus is at the screen again, clicking in, looking closely. 'I saw it ages ago. Great film.'

'What's the film about?' she asks.

He looks at her as if he'd forgotten she was there. And then a worried expression crosses his face. He does a few more things at the computer and comes and sits down in his chair. The triangle is filled with denim again.

'Is this really what you want to talk about today?' Gus asks.

Pearl nods her head.

'Are you sure?'

'Yes.'

'OK,' says Gus. 'The film is about a taxi driver. Travis Bickle is the name of the taxi driver. It's set in New York.'

In her mind Pearl sees blue sky and the two towers falling.

'What happens?'

'I'm trying to remember exactly. The taxi driver is a lonely man and he's troubled. He drives all over the city at night and he's disgusted by all the crime and violence that he sees. He likes a girl but she doesn't like him and he just gets angrier and sadder, driving all over the city.'

'What else?'

Gus looks uncomfortable. 'It's a long story,' he says.

'What happens?'

'All right,' says Gus, sighing. 'He starts to sort of change, he buys lots of guns and gets ready to do something violent himself. Then he meets a young girl, only a few years older than you – that's Jodie Foster. Do you know Jodie Foster?'

'No,' says Pearl.

'Well, he meets this young girl and it's really bad because she's a prostitute who takes drugs and the people around her are terrible people.'

'Why is she doing that?'

'I guess she ran away from home. The people pretend to care for her but really they just want her to make them money. And Travis Bickle tries to help her get away but he can't – a few other things happen that I don't remember. He tries to kill a politician . . .'

'Why?'

'I'm not really sure. The girl he liked worked for the politician.'

'Was he her boyfriend?'

'No – but that's not the important part. The important part is that it just gets worse and worse in the taxi driver's mind and he goes and kills all the people who are mistreating the young girl.'

'How does he kill them?'

'He shoots them.'

'And does Jodie Foster get away?'

'Yes, she does.'

'And what happens to him?'

'I think he gets wounded in the shooting but he gets better and goes back to driving a taxi. And the girl's parents thank him for rescuing their daughter.'

'Is it a happy ending?'

'Not really, because you know that there's still something wrong with Travis and still a lot more suffering on the streets. You're just left thinking: What's going to happen now?'

Pearl tries to put all this together in her mind.

'Does the taxi driver have no hair?' she asks.

'Well, yes, he does,' says Gus. 'How did you know that? He starts off with hair but later on he shaves it and leaves just a strip of hair down the middle of his head. It's called a mohawk.'

'Why does he do that?'

'It's like he's getting himself ready to kill. He's not going to be a normal man anymore, he's going to be a murderer, and shaving his head "symbolises" that. Do you know what symbolises means?'

'Sort of. So did he know he was going to kill all the people?'

'Yes, he thought about it, he planned it all out.'

'Is it a true story?'

'No, Pearl, definitely not. Travis Bickle is just an actor.'

'What's his real name?'

'Robert De Niro.'

'Is he famous?'

'Yes.'

'Is it an adults' film?'

'Yes, Pearl, it's only for adults.'

Gus's briefcase starts ringing. He says, 'Excuse me for a second,' and reaches behind him and answers the little pink phone inside.

Pearl rests her eyes on the picture of the house. She thinks she understands now. On television the man with the bow-tie sat with rows of books behind him and talked about the person who killed everyone at the oval.

'He had shaved his head,' the expert said. 'It's well-recognised psychopathic behaviour.'

Pearl didn't get it. The man had shaved off his hair because the twins had messed it up, which was like starting all over again when you did a drawing, rubbing out the mistakes and going back to the blank page. What had the expert meant?

But then one day, just before all the talking stopped, she was riding in a taxi with Lily when the expert came on the radio.

The taxi driver liked Lily, Pearl could tell. Normally Lily could tell too, but in the days after Riley's death she didn't notice anyone, she just stared ahead. The taxi driver had the sleeves of his T-shirt rolled up to display his muscles, and he was chewing gum. Pearl showed him the card that Lily had been given at the hospital, with the doctor's name and address on.

Pearl and Lily sat in the back of the taxi and Pearl held Lily's hand. At first there was music on the radio but then people started ringing up, and Pearl realised they were talking about what had happened at the oval. Pearl glanced over at her mother but Lily just stared out the window as if she was deaf. Pearl knew when she heard the man's voice that it was the expert from the television because he was saying the things he always said, about the killer's shaved head, the psychopathic behaviour. And then, in the middle of the expert speaking, the taxi driver looked laughingly over his shoulder and said something to Lily that Pearl didn't understand.

'Sounds like the weirdo thought he was Travis Bickle,' he said. And then, when his eyes were back on the road, the taxi driver spoke in a different voice: 'You talkin' ta me? You talkin' ta me?' It reminded her of the way that Riley chatted to himself when he was playing.

Lily said nothing.

Outside the doctor's, as she watched the taxi speeding away, Pearl asked Lily what the man had meant.

'I don't know,' said Lily quietly, staring at the ground. 'I think he was on drugs.'

Gus finishes on the phone and turns to her.

'Why did you want to know about Travis Bickle, Pearl?'

'I just heard something,' she says.

'Why is it important to you?' asks Gus.

Would she tell him? He had taken the time to answer her question but he might be disappointed – he might be angry, even – to hear what it was all about. The story of the man's shaved head seemed important to her, and that he had not planned to kill, but she knew that Gus thought she was particular, and maybe that meant she was just being fussy. She didn't know, she couldn't tell. Nothing that happened at the oval had been important to the taxi driver who spoke to Lily that day; he was just trying to tell her that taxi drivers could be like film stars too.

'It doesn't matter,' she says.

'You sure?'

'Yep.'

'OK,' says Gus, 'let's leave it there for today.'

The Taste of Others

EVERY MORNING NOW THE surface of the pool is covered with leaves. Sonia drags the scoop through the water and thinks of the cleaning and the chemicals, all the effort poured into maintaining something so remorselessly blue and silent. But she does it in the hope that one day soon the pool will be used by the two little girls she has never met. They will go in with their floaties and blow-ups. She doesn't know how Karl has managed his anxiety enough to have children, but then, of course, she doesn't know their mother, the woman her son has chosen to love; perhaps she manages it for him.

The pool had gone in after Pieter's first heart attack. They were reluctant to clear the lemon-scented gums, but it was going to save his life. For years she'd had the habit of pausing at an upstairs window to look down through the trees at Pieter while he worked. If he lifted his head, to follow the path of a bird perhaps, or because he could feel the light press of eyes upon him, she hastily withdrew.

She might have looked all she liked, when the pool went in. Every day he swam back and forth. The blinds in the workshop were down, and the door locked. His work had been blamed for the problem with his heart; the long hours, and cigarettes, the intensity. She might have watched his strong overarm strokes moving him quickly through the water, but he was engaged in something private then, a wager with his own mortality, and she didn't wish to see.

She walks slowly along the side of the pool, herding brown leaves. She never swims in the pool herself. She's never learnt to overcome the moment of entry, the cold that shocks awake some soft, slumbering part of herself, something inside her that is like the pink of a fingernail, that needs protection, that needs not to stir.

She lifts the scoop and tips the leaves into the garden. Autumn presses on her heart. Prepare yourself, it seems to say, soon it will be dark. Soon it will be time to go in.

There are things to do today. She drinks a second cup of coffee and swallows a multi-vitamin. For the visitor she will receive in the afternoon she dresses in black trousers, black jumper and low black boots, slips on her wristful of silver bracelets. She wraps her dark hair into a loose knot and draws a line of smoky colour across her eyelids.

She was relieved the previous day when she dropped the glass and it smashed on the floor. Now she had a reason to visit Ikea. Of all the ways she has sought to occupy herself since Pieter died, it's shopping that works the best. She can't sit alone in a cinema while it's daylight outside, and walking only amplifies the monologue that already cramps her head. Even galleries are not the same, now that there are only her own eyes with which to see.

She hadn't been in love with him when she first dragged him down and stripped him of his clothes on his mattress on the cold floor in Copenhagen. And she wasn't in love with him the next morning either, when he called her from over the little stove where he was cooking their breakfast.

'You must look at this,' he said. 'Sonia, please. Look at this.'

She wrapped a blanket around herself and went to stand by his side.

'Look how beautiful this is,' Pieter said, pointing with a hand comfortably holding four eggs.

She did as he asked, she looked down at the chipped red saucepan with half a handle.

'Look at the water, isn't it beautiful?' he said.

She looked again at the boiling water. She looked longer, remembering their bodies together the night before, and slowly the world inside the saucepan came to look like a bustling, glistening, crystal city.

'Yes,' she said.

She had been to Ikea with Pieter only once. They wanted real candles on the Christmas tree that year; a tree like the ones they'd had when they were both children, with a bucket of water and ladle standing by in case a branch caught fire. Ikea didn't have the candleholders they were looking for but they bought a bag of tea lights.

Pieter was enjoying himself. 'This is a clever design, and funny too,' he said, switching on a child's lamp in the shape of a spaceship. 'And this is a handsome eggcup. Look, Sonia, look at this eggcup. Acacia, made in Vietnam.'

'How much?'

'Fifty cents.'

'Fifty cents?'

'On special. Perhaps they weren't popular. But the wood is lovely. Let's take four.'

'Let's take another two for Gabriel.'

'But they'll cost more to post than to buy!'

'They don't weigh much. They'll encourage him to eat properly, now that he's a vegetarian.'

'But they have Ikea in London.'

'He doesn't look after himself in that way, you know that.'

'Should we send some to Karl too?'

'Karl will already have good eggcups. And the children too, those ones with the rabbits. Gabriel will use them, but Karl won't see the point. They don't have to be even all the time.'

'It's hard to get out of the habit. You'd just never want one to feel left out in any way.'

'I know. But no-one's being left out. Two more for Gabriel.'

'Look at this little table,' Pieter said. 'The top comes off for storage. Look at the price. One person with a lot of money can have one of my tables, but lots of people can have these tables for little money!'

'But then everyone will have the same table. In Helsinki and in Rome.'

'Does that matter?' he said, stopping at the rack of shower curtains.

Sonia felt that it did matter, and that in particular it should matter to him, but this was the kind of thing he said sometimes, now that his work was over.

'Does this remind you of that fabric I used on the Halifax lounge?' he asked, pulling out a white shower curtain with a buzz of intersecting black lines. 'We had to wait months for it, do you remember? It got stuck on the docks or something. What year was it? Gabriel wasn't walking, I remember that.'

'Nineteen seventy-two?'

'Yes, probably around 1972.'

Pieter found her hand and held it at his elbow as they made their way through the bathroom fittings.

'That was a beautiful lounge,' she said.

'Yes,' he said. 'Yes, it was.'

'I wonder where it is now.'

'I wonder.'

They moved silently amongst the bath mats and towels.

'If I was working today,' said Pieter, 'if I was starting my career again, I would simply be a designer. I'd work on a computer.'

'But what about your hands?' asked Sonia with surprise.

'I would specialise in kettles,' he said, as they moved into the kitchen area. 'My kettles would be world-famous. It's a Pieter Marstrand kettle, people would say. Some kettles would look like boats, some like mushrooms. There'd be a rustic design for camping. And a very expensive Special Edition kettle that was Perspex – transparent – so you could see all the lovely stuff going on inside. I would be in the weekend newspapers. I take my inspiration from the world around me, I would say.'

He picked up a nest of plastic tumblers.

'These would be good to have if we ever see those little girls of ours,' he said.

Sonia took the tumblers from him and put them in the big yellow bag she carried over her shoulder.

'You're teasing me,' she said.

'No, I'm teasing myself,' he said, smiling.

Careless

He is happy, she thought. He'd been lost, but he had found his way back. Now he didn't mind not working; he knew what he'd done. He had worked hard and cared well for them, and now he could rest.

They bought a garlic press that was better than the one they already had.

In the end, Pieter fashioned some candleholders and they had real candles on the tree. On Christmas Day they sat down to a crayfish lunch. They had decided against presents and gave instead to a charity. Gabriel and Karl rang, from London and Brussels, and they heard the light, sweet voices of their granddaughters on the phone.

Next year they would all be together, they decided, and raised their glasses in a toast.

Early in January, Pieter moved a chair into the shade at the side of the pool and opened the abridged edition of Manning Clark's *History of Australia*, while Sonia began her yearly overhaul of the house.

One day while she was laying new Contact in the kitchen cupboards, cream with a fine grey check, Pieter suffered his second heart attack and died, close to the end of his book.

For a while, this alone consoled her.

The Ikea bag on her shoulder is reassuring. Her life will be added to. When she has chosen something and placed it in the bag, its substance will be greater than the weight of the thing alone.

Just why Ikea's small rooms calm her, she doesn't know. She never returned to Denmark. Pieter's family had visited and he'd gone back as, one by one, they all passed away. Her own mother had been dead for a year before she learned of it. But when she looks at the imitation books with their Swedish titles on the shelves of the small rooms at Ikea, she wonders if there are not, in fact, Northern molecules that draw her here, something that speaks to her of the place that once was her home.

She strolls through all the possible rooms of a house and sees suggestions for work, sleep and play. She never had a doll's house but she imagines the pleasure is much the same: the intimacy of things miniature, of peering in, of practising for a grown-up life. Here she can watch people, they don't mind being watched, they don't even seem to notice. At galleries she can only look at the art on the walls; she has to look away from others, others are not supposed to be the object of her interest. If only they understood that she does not want anything, that she is only looking.

Can I help you with anything?

No, thank you, I am just looking.

Are you looking for anything in particular?

Well, yes, I am looking . . . I am looking for the human flavour.

The taste of others, madam?

Yes, that's it, the taste of others.

In front of her in a bedroom of coffee colours are a man and woman, and a small child. The couple are not young like she and Pieter were when their boys were this size; the man has a receding hairline, and the woman looks irremediably tired. She is inspecting some vanilla curtains hanging over an imitation window. On a tufted rug the man crouches to help his son take a small straw from the side of a carton of fruit juice. Sonia watches them, drawn by the child's plump cheeks and his focus on the difficult task of inserting the straw into a small hole in the top of the container. The man's hand hovers over his son's paw, willing him to succeed, but ready to guide him too.

This man had a different sort of father, thinks Sonia. He doesn't speak of it often because surely his father was not unusual? Surely his silence and his great, great distance were the silence and distance of all fathers? Unpraising, unwatchful, very nearly – but not quite, you could not accuse – unkind?

She feels the little wave of satisfaction that moves through the father and son as the child successfully pierces the foil with the tip of the straw and slides it into the container. She tries to imagine what it is like to be a two and a half year old standing in the full sun of his father's attention with his own small carton of juice on a wool/nylon mix rug that tickles his toes through his sandals.

The man presses his lips to the boy's creamy forehead.

Life gets better, she thinks, life makes its reparations. She walks on, feeling, as always, the empty space at her side.

There had been months when she could not comprehend how her body withstood its sadness. She thought then that she understood why someone might take a blade to their own flesh, not to end their life but simply to set loose some of the terrible weight within.

A voice reaches her and she turns her head. In a country-style kitchen a woman is speaking to her friend. They're young, thinks Sonia, but they won't be for long.

She has never shopped with another woman herself; the idea of it is unthinkable to her.

The young woman is speaking to her friend about the benefits of a breakfast bar. 'It would be so much easier to load the dishwasher,' she says. 'You know how at the moment I have to turn and bend . . .'

The friend nods her head in sympathy. The young woman speaks loudly, one plum-nailed hand on a denimed hip and the other worrying a short gold chain around her neck.

'And the square barstools would be best, you know how my back ...'

Suddenly Sonia hates her, voluptuously.

'And the cream plates to go with the brown wood, you know how dark colour affects me ...'

Her voice is one that Sonia feels she hears everywhere now: the voice of young women who have been taught that their every thought, and utterance, is important.

'I'm not sure, though, you know how I am at this time of month, I'll have to check with Rick ...'

There is a thrill in this hatred, Sonia realises; the heat and the vividness of it; the purity; the conviction. It feels strong. It feels like a passion. The young woman thumbs her mobile phone and tucks her hair behind one ear. Sonia watches her closely, eager for the phone call, for more to feed upon. But as she watches, she notices on the inside of one of the woman's elbows a small strip of white gauze over a tuft of cotton wool, the certain sign of a recent blood test. Suddenly the arm seems pale and sore to her, and the young woman vulnerable. Recently a needle had pricked her skin. It might have hurt. She might have experienced weakness when she saw the vials of her blood lined up on the counter, feeling she could not spare that much. She might be waiting; she might even be afraid.

Sonia walks on.

For more than forty years she has lived her own life around a breakfast bar, although it was not called that, it was not called anything that she remembers. It was where her boys sat for their cake after school, where Pieter poured wine while she cooked. Why does she want to judge a young woman's desire for something she herself has?

This can only be doing me harm, she thinks, this will only give me cancer. What is this black stuff inside me, squirting like ink from a squid?

It would have been different if she'd been with Pieter. Sonia imagines walking with him along the Ikea aisle. The young woman's voice causes both of them to turn their heads and they silently observe her. They walk on a little way and then Pieter says, 'What a cutie,' and she laughs with him and the young woman is forgotten, in an instant.

She fears that her mother's darkness is colouring her blood, now that he is no longer there to lighten it.

Sonia turns the corner and finds herself in front of a wall of glassware. This is what she needs, what she is here for. Her heart lifts. She can look, choose, have. She can forget.

It's only glasses for the kitchen that she wants, something for taking her vitamins in the morning and her sleeping pill at night, her six drinks of water a day, but she passes over the boxed glasses that are on special and reaches for a large tumbler that has caught her eye. She likes the smoky grey of this glass, the way it darkens at the base, and the heaviness in her hand. It suggests hard liquor and ice, warm nights, good times. It is the most expensive glass there, she notes, but she'll take six.

The woman from the museum is coming at two. She needs a new tea strainer and tea towels and a bud vase, it occurs to her, something for a single flower to put beside the bed. The curator wants to see the bed, and a bunch of flowers is harder than she wants to try. A single red geranium from one of the pots by the pool is the precise amount of trying she will do.

She had asked for time when the museum approached her a month after Pieter's death to request her cooperation in staging a retrospective of his work. She hadn't been ready then for anyone to consign him, no matter how reverentially, to the past. And she was certainly not going to take on the role of a famous widow.

'Mrs Marstrand,' the curator said, 'we're particularly interested in a number of pieces we understand your husband made for your own home. In particular he spoke of the Butterfly Bed as being the first instance of the use of the wing that later became such a distinctive feature of his design.'

Sonia finds the things she needs for the curator's visit. She has reached the rug section, which means that she is nearing the exit. Every time she reaches this point in her journey through Ikea, she remembers Karl's attempt to reassure his younger brother the first time Gabriel rode the ghost train at Luna Park.

'Once you see the big green skull with the red eyes,' he said, 'you know you're nearly out.'

She must get home. She must get ready. She has to lead a stranger through her house.

The curator asks if she can see the Butterfly Bed first. Sonia has not found it easy to be with the young woman called Natasha, with the asymmetrical haircut and maroon lips. But they have had tea and poppyseed cake, and Sonia has answered her questions. Now as they climb the stairs and Sonia leads Natasha past her sons' bedrooms and Pieter's study, she realises that this is the first time she can remember that another woman has been in this part of the house.

She opens the door to her bedroom and gestures the curator inside.

'Of course, it's a quiet bed now,' says Sonia. She says it without thinking, because suddenly it seems that way to her; the charcoal blanket and sheets so austere and hospital-cornered, all but one of the wings folded away.

The extended wing holds the single red geranium in its test-tube vase and her reading glasses and the biography of Patrick White that she has carried from room to room for many months now, opening it and giving up again. While she was preparing the bed for the curator's visit, she worried suddenly that it might seem the book had been placed there decoratively, like the false books at Ikea, and she moved the bookmark from page fifteen to a place two-thirds of the way along, feeling like a fool, but doing it anyway.

Quiet? She remembers a time when all four wings of the bed were opened, each at a different angle, the room full of bed and wings, the bedclothes swirled, semen drying on the sheets, pillows stacked against the headboard so the children could see the pictures in the books being read to them.

She remembers the wings holding boys' grubby T-shirts and cold cups of coffee, wine glasses, ashtrays, cigarettes, novels, dictionaries, atlases, pencils, paper, juices and fruit; holding Big Bird, Bert and Ernie; Matchbox cars; tubes of Savlon; bottles of calamine lotion; bottles of Mercurochrome; blue, black and silver Rive Gauche; Chocolate Mint Dessert; Band-Aids; Butter Menthols; *Cosmopolitan*; *Belle*; the *National Times*; lipsticks, cuff links, earrings, shoelaces and the buttons that came loose from all of their clothes . . .

Now it's a square bed dressed in grey, and it seems quiet to her. But no sooner is the word out of her mouth than she understands that the curator, because she is young, will take this to mean that it is a bed in which sex no longer takes place.

'It was a bed that came to life,' she says hurriedly, unable to free herself from the use of the past tense. 'I'll show you.'

Sonia moves to her side of the bed and reaches for the hollow in the underside of the wing where the fingers rest in order to glide the wings into place. The curator is looking on, aerating her thick fringe with the tips of her fingers.

'Can I pull out this one?' she asks, indicating the bed's other side.

'Please,' says Sonia. The wing with the cigarette burns, she thinks. Does anyone still smoke in bed?

'It's beautifully made,' says the curator, drawing the wing out slowly. 'Of course, the wings will be open when it's displayed but we won't let people touch them.'

Sonia looks at the young woman.

'I don't recall agreeing to the bed being in the exhibition,' she says, hearing her surprise.

With her maroon lips, the curator makes her pitch. Somewhere in all her words Sonia hears mention of the Opera House, and the Danish contribution to the nation's culture.

'My husband thought of himself as Australian, not Danish,' Sonia says.

'But he was Danish-born and he trained in Copenhagen,' says the curator.

'But he didn't bring his ideas from Denmark, it was this place that formed them. The native timbers he found here. This bed was only possible because of the space around us.'

Even as she speaks, Sonia knows she will let the bed go. She will give this young woman the bed for her exhibition but she will not make it easy; this is what her marital bed is worth. The curator is still speaking of culture and identity. Why doesn't she just say the work is good and original? thinks Sonia.

'How long would you need the bed for?' she asks finally.

'About four weeks,' says the curator.

Say please, thinks Sonia. This is the bed where my children were conceived. Just say please.

'And will you collect it and deliver it back to me?'

'Those arrangements can be made,' says the curator.

Sonia looks at the bed with its wings spread. He is not here, she thinks.

She is about to ask another question when she catches a sign of strain in the curator's eye, and realises with shame that she has been making it difficult for her in order not to feel the difficulty herself. The curator is merely a young woman with misbegotten hair and prepackaged ideas, both of which are sure to grow out.

'You can have the bed for the retrospective,' she says. 'The bed belongs there.'

'Thank you,' says the curator.

The cocktail cabinet downstairs is tall and narrow, made of red and gold woods that Sonia can't remember the names of.

'We can look it up in Pieter's records,' she tells Natasha. 'He was meticulous. It's all in the workshop. I'll take you there later if you're interested.'

It's been a long time since she opened the cabinet. When Gabriel was small he begged to be given its key, kept in a high place in the kitchen. He stood on a chair, holding his breath, and carefully turned the key in the cabinet's brass-edged lock. She feels it now as she opens the cabinet for Natasha – the erotic sliding and fitting and releasing – and she recalls Gabriel's solemn little face as the door folded down to reveal its sparkling cave.

The cabinet opens with the sweet, delicate smell of wood,

glass and liquor. The mirrored surfaces of the interior multiply the rows of drinking glasses and the bottles with their jewel-coloured contents.

'Pieter loved the inside of Thermos flasks,' says Sonia. 'Have you ever looked inside one?'

'Only a stainless-steel one,' says Natasha, peering inside the cabinet.

'No, not those. Earlier ones. We had one that was pink and brown check on the outside with a white plastic cup on top. When you looked inside it the insulation material was like a little world, all shiny and reflective. Pieter made the inside of the cabinet to resemble that.'

'He was a Romantic,' says the curator.

'Is that what you call it?' says Sonia. 'I don't know. He just knew how to look at things.'

'We actually have permission to exhibit another drinks cabinet, earlier than this one. The one your husband made for Hans and Maria Engelbrecht.'

'Really?' says Sonia. 'That huge thing? Very pretentious people, the Engelbrechts. Very demanding.'

'But it's a beautiful piece.'

'Yes, I suppose it is. Do you want to see the sideboard?'

'Yes, please.'

'It's in the dining room,' says Sonia. She decides to leave the cocktail cabinet open. She will come back later and make herself a drink; she will need to sit, and think about him quietly, after the curator has gone.

'I remember the timbers he used for the sideboard,' she says, leading the curator out of the lounge room. 'Queensland and New Guinea walnuts, and silver ash. I'll show you something I think is special about it.'

As Sonia opens the door to the dining room, she realises that she has left this room in mourning. Light falls in small, pale squares through the loosely woven curtains. In the days after his funeral she had wandered the rooms of the house, observing all the flowers. In most the green was quickly spent, and they sighed and darkened and rotted in their deaths. The tedious work of the disposal, all the smelly water. But there were a few that had no feeling for melodrama, that held firm. These flowers dried and faded, and settled instead into a new, brittle beauty. She piled the kangaroo paws, banksias and grevilleas at the centre of the table, locked the windows, drew the drapes, and left the chairs sitting straight. She eats her meals in the kitchen now, and sometimes in front of the television.

The sideboard is just a long plain box, made elegant by high legs.

'Look at the wood,' says Sonia, running her hand over its surface. The grain is long and sinuous, with an occasional seam of deep apricot.

'Have a look inside,' she says, bending to open one of the doors. On the inside of the door the grain runs horizontally and the single flash of apricot brings to mind a sunset, the last glimpse of a dying sun.

'Gorgeous,' says the curator.

'Yes,' says Sonia. She is about to close the door when she realises something about the glasses she bought that morning. She remembers sitting on the patio with Pieter, drinking beer. It was a hot, black, close night. Karl reached up from where he was playing on the ground, his small hands opening and closing like stars. It was the time of day she leaned upon: when her child went to his father.

'Me?' Karl said. 'Me?'

'Just a sip,' said Pieter, bending towards him.

She remembers her son tugging at the glass, demanding, and Pieter holding on, urging him to be careful.

'Me!' Karl said again, his fury rising. She wanted to speak, but it was the time of the day to let go.

'It's too heavy,' said Pieter.

'*ME!*'

And then, because he was who he was, Pieter gave it him. The glass dropped from Karl's hands, smashed at their feet, and she had dragged her son, howling fit to die, onto her lap.

There was no letting go.

Sonia gently closes the sideboard door. The glasses she chose are almost exactly the same. Time doesn't change you, she thinks, not really.

It's dark when Sonia first wonders if she has remembered to lock the workshop door. She stands at the kitchen bench, dicing salmon for an omelette, shifting her legs now and then to ease the pain in her back. She will have to wash and dry her hands, and go out into the night to check.

'It's big,' Natasha had said as they stepped into the workshop at the end of her visit.

Sonia lifted the blinds and the late afternoon sun fell across the empty workbenches and hulking tarpaulins. There were no cobwebs and, oddly, no dust.

'It smells wonderful,' Natasha said.

The cold, clear paradox of Pieter's presence in every atom, and his not being there at all.

'I should do something about this place,' Sonia said.

She looks down at the cutting board and sees that she has

prepared far too much salmon. Sometimes when her mind wanders, her hands still cook for two. Everything inside her feels as fixed and trapped as a pane of glass.

As she scrapes the fish into a bowl of beaten eggs, the possibility of another carelessness occurs to her. Perhaps she would not check the workshop door. What could happen? What is the worst?

The egg foam laps at the edges of the hot pan. She tears parsley from a pot on the windowsill, and switches off the woman who is speaking about religion on the radio.

She wonders about the six Ikea glasses in the cupboard above her as she flips the omelette – for a time in life all fashions are new, but beyond a certain age are they always a return to the past? – but as she reaches for a knife and fork and turns to plunge the pan into water, she clips her hip hard on the edge of the open drawer and the pain is sharp and insulting. Everything hurts more without his laughing sympathy.

Her thoughts tumble inside her tears. This is the time of day she misses him the most: the difficult passage into night, sitting down to a meal alone. She had spent her day shopping, showing furniture, thinking about drinking glasses. Is there nothing but objects now – unmeaningful, unloving things?

She wipes her eyes and reaches for the phone when it rings, her hands trembling.

It's the young curator again.

'Thank you for your time today,' says Natasha.

'You're welcome,' says Sonia. She can smell fish on her hands.

'I'm calling because I wondered if you'd ever considered renting out your workshop.'

'Pieter's workshop?'

'Yes. You know, to someone who could use that kind of space.'

'Another furniture maker?'

'Well, yes, or someone else. A sculptor? I know a sculptor – he's looking for a new place to work.'

Once she might have told the curator that just a short time ago she had thought of leaving the door of the workshop unchecked – unlocked, perhaps – and wasn't this a coincidence, wasn't this a sign? She remembers moments such as these from earlier times, but she no longer believes in mysterious design. Pieter's death changed all that, and it troubles her to think that the curator may already have been thinking of this sculptor and his needs as they stood amongst Pieter's things in the place Pieter had most keenly been.

'It's just that the workshop seemed a bit of a burden to you,' says Natasha.

That is true, thinks Sonia, that's an honest insight. There is still that little opening within her; that aperture of possibility.

'Who is this sculptor?' she asks.

'His name is Adam Logan,' says Natasha. 'He's very good. I think you'd appreciate his craftsmanship.'

'Does he work in metal?' asks Sonia. 'I wouldn't want welding.'

'No, only wax, resins, clay. He wouldn't make much noise.'

'And he wants a place to rent?'

'Yes. He hasn't got a lot of money but he needs to find something.'

Sonia doesn't want the trouble of money. 'Do you think he'd be prepared to look after the pool – instead of rent, I mean? That's really what I need, someone to help with the pool.'

'That's very generous, Sonia. I'm certain he could manage the pool very well for you. But are you sure that's all you want?'

Is that all she wants? Is that all that is left?

'I'm sure,' she says.

'I'll speak to Adam and get back to you,' says Natasha. 'Is that all right?'

She wants this to happen now; she wants the pool and the workshop taken care of. This much will help, she thinks.

Sonia says goodbye to the curator, runs a cloth under the tap and wipes the phone. She pours a glass of wine and turns from her cold meal and the unwashed dishes.

There are three hours before bed. She has a video.

The Stakeholders

LILY HAD RECEIVED AN invitation to a meeting of stakeholders. Pearl listened to her mother reading the letter to Anna. 'The recent tragic deaths of six young children have sparked an urgent debate: How does our nation come to terms with a history of children lost, stolen, worked, hurt, abandoned, detained and dispossessed?' she read. Lily's cheeks were pink with the discomfort of reading out loud. 'Perhaps it is time to recognise all the children who have suffered, and remember all those who have been lost? Perhaps it's a time for healing?'

The government was implementing a consultation process – and it was thought that a memorial might be what was needed. A big, important memorial; a memorial like other countries had, one that people travelled to see; one that told stories, bore witness. A children's memorial.

The seating for the audience at the meeting has been divided into four sections. Lily and Pearl have been directed to their seats in the third row of the second section. If Pearl looks between people's shoulders she can see the people seated on the stage at the front.

The chairperson introduces the politician, the psychologist, the architect and the father. Each of these people has something to say about the proposed memorial, the chairperson says, and then the discussion will be turned over to the floor. Pearl looks quickly around her and finds that no-one seems surprised by what has just been said. Then she remembers Anna telling her that everyone at these meetings can speak if they want to, and she concludes that *the floor* means those sitting in the chairs. It's a puzzle to her, how these expressions come to be, and how everyone agrees on their meaning. No-one seemed to think that *stakeholders* was funny either; she didn't know why, when there were so many words to choose from, someone would use one that obviously made you think of barbecues, or killing vampires.

Lily had been at the hairdresser's for most of the morning, and when she got home she looked so different with her hair golden, and as straight and silky as ribbon, that Pearl felt almost shy for a while.

All afternoon Lily sat on the couch reading magazines while Pearl drew at the table. Sometimes they looked up and smiled at each other without saying anything, Lily's hair floating between them like a messenger of peace.

The politician is speaking. He is sitting on one buttock, leaning all his weight on the arm of the chair, as if there is chewy on its seat. Pearl listens carefully. He's talking about the large sum of money that his government is willing to invest in the proposed memorial.

'In recognition of the children's history of our country,' he says.

Pearl feels the crackle in the air a moment before the voice yells angrily from the audience. It's a man's voice, coming from the other side of the room, from the last section.

'If you care so much why don't you give your money to living children?' the voice demands.

There is murmuring and shuffling. Pearl's heart pounds. Don't fight, she thinks, please don't fight. People are turning their heads, trying to get a look.

'I think that comment risks being highly offensive to a great many people here,' says the Chair. *He is the Chair, they are the Floor*.

There's a small amount of applause.

'Perhaps the Minister might be allowed to continue?' the Chair says, but he's not really asking a question.

Pearl looks at the politician again. He is sitting differently now, as if leaning away from the attack, although he smiles as if he's not concerned.

'What could be more offensive than the state of our hospitals and schools?' the man yells loudly again.

People groan and swivel to look at him once more.

'Why don't you shut up and listen?' a woman calls out, her voice shaking, as if she didn't want to call out, but she had to.

Pearl reaches for Lily's arm.

'Ow!' says Lily, slapping her hand away. 'You scratched me!'

'I didn't mean to,' says Pearl.

'But you did – look!'

There might be a tiny red mark on Lily's arm.

'It was my bangle,' says Pearl.

'Give it to me,' says Lily, holding out her palm.

Pearl works the twisty pink bangle that Anna gave her over her hand, and passes it to her mother.

'Thank you,' Lily says, throwing it into her bag.

Pearl's wrist feels bare, but the man has fallen quiet.

Everyone in the room seems relieved when the politician finishes and the psychologist begins, but Pearl doesn't like her. She's wearing too many bright colours. She has too much kindness in her voice, and while one long feather earring hangs down, the other is accidentally hooked up and sticks out from her ear. And she doesn't even know, she can't even tell.

'She's nice,' Lily whispers.

'We expect the consultative process will bring up many issues for some of you,' says the psychologist. 'But we have a commitment to your input in this project. At the end of the day it's about us helping you to empower . . .'

Pearl's attention wanders. She's never been in a room like this before. A room in a big hotel, in the middle of the city.

When Lily and Anna talked about the invitation to the meeting, Lily said: 'I don't feel very good about myself.'

'But you should make the effort,' said Anna. 'It'll be good for you.'

Anna told Lily that she should take Pearl to the meeting, and that Anna and her husband would drive them in. David Jones would be open, so she'd take Leo to buy some casual shirts and then they would drive them home again.

Pearl gazes at the chandeliers hanging thickly from the ceiling. Lily has Anna's mobile phone in her bag and she'll call Anna on Leo's phone when they're ready to be picked up.

Pearl thinks of Anna and Leo now, shopping and waiting for their call. She thinks of the smooth drive home in the dark and the backs of Anna and Leo's heads and the lights on the dashboard. Already things have changed since Riley left. He would be bored if he was at this meeting, and she would have to take him outside to lean over the railing and look fourteen floors down on the tiny people below.

'Imagine if you dropped a rock,' he would say. 'Imagine if you dropped a bomb!'

Things were more – babyish then.

Riley had never known Anna or driven in Leo's car. It made her feel bad, this feeling of leaving him behind.

The walls of the room are cream and the curtains at the windows are a dark red velvet. Outside, the other buildings are sparkling with light. There's a diamond pattern on the carpet, and her foot, if she slips it free of her sandal, fits exactly from point to point. She is the only child at the meeting, although in the seats across the aisle a woman is nursing a sleeping baby.

Is a baby a child? She's not sure, exactly. Maybe a baby is a baby until it can walk and then it's a child. Babies die, so is the memorial for them too? Its pink feet are poking out of its blanket – is that all right?

As Pearl lifts her eyes from the baby she sees that a man in another row is looking at her. At first she thinks she has done something wrong but then she realises that really the man is staring at Lily, who is listening to the psychologist, unaware. When she is satisfied that the man has not noticed her at all, she looks at him closely. He has sharp angles of hair growing on the sides of his face, and although he is wearing a suit and tie he doesn't look like the politician or the other men in the room who are wearing suits. His suit is striped, and his tie is thinner. The other men look like they're going to work, but he looks like he's in some kind of costume, or dress-ups. He's looking at Lily as if he's got cigarette smoke in his eyes.

Adam Logan isn't really interested in what the politician and the psychologist have to say. He will listen to the architect and the parent of the deceased child, and later he'll look more closely at the photographs of the memorial site pinned on boards at the back of the room. He has already studied the topographical model, and felt inspired by the grandeur of the headland and cliffs and sea; their suggestion of eternity. The memorial would take its place against time and nature.

He takes a long, surreptitious look at the people seated around him. These are, he supposes, his competitors: other artists, architects, designers. Although nothing has been said about the seating plan, he detects its logic. In the first section, he thinks, are the people who, as children, suffered at the hands of church or state. Those who have lost a child are in the next section, and the last grouping – where the angry interjections had come from – he guesses might be termed community representatives.

He notes that there is more black being worn by those concerned with the design of the memorial than by those mourning their children. He, thank god, has worn his navy pinstripe.

He knows that everyone seated in his section has, like him, got through Round One. In order to be present at all that night, to be part of the consultative process, those interested in the job of creating the memorial have already been through a selection process. In their applications they were asked to include a discussion of past work (with supporting material), professional references, and a statement of philosophy regarding the proposed children's memorial.

Adam had thought of Wes Allen as he worked on his statement. Finally, in this memorial, he would reply to his critic. How could beauty ever be indecent? Art made the world's agony and loss beautiful, and once you had beauty, you had redemption, and people could be released from their suffering. All art was about redemption – how could he not understand that?

These thoughts on art, beauty and redemption, Adam put down in his statement. In support of his application he included a number of reviews of his past work. In particular, he highlighted with a fluorescent yellow marker the words Laura Benjamin had written about *Katy's Gone*: 'Many artists today would stand back from difficult material such as this, or mask it with post-modern irony or cool. But Logan leads you by the hand to a place of terror and pity, and from the terror and pity you simply cannot turn away. This reviewer must confess to having shed tears.'

Perhaps it took a woman really to understand what he was doing, thought Adam. Perhaps it was simply that Wes Allen's emotional range, like so many men of his generation, went all the way from A to B.

Adam sits with a notebook on his knee. He would chew off his right arm to know what his competitors have submitted. Not that he doesn't think he has as good a chance as any, he is there, after all, his submission has been chosen above many others. How many others? One hundred? One thousand? He wishes he knew. He should be allowed to know.

He would take down notes, if someone would just say something interesting. The woman sitting in front of him has an unsightly bump in her spine. What do they call it – a dowager's hump? She should do something about it, he thinks. Grow her hair, or try yoga or the Alexander Technique.

It doesn't matter that he does not yet have any real ideas for the memorial, beyond the idea that he is the best possible person to design it. It's as if all his work in Death Studies has been leading him here. It's the next logical step for him but it is, of course, like all art, a process and – doesn't he know it yet? – there is wisdom in having no knowledge; his task is simply to open himself to the darkness of all beginnings.

What he really needs is to learn about grief. He wants to create a memorial remarkable for its gravitas, he knows that much, and he wants those who visit the memorial to experience an aesthetic catharsis. The problem, as he sees it, is one of feeling. When he looked into Katy's dead face that cold afternoon, he knew instantly that what he felt had to be communicated.

The design for the memorial should be an embodiment of the structure of a feeling, and that feeling was grief. But what is the structure of grief? He had experienced only three deaths personally, leaving aside Katy: the death of a grandmother, a classmate who fell off a cliff on a school excursion, and a girl who had a fit at a party and hit her head. In his mind he has images from these deaths, but there is little feeling to go with them. If he wants to examine grief, maybe he will have to go to his break-up with his only real love, Zoe, and how he had wanted to die. In the absence of direct experience this is what artists do: they mine their own feelings. But even Zoe might not be enough: when he ran into her on the street recently she was no longer luminous; he'd moved on, he could see that, and his earlier feelings, those he had been so sure of, no longer seemed important to him.

What he needs, therefore, is access to someone else's grief. If someone could express their grief to him – in their words or gestures or body – then perhaps he could shape that grief, like he would a very good clay, or expensive resin.

The bereaved father, who is going to speak soon, might communicate his grief in such a way. In the meantime the other half of the room, Sections One and Two, is occupied by people who have known grief. There is old grief there, he knows, and new grief.

He's been doing some reading, and thinks he has learnt a few things. The old grief – of having been taken as a child from family or from the place that one knew, or of having been subject to the cruelty or depravity of those who had power over you – was a grief that infected the flesh. The bodies of those suffering old grief were hurting, and their addictions and illnesses and dysfunctions were simply coded expressions of mourning. The new grief – that of the parents of children snatched away by the hand of fate – is blood-bright, blade-sharp, caterwauling. It's the new type he thinks he needs.

It's her hair he notices first: a pour of gold down her slender back. She is sitting with the people who have lost a child. There's no man beside her but the small girl is probably her daughter because their clothes have the same op-shopness, not retro like his own suit, just second-hand; cheap even the first time round. There is something about the woman, though; something about the way the sleeves of her pale blue cardigan are rucked above her sharp elbows, the slow swing of her sneakered foot, her long loose ankle. She is bereaved, and alone.

The psychologist finishes speaking and returns to her chair, and the architect stands to speak. There has been a question in Pearl's mind since the day that Anna first showed her the picture of the water-wheel that is the Memorial for the Unre-covered. Pearl would never say this to Anna because she knows it would hurt her, but she thinks the memorial is horrible. The huge wheel with the water doesn't remind Pearl of any of the things that Anna has told her about her daughter. It doesn't seem sad, and she thought a memorial was supposed to make her feel sad. So there was the question she wanted to ask about memorials: *What if you don't like it?*

She thinks that the architect might talk about this in some way – Anna told her that the architect is the person who thinks the memorial up. How will the architect know how she and Lily feel about Riley? How will the architect know what she has never told anyone, not even Gus, that Riley doesn't live on inside her, as the man who spoke at his funeral said he would? She can make him up in her head, and she can move him around and get him to say some things, but really she knows that it is just like working a puppet, and there will be no surprises, no new things. She's sure it isn't like this for Lily; that Riley is still inside Lily like he was when he was a baby. It's only she who has lost him, and she can't tell anyone, because she's ashamed.

The architect speaks softly, as if commanding her audience to draw close. She is tall, but Adam notices that her thighs and upper arms are disproportionately longer than the lower part of her limbs, as if they'd run out of material when making her.

'There are many different experiences of loss in this room tonight,' she says. 'Some of you have lost your own children, and some of you had your own childhoods stolen from you.'

Pearl feels as if everyone has taken a sudden, sharp sip of air, and there is now less of it.

'Each one of you will have your own memories,' says the architect, 'and you will want to see those memories recognised by this memorial.'

Adam doesn't want to go down this road. Down this road lie politics and difference, and he cannot create a memorial to politics and difference. It's his task to lift people above these things and to find what is universal in their experience; the particular is of no concern to him. He thinks that the architect should be preparing people for unification, not pandering to the individual.

The architect is speaking about the controversial histories of some famous memorials. The Ground Zero site in Manhattan, of course, with its clash between aesthetic ideals and the price of real estate.

The Holocaust Memorial in Berlin: does it really remember six million victims or does it, rather, serve to close a chapter of disgrace in a nation's history?

The Vietnam Memorial in Washington (DC), designed by twenty-one-year-old Chinese-American Maya Lin: a simple black gash in the ground that infuriated some patriots but, for so many of those whose lives had been marked by it, represented truly the open wound of that war.

Adam wonders how many mini-Mayas there are in this competition. He's tired of all this abstraction and minimalism, all this quietness of memorials. Death deals in bodies; that is how it makes itself known. He wants to bring the body back to the memorial; restore some grandeur and heroism. This is why talk of difference doesn't help him. He cannot dare to design his memorial around the figure of a boy, for fear of leaving out a girl. The child cannot be Aboriginal, because the lives of European and other children must be shown also.

And he does not want a group of children, a representative mix – like a Benetton ad – because that is not art, that is politics again; that is selling something.

The architect is of no help to him. He puts his pen to his notebook, and doodles.

Pearl feels like the architect has been reading her thoughts. It's as if she understands that the wrong memorial will make Riley's death worse, not better. She wants to know how the young Chinese girl the architect talked about knew what it felt like to be in an American war. Was this what architects learned, how to understand other people's minds?

A door opens at the side of the room and a woman wearing a black skirt and white blouse appears, carrying a tray of glasses. The waitress sees that someone on stage is still speaking, and she grimaces in embarrassment, as if the whole room has observed her, Pearl thinks, although it is only she and Lily who have turned in her direction.

The architect finishes and the last speaker stands.

This is the father of a child who has died. He's a large man with a thin line of beard, but it's only when he begins to speak that Pearl realises that he is the father of Courtney, who was killed at the Eric Cahill Oval. She watches the side of her mother's face to see what is happening.

Adam has his pen at the ready. The man is telling the story of his daughter's murder. His daughter had been killed by a sicko, he says. In his twisted mind the sicko had seen the children playing on the oval and carefully planned how to get them.

Adam recoils from the man's words. It is illumination about grief that he wants; a taste of its beautiful blacks and slow, stirring music.

Anger is of no use to him.

Lily holds Pearl's hand in her lap. There's a pulse inside their hands, but Pearl doesn't know whose body it is.

As Pearl listens to Courtney's father she realises that he's heard the Travis Bickle idea from the man on television, and he believes that Courtney was hunted, like someone hunts an animal. Inside her it feels like a tiny doll is quietly sobbing. She would like to tell Lily that the things the man is saying are not the truth, but she's not sure that Lily would want to know. She doesn't know how much the truth matters, and if it matters, why.

Pearl looks at her mother and follows her gaze back to the front of the room, where she sees that Courtney's father is crying.

'And if a memorial can help us deal with some of these terrible feelings,' he says, tears streaming down his face, 'then maybe it's a good idea.'

Adam looks up when he hears the man's voice break, and jots down his words.

Pearl waits at the serving table for a glass of wine for Lily and an orange juice for herself. While she is waiting, she looks around at the room. After the speakers finished, the people sitting in the chairs were allowed to ask questions or say what was on their minds. Although nothing had really happened, it felt like any moment there might be a fight.

Now that the discussion is over, the mood has changed. Pearl fills her palm with small star-shaped biscuits from the table, and watches the people sitting and standing, talking quietly, smiling at each other. A waitress moves through the crowd close to Lily, and Pearl watches as her mother reaches for a glass of wine from her tray. Now she will have to say to the man serving the drinks that she only wants the orange juice after all.

As she steps away from the table she sees the man wearing the striped suit walk over to Lily and say something, and her heart sinks. She watches as her mother raises her eyes to the stranger's face. Lily sips her wine, her lips lingering at the edge of the glass, as if she is thinking about the taste, as if she is humming 'Mmm'.

Lily and the stranger smile at each other and Pearl sees that her mother and the man are similar in some way, and she thinks that they feel it also, and although she doesn't know exactly how they are similar, she knows that the stranger, too, would send someone away for a glass of wine but take another if it came to him first.

The psychologist's earring is still sticking out as she talks to Courtney's father, who slowly turns a glass of beer around in his big hands. Pearl holds her breath as she weaves her way past them, through the knots of bodies, her hand closed tightly over the little biscuits, taking extra care not to spill her orange juice on herself or on anybody else.

Lily's face is flushed and her glass is nearly empty.

'This is Adam,' says Lily, putting her hand on Pearl's shoulder. 'He's an artist. He's going to design the memorial.'

'Isn't it a competition?' asks Pearl.

'That's right,' says Adam. 'I'll be submitting a design.'

Pearl opens her palm and offers one of the delicious biscuits to Lily and her friend.

'Ah – I don't think so,' laughs Lily, looking at Adam.

Adam shakes his head.

'Not for me, thanks,' he says. He meets Lily's eye and laughs too.

Pearl puts one biscuit after another into her mouth until they are all gone and then she wipes the grease and crumbs on her skirt. Above her, Lily and Adam talk on, and when a waitress comes by he reaches for two more drinks.

She is wondering what to do with her empty glass when Lily says: 'Adam's offered to give us a ride home.'

'But what about Anna?' asks Pearl. She pictures Anna and Leo in David Jones, their shopping finished, just wandering and looking, waiting for their call.

'We won't have to bother Anna,' says Lily.

'But how will they know?'

'I'll call her.'

'But then you'll have her phone. She might need it.'

'I'll get it back to her,' says Lily, separating the ends of her hair. 'Anna won't mind.'

Pearl feels an ache for Anna. It's just like the glass of wine, she thinks.

Adam's car is old, with two sharp wings at the front, and two at the back. As they drive through the carpark beneath the hotel, Pearl wishes that she hadn't worn her denim mini, because the backs of her legs are touching Adam's seat.

Out on the city street, two girls are sitting on the kerb smoking cigarettes. They just had to sit down, Pearl thinks, so they sat there. She wants to listen to what Adam and Lily are saying but her mother sounds as if she's talking into a tape-recorder, trying to sound as good as possible so she won't feel embarrassed when she has to listen to herself later. Although the night is cool, Lily's window is down and her elbow rests on the door. As she speaks to Adam she runs her fingers through the breezy side of her hair. She has taken her cardigan off and her arms are bare and the tag at the back of her top is sticking up.

Anna and Leo are probably driving these same streets, going home alone. She's not leaving Riley behind now; now things are just like they were when he was with them, and Lily was interested in something else. There's no Anna; no smooth, clean car to ride in. Nothing is different, except that she is in the backseat without him.

Adam stops the car in an unfamiliar, busy street, and opens his door. Pearl reaches up quickly to tuck in her mother's tag but when Adam's head reappears suddenly through the window she gives a little cry of surprise and jumps back in the corner, her skirt exposing even more of her bottom, her heart beating wildly.

'What do you want to drink?' Adam asks Lily.

She'd missed the moment when this had gone from Adam giving Lily a ride home, to Adam coming inside to drink. She knew this meant that Adam might be there in the morning, that there might be a smell in the toilet.

'Bourbon?' says Lily.

This is Lily's favourite but she can't afford it. She's leaning across the seat towards him and Pearl knows Adam can see her bra.

'How about vodka?' asks Adam.

'OK.'

Pearl and Lily watch him as he turns and jogs across the road, the jacket of his suit flapping behind him.

All of a sudden a memory of Riley comes to Pearl. It's not like the pictures she has to make an effort for, the stiff images that will only move if she pulls the strings. It's a memory as free and surprising as Riley was when he was alive.

She remembers him in the food hall of a big shopping centre. They had bought chips. His elbows were on the table, the little bucket with the black and red writing in front of him. His eyes were dark and soft, like they always were when he was hungry. But it's the way he ate the chips that she remembers. He picked up each chip by its very end; carefully, delicately, as if it was a little creature he would sadly have to eat, but not needlessly hurt. Maybe someone else would say that the chips were just hot, but they wouldn't know.

'When we get home you'll go straight to bed, won't you, Pearlie?' says Lily, checking her lips in the rear-vision mirror.

'Yes, Mum.'

'Good girl.'

Adam watches her long fingers reach into the bashed-up packet of Drum.

'Only when I drink,' she says.

Even though he gave up smoking years ago he still likes to watch a woman making a cigarette. She has oval nails, painted pink, and she rolls the tobacco into the little paper slowly, with promising sensuousness. The tip of her tongue darts along the edge of the paper and she seals the cigarette and places it between her lips and lights it with the blue interior of a flame. And then, he can hardly believe it – it's the sexy gesture of women smokers in old movies, or in new movies in which an actress is playing the sexy past – after the first exhalation she lifts elegantly, between two fingers, a strand of stray tobacco from her tongue.

Somehow they have ended up sitting on the floor with their backs against the salmon couch and the bottles of vodka and tonic between them. It's their second drink; the child has flickered past the open door in a pale nightie and disappeared into the dark at the end of the corridor, and he has adjusted his sensibilities to the place. There's not a decorative touch anywhere; no moment of wit or loveliness, no trace of memory; just the brown carpet and the bare blonde brick and the subsiding eighties furniture like a pornographer's hand-me-downs. But surprisingly, enviably, there's a brand new, fuck-off, flat screen TV.

He's loosened his tie, and she has kicked off her sneakers. The nearness of her bare feet to his booted ones excites him. She has a small, crude tattoo of a bluebird below the bone of her ankle.

He asks her about her childhood, and she waves the question away with her half-empty glass.

'My parents didn't want me to leave school,' she says. 'They didn't want me to become a model.'

He looks at her long, smoky eyes and soft, kittenish mouth. Maybe, he thinks, at a pinch.

'You were a model?' he asks.

'It didn't really work out,' she says, drawing deeply on her cigarette. 'Some bad things happened.'

He pours more vodka into his glass and his hand hovers with the bottle until she throws her head back and drains hers. He wants her to move on, to get to the bad things that have happened more recently.

'Tell me about your little boy,' he says, and then pauses. 'If it's not too difficult.'

'Riley?' she says.

She has lovely shoulders, he thinks. Knife-sharp clavicles.

'Yes,' he says.

'Riley. Well, Riley was *my* boy, he was like me.'

She draws her knees to her chest and circles them with her bare arms.

'Is his father around?'

She shakes her head slightly as she takes a drink, and it seems she's not going to say more.

'What was Riley like?' asks Adam

'He was a free spirit, you know?' She looks at him. 'He was artistic – like you.'

She shifts awkwardly, and then she's on her knees.

'He did great drawings. I'll show you.'

With a long stretch she reaches over to a pile of magazines and papers that are stacked against the wall. He looks at her lean, denimed arse.

'I'm sure I kept some,' she says.

She glances at a large sheet of paper that has come free in her hand, and then tosses it behind her.

'Pearl isn't like Riley and me. She's sort of . . . tight. She uses rulers and things to draw. I'm sure his stuff is here.'

Even from where he is sitting, he recognises the subject of the drawing that she's discarded. He puts his glass down and reaches for the sheet of paper as she continues her search.

'Your daughter did this?' he asks.

She looks quickly over her shoulder. 'Yeah,' she says.

The page in his hands has been torn from a large, cheap sketchbook, but Lily's daughter has turned the page around to allow for the descent of the drawing. He can't quite believe what he is looking at. It's a drawing of the Frank Lloyd Wright house called *Fallingwater*. He can see that a ruler has been used to outline the house's great cantilevered terraces and its stepped foundations of rock. She has used the edge of a green pencil, he sees that too, to suggest the delicacy of the forest foliage surrounding the house, and the falling and pooling energy of the water below it has been drawn in quick, light, lead strokes. She's been frustrated by her materials – it looks like she's had no more than five or six coloured pencils to work with – because he can see the layers of colour she has used in an attempt to achieve the ivory of the concrete terraces and the subtle dove greys of the house's rough stone core. He can almost feel the girl's hand and eye, close to the page, striving. As an architectural drawing it is, of course, imperfect, but she has recognised the beauty of the house; its boldness, its lyricism . . .

Perhaps he's pissed. He lowers the drawing to his knees, unscrews the top of the tonic water and takes a long drink.

Lily is resting on her heels now as she continues to sort through the pile against the wall.

'I can't believe it,' she whispers. 'I can't believe it.'

They're only minutes away from fucking, he's sure of that. He picks up the drawing again. It would be better not to say anything. Better not to tell her that her daughter, so unlike her, has drawn what he has always thought of as life's perfect house, the place where he had always imagined he might most perfectly be.

'I can't find Riley's drawings,' she says, turning to him, a wretched look in her eye.

He puts the drawing aside.

'It doesn't matter,' he says, pulling himself onto the couch. 'Come and sit here, where it's comfortable.'

Sex on the salmon couch is constrained but there's the heat and fervour of her mouth and her bare arms and her thin, struggling legs. When she slips sideways off the vinyl he has her pinned, her hair and throat and breasts falling below him, in the drink and the ashtray, and he can see them both, in the wide TV screen, the long pale fall of her upper body and his hips and chest rising above. It reminds him of an awful painting of a nymph and a satyr, but he can't think of which one.

He seizes her below the shoulderblades and hauls her back to be with him, to kiss him again, and they're rolling and she's above him, and when she reaches down to touch herself he cuts himself free and focuses on his own coming, which he knows is only moments away if she keeps doing what she's doing.

'Fuck!' he says, wiping his hair from his eyes.

He expects her to lift her head now and to look him in the eye, wipe her hair back too, share with him a knowing look about this animal thing they have just done. But her bony back lies splattered across his chest, moving in an awkward rhythm, and then he feels wetness on his shoulder.

Where has she been? he thinks, sober suddenly, condom-less. His hand caresses the puffy pink back of the pornographer's couch and then sound meets the wetness on his shoulder, and he realises she is crying. He brings his hand down to her back and counts her prominent, heaving vertebrae. She will stop, he thinks, by the time he reaches the top of her spine, she will stop. But she doesn't stop; his hand circles the back of her neck and still she's crying, and he realises she won't stop, not yet, and that this is why he is here, for her grief, for its inspiration, and he wraps his legs over hers and winds his arms tightly around her and takes it all in; all the sadness, the whole bad experience, feeling its shape, its limits, its volume and texture and mass; thinking, I am blessed; thinking, *this* is how art begins.

Careless

She lifts her head from his shoulder and swipes at her eyes with the backs of her hands. Clear snot runs from her nose.

'I need a ciggie,' she says, and pulls clear of him.

At the door she clings to his neck for one second too long as he fumbles his tie into the pocket of his jacket.

'You've got my number?' she asks.

'Right here,' he says, patting the other pocket.

He thinks to say, one last time, your daughter has done something special, but perhaps he should not correct her, hurt her in this way.

'I had a really good time,' she says.

'So did I,' he says, without lying.

Outside, the air is cold and clear. He hears the door close behind him. There are lights and lives as far as he can see. Stars but no moon. His old Valiant is waiting below. The stairs zigzag to the ground and he takes them two at a time.

He is empty, and full.

He doesn't know if he will see her again.

141

Hansel

SONIA HAD SLEPT THROUGH the storm. It was the sleeping tablet, the second one.

She sits at the dining room table with coffee and a piece of warm apple pie and unwraps the wet plastic from the rolled newspaper. She'll have to call someone about the tiles that have blown off the roof, and when Adam arrives there's the old leak in the workshop to be checked. But it was a bad storm, she's heard on the radio that all the emergency workers are out. She can wait.

She's using the dining room more now, since Adam moved into the workshop. Sometimes he eats lunch with her there or they sit down for afternoon tea. It has to happen by accident, she understands that. She has to catch his eye as he moves about in the workshop, while she is hanging out washing, perhaps, or tending something in the garden. And after she catches his eye, her tone needs to be light.

'I've just heated up some soup for lunch. Hungry?'

She finds that a simple lift of her hand is best – a nonchalant acknowledgement, she has things to get on with anyway – if his answer is in the negative or if she catches that note of male irritation in his reply, that note she sometimes hears in the voices of her sons, travelling the thousands of miles down the phone.

'What do your sons do over there?' Adam asked one day as he took a bite of her orange cake. He'd eaten all the icing first.

'Karl works for a pharmaceutical company. He's in Brussels.'

'What does he do with them?'

'I think he's called the chief business executive.'

'The chief executive officer?'

'Yes, maybe, I don't know.' She sipped her tea. 'And Gabe's in London. He works as a sound engineer but he's really a composer.'

'What sort of thing does he compose?'

'Oh, modern stuff. Electronic music, I think.'

'They sound quite different.'

She thought of saying *they hate each other* but, although that would impart the flavour of their relationship, it wasn't the whole truth of it.

'They're very different,' she said. 'My husband used to say that Karl makes drugs and Gabriel takes them.'

When Adam laughed, the subject felt so much lighter.

'Do they have children?'

'Karl does. I don't know that Gabe will have any. He keeps to himself more. Karl has two little girls, Poppy and Lottie.'

'Cute names.'

'Do you think so? I think they're silly. Their mother is German.'

'What are they like?'

'I don't really know. I haven't met them, but they look lovely in photographs. I might go and visit them soon.'

She hadn't been thinking of it. She couldn't imagine packing and flying and being in strange places, but she had said it and perhaps just saying it made it true. How much became true simply because it was spoken, and what happened to all the potential truths that went unsaid?

'When did you see your sons last?'

'A little over a year ago. They came home for their father's funeral.'

'What was the funeral like?' asked Adam.

She was getting used to his questions. At first they had seemed like a trespass, but she told herself she had been away from conversation for too long and, besides, he was working on a memorial, she knew he was thinking about death.

'I can't remember much of the funeral,' she said. 'Karl and Gabe made all the arrangements.'

Adam drank from his cup and looked at her, as if wanting her to continue.

'Lots of people spoke. Friends and clients. Clients who'd become friends. I didn't really hear what they said. Karl and Gabe spoke.'

Sonia remembers the argument that took place just before they left home. Karl insisted Gabriel wear a jacket over his red shirt, and she had to find one of Pieter's for him even though it didn't really fit. She remembers their men's dark shoulders as they stood at the front of the chapel speaking about their father, saying important things probably, but she didn't hear them, she was looking at her sons' bodies and the space between them, how important it was not to touch.

She sensed her answer had disappointed Adam. He had finished his cake and was making the movements that meant he was getting ready to leave.

'I suppose it's stupid, but I sometimes wonder what Pieter would have thought of his coffin,' she said. 'After all those years, working with wood. We'd never talked about it, we weren't prepared. It's just one of those conversations you never have.'

Adam poured some more tea.

'Tell me more about the coffin,' he said.

She looks at the photographs of the storm on the front page of the newspaper. There's a small map charting the path of the storm's destruction.

All the time she is listening for the sound of the gate opening at the side of the house, which means Adam has arrived. She has good reason to seek him out today. There's the damage from the leak to talk about, if there has been any. She wants to tell him too – she will cut out the story from the newspaper – about the two small brothers who have gone missing in the storm. They were seen at their local skateboard ramp, and later playing near a construction site, but they haven't been seen since.

Adam has told her that he's working on some ideas for the children's memorial. She's heard about the memorial on the radio and read about it in the newspaper. She knows that the competition for the design closes in three months, and that the building of the memorial will begin in early summer.

She was watering the geraniums by the pool the day the

honeyeater flew at its reflection in the workshop window and dropped to the ground. Adam opened the door of the workshop and together they looked down at its lifeless body.

'This is weird,' Adam said, bending and lifting the bird onto the large book he was carrying.

Sonia saw that the book was a volume of Grimm's fairytales. He spread the bird's wings with the tips of his fingers. There wasn't any blood. She thought of the bird's brain and of the stones inside small black olives, the cheaper Spanish ones.

'I've been reading these fairytales,' Adam said, 'thinking about children and stuff. I was just noticing how in so many of the stories animals are associated with the protection of children, especially the ones that warn them of danger and harm. Mice and squirrels do this, and birds, of course. I was just thinking of birds when I heard the thud at the window.'

'Uncanny,' said Sonia.

'It's hard not to see it as a sign,' said Adam.

'Of what?' asked Sonia.

'Oh, you know, that I'm on the right track, moving in the right direction.'

Interesting, thought Sonia, how he'd allowed himself to sidestep the danger and harm. We think we believe, but only if we can interpret the signs in any way that we wish.

Adam said goodbye, and perhaps they could have tea later? After he closed the workshop door, Sonia looked at the tiny smudge on the window, as if the bird's eye had grazed the glass just before it fell to its death.

As Sonia wiped at the glass with her tissue, the image of a man jumping from the World Trade Center came to her. Again and again he fell through her mind, as engraved as any of her own memories. The man at the window's edge was dressed for a normal day, wearing a light-coloured shirt. A light shirt for a blue-sky day. This is what always hurts; that he hadn't known it was his last shirt, chosen carefully or in haste, but chosen freely. Later, all his choices would be gone.

Adam stayed late that night, casting the body of the dead honeyeater. Small wax, resin and plaster birds appeared along the windowsills of the workshop. He was focusing, he told Sonia, staying in touch with his materials, following the threads of possibility. Did she have any mousetraps?

Sonia has found the scissors, so she can cut out the story about the two missing boys. She looks at the face of the boys' widowed father in the photograph. How do people bear it? she thinks.

She has seen the research about children – printouts from the Internet, mostly – that Adam has taped to the walls of the workshop: the murders and abductions of children, the animal attacks, the children burnt, the children lost in the city, the desert, the bush and the sea. But if she were designing a memorial for children, she thinks, it's the image in front of her now that she would turn to; the stricken face of a parent. If she were searching for a form that might commemorate loss, she would have to ask that face again and again, how do you bear it? *What can I do to help you bear it?*

There it is, the sound of the bolt sliding heavily and the gate creaking open. She can't help it, her heart quickens. She waits to hear his footsteps across the patio, followed by the silent seconds as he circles the pool, the unlocking of the workshop. But suddenly there's a loud knocking on the back door, and the surprise of it lifts her out of her chair.

Adam looks tired and cold. He has just washed his hair, she thinks, it's damp and hangs in his eyes. Of course, this is what people do after a storm, she realises this is what she had hoped for; a discussion with another person about general and specific damage, a check on well-being.

'Hello, Adam,' she says, opening the screen door.

'Hi, Sonia.'

'Do you want to come in?'

'No thanks, I want to get straight to work. I just came to see if you've got those rags you said you'd put through the washing machine for me.'

She'd forgotten. She reaches into a cupboard behind her and takes out the plastic bag that contains the clean, folded rags. As he reaches for the bag she smells his shampoo, like apples in the cold, clear air.

'Thanks a lot,' he says. 'Do you know how the workshop fared last night?'

'I haven't been in – I wouldn't,' she says. 'Let me know if there's anything that needs work. I have to get someone out to do some work on the roof anyway.'

'OK, I'll let you know.'

He turns and looks out over the backyard.

'Do you mind if I get to the pool later? I was hoping to get stuck into some work.'

'It can wait,' says Sonia. 'I've cut something out of the paper for you. About some boys missing in the storm.'

'They found them,' says Adam. 'I just heard it in the car.'

'They found them? Were they – alive?'

'Yeah, they had a rough night but they're alive.'

'Thank god,' says Sonia. She's aware that she has placed her hand over her heart.

In the dining room she picks up the newspaper cutting. She will have to listen to the next radio news, just to hear it herself.

It doesn't matter now. The long day in front of her, the heavy blocks of time. The brothers are alive; none of it matters.

But she will keep the cutting anyway. She pulls out the drawer of the sideboard where the serviettes are kept. There is something consoling in a drawer full of table linen: the silence of all the soft folds.

She places the newspaper cutting inside the drawer and closes it gently.

The next time she looks at the photograph, it will be for her the face of a man who has found his children.

Adam's gut churns as he steps into the cold, dark workshop. As he moves slowly along the windows, raising the blinds, a watery light settles over the room.

He misses his studio in the warehouse, its view across rooftops and down onto the street below. He still smarts at the injustice of his eviction; the landlord didn't want a tenant who worked with dead bodies, he was told.

He'd argued back, but only in his head. He wasn't, in any ongoing way, working with dead bodies. He was *interrogating* death, because how we die might just tell us something about how we live, and Katy had been a spontaneous, inspired moment in that interrogation, an opportunity he believed he was not meant to refuse, and he had received applause for his daring, might even receive a lot of money for it one day.

How had the landlord made *his* money? What else had he made apart from money? It was the landlord's warehouse that Katy had died in, anyway; his warehouse and his cheap-shit conversions.

It's better here, of course, in the workshop of the old carpenter. He walks around the room looking for signs of the storm but everything is dry and tight. It's just that sometimes he feels superstitious about the comfort that surrounds him now: the trees, the pool, the house, the elegant Dane.

He stands at the window and looks out at the leaves and bark floating on the surface of the pool. When this workshop became available, he read it as a sign – a new place for a new project. But the work isn't moving as he thought it would. The design for the memorial is eluding him, and he can feel anxiety – lack of money, uncertain future, just who the hell he is – white-anting him from within. This is the project for him, he is sure of that, but he can't get a grip on it, he feels like he's spinning his wheels in a bog.

He stayed too late at Lily's again. He should not have allowed the storm, or her, to keep him there. It's already late morning.

He can remember times when he felt as powerful as a blade: when he worked precisely, forensically; cutting through obstacles; everything that was within him gathered on a fine, sharp edge.

His eyes move from the swimming pool and up the steps of the patio to linger on the windows at the top of the house. If he had a house like this everything would be different. He imagines waking in the morning to the certainty of his own walls, with work the first thing on his mind. A swim, whatever the weather, and then into the studio.

But he has to keep going, turning over the problem of the memorial, believing in an unlocking, a key.

He had been wrong about Lily and the benefits of being close to her grief. He thinks of her the night before, standing over him on her messy bed, her feet locking his hips, breasts bare and slightly asymmetrical, g-string askew. The pink, wet, private view.

She held a pillow above her head, laughing down at him. 'If you don't stay, I'll smother you,' she threatened.

Oh Christ, yes, smother me, he thought.

After the first time, when Lily lay on him and cried, he had seen no further signs of her sadness. As soon as they were alone they took off their clothes, and she began laughing. Her daughter sometimes flickered like a ghost at the edge of his vision, or stared at him with her grey eyes, but no-one talked about the boy who was not there.

Every time he leaves Lily's flat he thinks he is leaving for the last time. He'll have to get a handle on it, he can't afford the late nights and the slow starts to the morning. Tomorrow, to make up for it, he will be here by eight.

He turns from the window. He'll go back to the drawing he started yesterday. He has been sketching scenes from the book of fairytales – for stories of cruelty, and the abandonment of children, there's nothing like the Brothers Grimm. He's chosen moments that stand out for him, ones that resonate in some way with the contemporary stories about children that he has stuck on the wall. Some things change, and some things remain the same.

The sketch he returns to is a scene from Hansel and Gretel. The witch has placed Hansel in a cage, for fattening. Gretel prepares rich foods for her brother, while she survives on crab shells alone. Each day the blind witch commands Hansel to put his finger through the bars of the cage, so that she can feel if he is plump enough for the pot. But Hansel fools the witch each time – instead of his finger, he extends a bone from one of his meals. Bah! the witch spits. Still too skinny for slaughter.

In this scene it's Hansel's ingenuity and resilience that

interest Adam. And this is partly the difficulty of the memorial's design, he thinks. There are dead children to be commemorated, but there are also children who have survived separation, violation and fear. How can the memorial represent these Hansels and Gretels, while at the same time mourning those children who were unable to prevail?

He pulls up a chair and opens the sketchbook on the bench in front of him. He takes a pencil from the jar on the windowsill and props the book of Grimm's tales against the window.

But surely he's getting a cold? He swivels around in his chair. The echinacea tablets and vitamin C are on a shelf above the washbasin at the end of the room. He gets up and walks over and fills a glass of water from the tap. Three echinacea are advised so he takes five, and then he fills the glass again and drops a vitamin C into the water and carries it back to his chair and sets it down on the bench.

He's already drawn a wide view of the scene that interests him. He studies it closely, trying to anchor the anxiety surging through his body. The glass of water fizzes orangely. He is aware of the pearly light on the page and the oblong of blue water that hovers just outside his vision.

He has drawn the witch to look like a woman he often saw in the street outside his old studio in the warehouse. The woman's head was shaved but for a mangy, tri-coloured tail that hung the length of her spine. A blue tattooed flame emerged from between her heavy breasts, snaked its way up one side of her neck and lapped at her skull. She wore string vests over lurid underwear, tight workman's shorts, and biker's boots that strapped and buckled to the thigh. He studied her closely whenever he could, looking down from the studio window.

One day, as they both reached for the same bag of plums on a table outside a deli, she held his eye with a furious, kohl-ringed stare. I know you, lump of shit, her stare said.

In his drawing, the bald witch gropes blindly towards the boy in the cage. He's drawn the boy with a look of concentration on his face, as if searching within himself for a way out.

Adam picks up the glass and drinks the vitamin C. It's the bone that interests him – the little bone that Hansel pushes through the bars of his cage in imitation of one of his own fingers. He's a clever boy, thinks Adam, a boy who can outwit a hag.

He decides to begin a new drawing, but this time he'll draw only the bars of the cage, the child's hand and the bone. This is what Adam feels he knows best: the tight, close view, the telling detail.

His hand moves quickly over the centre of the new page. With hard downward strokes he makes the bars of the cage. There's something about this finger, this bone. Something he needs to understand. How would the boy hold the bone, what shape would his hand make?

He begins with the wrist.

Adam is aware of the empty glass at the edge of his vision. Sonia had given him this glass for the workshop. And then she'd told him a story, although he hadn't really been listening, he'd been pondering the handsome glass, and how it reminded him of James Bond. What was the story about? New glasses that were, in fact, old? A memory she'd had of her son?

Hansel's wrist had to be thin but not too thin, it had to be more substantial than the bone.

Her small son had broken a glass, that was it. But what *is* the deal with that bone?

Adam puts the pencil down suddenly and leans back in the chair. He, too, has remembered something. He could tell Sonia a story about the things a boy breaks.

When he was small he stayed at home with his mother and she explained to him all the things that existed in their world. This was your great-uncle's desk, when he was a scientist at Oxford. This is Aunt Jocelyn's armchair. This footstool was made from a ship that Cousin Iva found wrecked on the beach.

He learnt the story of each item and he understood how much his mother loved them and how, in their own silent way, they expected something of him.

His mother called these things her heirlooms, but when his father came home he called them her ghosts. They argued above him. His father explained to him how the things had been made. He learnt how a table was cut from a tree. He learnt about glass, metal and fabric, and how colour came to be. With each explanation, and every new fact, he felt the power the things had over him lessening. His mother watched silently as the stories of her family were replaced by knowledge of another, unassailable kind.

Grandmother's bone china was kept in a cupboard in the hall. He accidentally broke a teacup, because he was nervous – a little frightened of it – before his father laughed at him and told him that this pale, eerie, fragile substance was made from mixing the ash of animal bones with different types of clay, and had nothing to do with his grandmother's bones or the bones of any old lady. He understood then that when he put his fingers around the delicate handle of one of these teacups it was simply baked earth that he held, and he had no more responsibility for it than for the water that came out of the tap every day.

In fact, he had power over the teacup now. He was free to set the cup down carefully in its resting place in the saucer, as his mother had taught him to do, or he could let it slip from his hand and burst apart on the floor at his feet.

He didn't like the look on his mother's face when it dropped, but his curiosity was stronger than his feeling for her at that moment, and he learnt to cultivate a small, cold place in his heart in order to experience something that interested him. She never scolded him because he could not suffer censure of any kind, and he would have broken apart like the china itself. She loved him and she trusted him, the two were inseparable for her, and he saw that she chose to believe that every broken cup was an accident. She could not refuse him when he asked to handle the china because she would be denying him the experience of family, of all that was important to her.

He was careful and he wasn't greedy, but still the day came when the second-last teacup slipped to the floor.

'That's enough,' his mother said quietly, taking her hands from her face. She stared at him with searching, anguished eyes. 'That's enough.'

But she need not have said it, he had never intended to kill the last cup. It was beautiful, he knew that, with its white flowers and leaves of gold. When he held it up to the light, he could see through it. It was rare now; he would always value that teacup.

For a long time after, whenever his mother was away from the house, he went quietly into his parents' bedroom and took from a corner of her wardrobe the plastic bag that held the broken pieces of Grandmother's bone china. One by one, he emptied the pieces onto his parents' bed, and moved them around with the tips of his fingers. The beauty of the whole teacups was gone, but there was something in these fragments. Most of the handles had broken away from the cups in one piece. Lying there on his mother's brocade bedspread they looked to him like pale, bony, hooked fingers; beckoning. He tried to remember the recipe for bone china but there was something else in the pieces in front of him; something human. Something to do with him.

Adam stands and picks up the empty glass and walks over to the washbasin. He fills the glass and drinks from it. He thinks about the porcelain flowers that he made to surround Katy on her resting place. Porcelain was a good material for representing death: still and hard, but somehow ethereal. He had learnt a lot about it, working on Katy, and some day he'd like to use it again.

The workshop has a back door. He can go outside without being seen by Sonia, wander to the end of the garden, move his ideas around. He opens the door and smells the storm-disturbed earth. Long strips of bronze bark lie scrolled at the base of nakedly gleaming trees.

Perhaps the story of Grandmother's bone china is no more terrible than the stories of boys who pulled the wings off flies, but he would never tell it. It seems he has a chip of ice inside him – but perhaps it's what art requires.

He bends first one arm and then the other behind his head, stretching his stiff shoulders. The idea comes to him as he walks towards the back fence, unbuttoning his jeans. As always the idea comes quietly, announcing itself not with fanfare and lights but with a slight tightening of his gut, a new clarity in the air around him, a sudden calm conviction within. It's as if some strong, canny magnetic force has drawn from his life and thought all the necessary elements to set before him this concept; this wild and beautiful proposition.

He urinates to the side of the garden mulch that is piled against the fence. He rebuttons his jeans. He turns slowly, pushing up the sleeves of his jumper.

The idea presents problems, incredible problems; insurmountable ones, perhaps. His head swims and greys and then clears a little. But nothing was impossible, hadn't he proven that with Katy? You could not start with the problems; you had to believe that the idea would cleave its own path.

By the time he reaches the workshop he's sure. He fills the glass and drops another vitamin C into it. His design for the memorial will contain porcelain; may indeed be porcelain alone. Except that this will be no ordinary porcelain. This porcelain – and he would strive to make it sublime, the deepest remembrance – this porcelain would be made from the bones of a child.

In Black and White

EVER SINCE THE STORM there has been something wrong with the TV. Lily told Pearl that Adam had said the storm wouldn't have had anything to do with it, but Pearl thinks he's wrong.

All winter, Pearl has been watching *Frasier*. When *Frasier* begins there is still some light left in the sky, but by the time it's finished the lights have to be turned on. It's the saddest part of the day. She likes everyone in *Frasier*, except for Roz and Bulldog, and there's a little dog, Eddie.

Since the storm the channel that *Frasier* is on has changed to black and white. It's only that channel, all the others are still in colour, and it makes her feel like someone is being deliberately nasty to her. *Frasier* isn't the same in black and white, everyone seems further away.

'What do you expect me to do?' said Lily. 'Watch *The Simpsons* instead.'

She tried to explain to Lily that *The Simpsons* made her feel nervous, and about the time of day, but Lily left the room.

'Tell Dr Gus about it,' she said. 'I've got other things to worry about.'

Lily worries about when she will see Adam again. After Adam has been she is happy for days, and she'll talk to Pearl and sit on the couch. But as the days wear on and Adam doesn't knock on the door, Lily becomes quiet. She lies on her bed holding her old teddy bear, and cries about Riley.

Pearl is watching *Frasier* in black and white when Lily comes into the room carrying the thing she straightens her hair with.

'Did you turn this off?' asks Lily, holding it up, the cord trailing to the ground.

'When?' says Pearl.

'Just now.'

Pearl looks at her mother. She has make-up on only one eye. The other half of her face looks as if it's disappearing.

'No, I've been watching *Frasier*,' says Pearl.

She expects Lily to start an argument, to accuse. But Lily's mouth just softens and she sits down on the end of the couch. She holds the hair-straightener in her lap and looks at Pearl.

'I think he's been here, Pearlie,' Lily says in a quiet voice.

Pearl thinks of Adam, but he has not been there for days.

'Who?' she asks.

Her mother holds her eye. 'Riley,' she says.

Pearl's heart sinks. On the TV screen, Daphne throws her arms around Niles. Daphne doesn't know that Niles is secretly in love with her and that over her shoulder his eyes are bulging out.

'Mum?' says Pearl.

Lily moves her head slowly from side to side. 'I think Riley turned off my hair iron.'

'But –'

'He's been doing things, Pearlie. Little things.'

'What sort of things?'

'You know, things. He's been playing tricks on me.'

Pearl has waited for Riley. For a long time she lay perfectly still in her bed at night so that, if he could, he would come to her. But now she understands that she will never know Riley again in the old way of him being separate, outside of her. If he could not reach them from his dead place with his loneliness and his sadness, he would not reach them just to play stupid tricks.

She looks at the straightening iron. 'Is Adam coming?' she asks.

'Yeah,' says Lily, as if remembering. 'He said he was.'

'You'd better get ready,' says Pearl.

'I am,' says Lily, standing. 'I am getting ready.'

Pearl turns back to the TV. There's Frasier and his father, and the dog, Eddie. The black and white is the same feeling as the sun going down.

'That was my twenty-dollar-a-pound, imported, hand-made German sausage!' says Frasier, looking at the empty bowl his father is holding.

'Then I guess Eddie just ate forty bucks' worth,' his father says.

In the kitchen, Pearl takes the pizza pockets from the fridge and puts one on a plate and places it in the microwave. She can hear Lily in the bathroom. Time goes more slowly when she watches it, but she doesn't understand why.

As she waits she thinks about her visit to Gus that day. She sat down in her usual chair and looked at Gus on the other side of the coffee table.

'How is Lily?' he asked. 'How is Anna?'

'Good,' she said.

Gus was wearing a brown leather jacket but underneath it his windcheater was twisted, and he looked uncomfortable. She thought he should take everything off and start again.

There was something she had been thinking about.

'Was it ever worse than now?' she asked.

'Was what ever worse, Pearl?' Gus said, tugging at the front of his windcheater.

'The world,' said Pearl. 'Was the world ever worse than now – or is this the baddest it's ever been?'

'What do you think?' asked Gus, settling.

'I don't know. I've only lived in this time,' said Pearl. 'There are terrorists now.'

'There have always been people who harmed others because they believed they were right. You know about Hitler?'

'Sort of.'

'He killed many more people than Osama Bin Laden.'

'Is that how we know it was worse?'

'Well, maybe. No-one today could kill all the people that Hitler killed.'

'Why not?'

'Because everyone would know about it. People would stop them.'

'What if it was some bombs?'

'There are a lot of people trying very hard to make sure that never happens.'

'But it could happen?'

She watched Gus's face closely. She could see he was thinking of what to say. She hadn't meant to lead him to this question but now that they were there and she was waiting for his reply, she could feel the tears in her eyes. She had learnt that anything in this world could happen, and that people could do anything. If Gus didn't know that too, and didn't know that she knew it, then she would not want to come here anymore, and she would be alone.

'It could happen,' Gus said finally, 'but that doesn't mean that everything is worse. For lots of people the world is much better than it used to be.'

'What people?'

'Well – sick people, for example. People can be cured of all sorts of illnesses now. They don't have to suffer as much.'

'Not all people.'

'No, not all people. But more people than ever before.'

'But what happened to Riley and everyone, that only happens now, doesn't it?'

Again she was somewhere she hadn't planned to go. Gus wriggled for a moment.

'Not exactly. They didn't have huge cars like that in the past, so the way they died is new. But there's always been murder.'

'But fathers didn't do that before, did they? They only do it now.'

Pearl knew that this was the first time she had ever mentioned the man at the oval. She knew from the look on Gus's face that he was thinking this too.

'There are different pressures on people today,' he said. 'Maybe there are different crimes because of that.'

Pearl realised that everyone thought they knew everything there was to know about what the man had done.

'Lily hates that man,' she said.

'How do you feel about him, Pearl?' asked Gus.

'It's good he's dead.'

'How would you feel if he was alive?'

'I'd wish he was dead.'

'What would you *feel*?'

'What I just said.'

'Would you hate him?'

'No.'

'Would you be frightened?'

'I don't think so.'

'What would you feel, then?'

'I would just feel him all around.'

'And because he's dead, you don't?'

'No.'

'Where is he now, do you think?'

'He's just gone.'

If there was ever going to be a time to say something about what she knew, it was then. She had a feeling that she and Gus would not talk about the man again. At night when she lay awake in the dark she thought about what it would feel like to tell. To her it was one of those small things that was also a big thing, but she didn't know what size it would be to others.

She looked at Gus. He was letting her think. Gus had told her he was trying to learn to write with both hands, to be ambidextrous, and on his pad of paper she watched his large hand slowly make words that looked like they'd been scrawled by a baby.

The room was quiet. The beautiful house was on the wall. Everyone was dead, so what difference did it make? The truth only really mattered to one other person and that was the man. It would matter to him that people thought he was like Travis Bickle; that he had planned to kill. She saw him clearly in her mind, as clearly as Gus in front of her practising to write with his left hand. She saw him smiling at his boys as they ran to him, and the wet patches on his T-shirt.

Pearl watched a bird settle on a bare branch of the tree outside the window, and decided at that moment she would never tell. There was nothing he could do. He would have to be what other people thought he was. And he would have to be that way forever.

Pearl eats the pizza pocket at the kitchen table. One by one she picks off the pieces of pineapple and puts them in a little pile on the side of her plate.

'You should eat those, Pearlie,' says Lily, as she enters the room. 'They're good for you.'

Pearl looks up at her mother. Her hair is as straight as paper; her eyelids are silver-blue, and her eyelashes dark and spiky.

Lily sits down at the table and picks one of the pineapple pieces off Pearl's plate and pops it in her mouth. She is wearing perfume and a top that falls off her shoulder.

'Do you want a drink, Mum?' Pearl asks, watching Lily's eyes on the clock on the wall.

'Adam left some vodka in the freezer,' says Lily.

'But won't it be frozen?'

'No, it doesn't freeze. It stays the same.'

'But how come?'

'I don't know, Pearl, it just does. I'll have it with tonic.'

'It's flat.'

'What is?'

'The tonic.'

'How do you know?'

'I had a little bit.'

'Didn't you screw the top back on tight?'

'The fizz had already gone.'

'I'll just have to drink it like that then, but it's not very nice.'

'I'm sorry.'

Lily sighs deeply and looks at the clock again. 'That's OK. Just so you know.'

Lily always seems calmer after she's straightened her hair. She sits at the table as if she's balancing a crown, and holds the drink that Pearl has made for her between two hands. Pearl scrapes the pineapple and the sharp crusts into the plastic bag that hangs on the doorhandle under the sink.

'Will you take the rubbish down for me later, Pearlie?' asks Lily.

'Yes, Mum,' says Pearl, and sits down again. The sounds of television come from the flats all around and down on the street dogs are barking.

'It's good how your headband always sits properly,' says Lily, her eyes scanning the top of Pearl's head. 'I had a fringe at your age. I've always liked to wear my hair on my face.'

'I like wearing it back,' says Pearl, feeling the warmth in her cheeks.

'Funny how we're so different, isn't it?' says Lily, sipping her drink.

'Yep,' says Pearl.

Sometimes when she smiles, when she tries to smile widely, something on the underside of her top lip gets stuck. She thinks it might have something to do with dryness, and she quickly licks her lip there, but you only get one chance at a smile, you can't try again.

'What's the time?' says Lily.

Lily can see the clock but her eyes are looking into her glass.

'Half-past eight,' says Pearl.

'Adam's late.'

'What time did he say he was coming?'

'He said he'd get here when he could.'

If he didn't say a time he can't be late, thinks Pearl, but Lily feels he is late, she understands that, and saying something might only lead to trouble.

'Do you want another drink?' she says instead.

Lily nods her head.

Pearl opens the freezer door and lifts out the vodka. It pours like water from the frosty bottle into Lily's glass.

'Would the tonic freeze in the freezer?' she asks, as she sits down again.

'It would probably explode,' says Lily, looking up at the clock.

'Why?'

'Oh, I don't know, Pearl, something to do with the bubbles.'

Pearl hopes that Adam will come soon.

'Did you talk to Gus about school today?' asks Lily, swirling her finger in her drink.

'No,' answers Pearl.

'Well, I want you to. Promise me next time you'll talk to him about school.'

'I promise.'

They sit without speaking. Lily sips her drink. Pearl counts all the green things in the room: the detergent in the bottle on the windowsill, the tea towel hanging over the oven door, every second square of lino, the frog magnet on the fridge. She places the different greens in her order of preference, beginning with the pale green that is on the floor and ending with the detergent green, which is too bright, too fake, too much like yellow.

'Will we ever move from here?' she asks.

'Oh, I don't know,' snaps Lily. 'Don't ask silly questions.'

Lily stands up from the table, holding her drink in one hand, smoothing the ends of her hair with the other.

'I'm going to watch TV,' she says.

Pearl walks to the sink and takes the plastic bag of rubbish off the door handle and ties it at the top.

Outside, the air is icy cold on her legs. But as she goes down the stairs she can look through the windows into other people's rooms. On the ground floor she puts the plastic bag in one of the bins, watching carefully for the rat that sometimes runs close to her toes.

She climbs back up the stairs, counting, until she reaches the landing outside her door. Through the window she looks at the kitchen where she and Lily sat a moment ago. There are sticky rings on the table, but everything else is just the same.

It's not as cold now. She sits on the top step and looks down at the carpark. If she sees Adam's show-off car she can hurry inside to her bedroom. But she doesn't think he'll come. She might hear him later, in the middle of the night when she wakes, or she might hear her mother crying on the other side of the wall.

She won't talk to Gus about school. She had promised but she'd lied. Everyone is waiting for someone else to do something about her going back to school. She looks down at the concrete steps and thinks about the children in her class and what they are learning and how they're becoming different from her.

She remembers the time she couldn't find Riley in his class-room at the end of the day, and how she wandered across the playground to the sheds where she found his class finishing their Tai Chi lesson. The children's backs were turned and a woman wearing a tracksuit stood at the front showing them what to do. It was cool in the shed and she sat down against the wall and drank from her water bottle. Now that the chil-dren were in rows she could see that Riley was one of the smallest boys in his class, just as she was the smallest girl in hers. She wondered if they would both always be this way. Lily had told them that she wasn't tall enough to be a model.

She watched Riley's concentration as he slowly lifted his arms in a circle, as the woman at the front was doing.

She tries to go further into the memory, to be back there with the hard school bench beneath her legs and no knowledge of being without him. It was perfect then and she hadn't known it. She tries to go further but she can't even get him to turn. Turn and smile and fly towards her, as he would at the end of every day. She can't get the bell to ring and the children to scatter like birds. Riley's back remains fixed. He is focused, as he has been told, on a point in the distance. There will be no new memories of Riley, she knows that. One day she will have remembered everything.

She hears a car pull into the carpark.

She looks down through the railings as a battered old station wagon makes its way into one of the parking bays. It's not Adam, it is just the refugee boys, and she watches their six thin, tall bodies unfold themselves from the dark interior of the car. The boys' strange voices disappear beneath her and she hears the slamming of a door.

The lights stretch on in the darkness: houses and flats and shops, and the roads in between. She had walked with Riley down these roads, talking and looking, going somewhere. Now she rides in the back of a taxi to see Gus, and rides home again. Everything is small. She is small too, may always be the smallest. She knows there is more, the sky and the stars tell her that, but she cannot reach for it, cannot stretch, like the refugee boys with their long arms and legs in the small rooms in the flat below.

One day she will have to stop going to see Gus. Lily has told her that the government won't pay forever. This is why she must keep drawing the house, trying to get it right. Every time she goes to Gus's office she studies the house, putting it piece by piece into her head. And then she starts a new drawing from the beginning again. She tears out the page on which she has made the old drawing and scrunches it and stuffs it into the rubbish. When she is not allowed to sit in Gus's office anymore, she will still have her perfect drawing of the house.

Lily is asleep on the couch, holding the remote. Her hair is messy but her eyes aren't smudged. Pearl sits at the end of the couch and draws her mother's cold feet onto her lap. Lily's shoes lie on the floor next to her empty glass. Sometimes it's embarrassing, to look inside someone else's shoes. She holds Lily's toes to warm them.

Law & Order is on the TV.

Lighting the Dark

HE FEELS FOR HIS watch on the floor beside her bed and strains to read it in the moonlight falling through the uncovered window.

It's late again. He pulls the watch over his wrist and lies back on the pillows. There's something lumpy under his shoulder – he reaches for it and flops it down on her bare stomach.

'Old Paddy,' she says, touching the bear to her nose.

Lily lifts her right leg in the air and flexes her foot. Like some kind of professional, Adam thinks. Her toenails flash metallic in the grainy dark.

'What have you done to my neck?' he asks, moving his hand to the patch of heat below his ear.

'You want me to kiss it better?' she says, raising herself on one hand and leering at him from beneath her long eyelashes.

'No!' he protests, seizing the teddy bear and pressing it to his neck.

She lunges at him, growling. 'Paddy won't help you,' she says, 'he's on *my* side.'

'It's late!' he cries, but his laughter disables him.

She is over him again, all over him, and he submits to her plundering hands and insolent mouth. There's a sound from the child on the other side of the wall as her cheek brushes his thigh and a memory of someone he once slept with a long time ago sweeps through him: a girl pregnant with a baby who was not his own; the interest of it, the oddity; the sharp, surprising loneliness when the fucking was done.

Lily draws her mouth slowly from his dick and rests her head on his stomach. As he reaches for her shoulders and lifts her towards him, wanting it to be over – the sex, the laughter, everything that is getting away from him – he sees that she is still holding his semen in her mouth, her lips sealed defiantly, like a child caught with a lolly. 'Spit it out! Spit it out!' he imagines a mother demanding, holding out her palm.

Lily's face draws near and for one ugly, gaping moment he believes that this is what she intends – to spit it; spit his own stuff at him; all her grief and bad experience; spit it like venom. But he catches the look in her eye and he knows that look by now; she's playing, it's his attention she wants, and she lifts away from him and straddles his chest and he watches her lean, hungry face as she pantomimes the pleasure of her mouthful and its slow slide to the back of her throat.

They lie side by side under the blankets without speaking. The moonlight is cold. He's growing to like this small, bare room with its pink candlewick bedspread and blonde, bashed furniture. He is accustomed to the bedrooms of girls with resources and an impulse to decorate: large, firm beds with high threadcount linen and big and small pillows and lamps that cast shadows over falls of jewellery and kimonos and photographs of holidays and loved ones and framed fruit and flowers painted by talented but unrecognised aunts and grandmothers.

Lily's bedroom is like a rock-bottom hotel room at the end of the earth. Sometimes it's good to be at the end of the earth.

'It's late,' he says.

He thinks of the cold on the stairs outside and the long drive home. He has to get to the studio early; Katy is packed away in a storeroom now, still unsold, and it feels like the final seconds of his fifteen minutes of fame are passing him by, tick tock, tick tock . . .

'Stay,' she says, in a sleepy voice.

The bed's soft centre rocks their bodies close. Her breath warms his collarbone. He drifts in the dark and the quiet.

There's a memorial he has been reading about; a memorial underground, in Jerusalem. He imagines the weight of the earth above, and the cave quiet, and in the darkness, mirrors and glass repeating the flame of a single candle, a point of light for each life; one and a half million child victims of the Holocaust.

Adam opens his eyes and folds his arm behind his head. And then, he thinks, there are the two immense beams of light projected into the night sky above Manhattan, each year on September 11 . . .

'I've gotta go,' he says, drawing himself to a sitting position.

'Stay,' she says, her hand trailing down his back.

'I can't. I've got work to do.'

He feels her tug at the bedclothes as his feet touch the floor and registers her hurt along with the cold. He shakes his jeans. He pulls on his boxers and socks and separates his T-shirts and drags one on after the other. His jacket, he remembers, is in the lounge room. He reaches for the boot on the floor in front of him and glances at her as he sinks his foot into its stiff leather. She is facing him, her head turned into the pillow, one huge eye staring at him in the semi-dark. He should kiss her, he thinks, make the leave-taking sweet.

'I can't find my other shoe,' he says, feeling amongst the shadows on the floor.

He clumps around the bed.

'It won't be on this side,' she says.

He clumps back and gets down on his hands and knees and peers into the blackness under the bed. There's a shape there that he reaches for, but it's just a plastic bag, containing something heavy.

Above him, she speaks.

'What did you say?' he asks.

'I said, that's my little boy's ashes.'

His hand feels suddenly hot.

'What is?' he says, knowing.

'In the bag,' she says. 'I heard you move them.'

He can't understand why he wants to yell at her. He's on his feet, dusting himself down.

Her eye is closed.

He sits on the edge of the bed, and slowly the feeling goes. The toe of his boot protrudes from beneath a chest of drawers.

'Why haven't you done anything with the ashes?' he asks quietly.

Her voice is slurred, she's nearly asleep. 'There's no hurry,' she says.

He turns and leans over her, and presses his lips gently to her cheek.

Wine

ANNA PULLS INTO THE driveway and parks behind Diana Kimble's yellow Toyota.

Anna has never told Diana that the sticker on the back window of this car fills her with pain and confusion every time she sees it. Since Tania's disappearance, the words in purple – *Magic Happens* – strike her like a hand across the face. When it's Diana's turn to drive, to lunch or Pilates or shopping, Anna sits in the passenger seat and feels the sticker's perky optimism preaching away behind her, and she wonders sadly if Diana's view of the world has really been so little affected by the murder of her only goddaughter.

Today when she sees the sticker her body runs hot, and she thinks of reversing her car down the driveway, into the street, and out of Diana's life forever. She questions whether she has ever really known her friend and if, for forty years, she has been deluded about the nature of their friendship. But her hands tremble too much on the wheel and she knows that she must keep the promise she made to Diana on the telephone last night: to be there at four. To talk.

Anna turns off the engine and collects her bag from the seat beside her. On the backseat are Diana's salad bowl, cardigan and copy of *White Oleander*. As she gathers the items, remembering what the chiropractor has said about her neck, Diana's violet perfume rises.

She takes the familiar tiled steps to her friend's front door, her heart thumping.

She knows it shows on both their faces: the shock of each appearing to the other unchanged – the same old beloved. She's thought so hard about Diana these past five days that in her mind she's almost become a stranger; but here she is again, with her difficult hair and smiling eyes, Diana the brave, silly girl.

They kiss lightly on the cheek, and Diana talks too much as she leads Anna through the house.

'You can feel spring in the air, can't you?' she says.

'I think it's still a way off,' replies Anna.

In the kitchen, Anna puts her handbag and Diana's belongings on the counter and stands in the familiar afternoon light.

Diana opens and closes the cupboard doors.

'So, what will it be?' she says. 'A cup of tea? Or shall we have a drink?'

She looks at Anna directly, her eyes brimming and defended. Anna knows that her answer is important. To agree to share a drink with Diana now suggests give, and possibility, while tea will signal battle. Her hurt heaves, pronged and bulky inside her, and it's a surprise, an answer to herself, when she replies: 'I think a drink.'

'Good!' says Diana, clapping her small palms together.

Anna leans her body against the counter, and watches as Diana takes two wine glasses from the shelf.

'Did you finish the book?' asks Diana.

'Yes,' Anna says.

'Did you like it?'

'Yes, I did.'

'It's sad, though, isn't it?' says Diana, opening the fridge.

'Yes,' says Anna. 'It's sad.'

What does she know about sad? thinks Anna. Magic happens, that's what she knows. She wants to leave – this gulf between her and her old friend is unbridgeable, her pain is too great.

Just at that moment, Diana emerges from behind the fridge door and Anna sees that she is holding, with a certain shyness, a very particular bottle of wine. Anna understands the meaning of this wine. But she doesn't want to show Diana the effect of the memory she has summoned. She doesn't want to acknowledge anything, yet.

The two couples went away together, just as they always had, except that the children were not with them anymore. They booked a cottage with an open fire and a spa on the deck, and bush all around.

Tania was alive.

Anna remembers the long drive there and how many times she and Diana needed to stop to go to the toilet, and the joking about it between the men and the women. Syd was funny, as usual, and Leo relaxed behind the wheel and joined him in the teasing, and in the backseat she and Diana ganged together as they had as schoolgirls, sticking up for each other, batting away the insults.

It rained for a while, and she wound her window down to smell the wet, green world. She was so innocent, she thinks now, as she watches Diana struggling with a corkscrew; she didn't have a clue.

The next day they visited the wineries. Anna had always said she didn't know anything about wine, that they all seemed the same to her. But late in the afternoon, at the last cellar of the day, she tasted a wine that made her sigh.

'It's heaven,' she said.

Although it was expensive, and the others didn't like it much – it was too sweet for them – Leo wanted to buy a bottle. He seemed proud of her, and Syd and Diana urged her to agree.

When they got back to the cottage, Anna's wine was put in the freezer, so that it would be cold enough to drink with dinner. The fire was lit and they sat down for a game of cards. Diana and Leo won – it was never any different. When they couldn't see their cards anymore they drew the curtains and turned on the lights, and decided on a round of drinks while Syd got started on his famous pork dinner.

Everyone was in the kitchen when Anna opened the top of the fridge to get the ice. Before she understood what was happening, her wine had slipped from its place on top of the frozen vegetables and was headed for the floor. Later they all agreed that it seemed to happen in slow motion.

Syd was the furthest away from the falling bottle but in a direct, unobstructed line, and everyone agreed that the wine was only six inches from the floor when he launched himself towards it. For one stretched, open-mouthed moment he flew parallel to the ground, and then he wasn't flying, he was crouching; he was there – and the gleaming green bottle fell gently into his outstretched arms like a baby dropped from a stork.

A loud cheer went up in the kitchen. Syd was somehow upright again, the bottle in one hand, a puzzled look on his face.

'What a slips-catch!' said Leo.

Diana put her arm around Anna's shoulder. 'You were meant to have that wine, Anna,' she said.

And because it felt true, Anna agreed.

They ate the field mushrooms bought from a roadside stall and then Syd served the pork. Anna's riesling stood on the table with the red wine the others were drinking. They made their toasts – to friends, to health, to happiness – but as they began eating, Anna noticed a piece of pork crackling on the serving dish at the centre of the table and she reached for it quickly , her mouth watering.

She felt her elbow brush something, but she didn't see the special wine fall.

They all heard it smash on the hard slate floor. There was silence.

'I don't believe it,' said Diana finally.

'I'm sorry,' said Anna, looking at Leo.

Leo smiled at her and shrugged.

'Don't be sorry,' said Diana. 'We're sorry.'

'I guess we'll call that the wine that got away,' said Syd.

Everyone laughed nervously. The women got up from the table and Anna picked up the pieces of broken glass and Diana found the mop on the verandah. No-one said, 'You weren't meant to have that wine, Anna,' and no-one would, although she felt it to be true.

Tania was still alive.

Here is that same wine now, standing on Diana's lace table-cloth, pouring into Diana's green glasses with the twisty stems. She'd had this wine since that night at the cottage, of course, on special occasions, and between the two couples the wine that got away had remained a fond joke.

Anna takes the first lovely sip, knowing it was thoughtful of Diana but thinking, you are thoughtful now? It's too late to be thoughtful.

She looks across the table at her friend.

'Oh god, I have to smoke,' says Diana suddenly. 'Do you mind? If I open a window?'

Anna says she doesn't mind.

'You sure?' asks Diana.

'I'm sure,' says Anna.

Diana disappears into the kitchen and returns with three cigarettes and a box of matches and an ashtray in the shape of a pineapple.

'I didn't know you'd started again,' says Anna.

'I haven't,' says Diana, 'just in the last few days.'

Anna sips her wine. So, she thinks, the last few days.

'I'm really, really sorry,' says Diana quickly.

Anna turns the stem of her glass between her fingers. She doesn't want to look up. It should be enough that Diana is sorry. She feels within herself for an opening, but she can find none.

Five days ago she woke, showered and dressed. She ate breakfast with Leo and they listened to the radio in silence. Before he left the house, Leo put his arms around her and held her tight. 'Try not to stay in the house all day,' he said. She kissed him goodbye and then she sat at the table again, the breakfast dishes in front of her, listening to the birds in the garden, the sounds of life.

She was still sitting there mid-morning when the phone rang. Thank god, she thought.

'Hello,' she said.

'It's me,' said Diana.

Thank god, she thought. 'I'm glad it's you,' Anna said quietly.

'Good,' said Diana. 'I've got some news.'

Anna was taken aback. 'What news?' she said.

'Jamie's getting married,' said Diana.

Anna pressed her fingertips to her forehead. Jamie had been in love with this girl for as long as Anna could remember. She had dated other boys, gone travelling, played fast and loose with his affections. But lately there had been a change, and they'd all been hoping.

'That's wonderful,' said Anna softly. 'I told you she'd come round. I'm so happy for him – and you.'

'I'm over the moon,' said Diana. 'Your heart aches for them.'

'Yes, it does,' said Anna.

'We're having a few champagnes at six. Just us, and her people. I want you and Leo to come.'

Anna didn't hesitate, she didn't pause. 'Of course,' she said.

She put down the phone. She breathed deeply and listened to her heart. After an hour had passed she picked up the phone again and dialled Diana's number. The answering machine took the call. Diana was probably shopping, Anna thought, looking for something to wear, fretting about her weight, nervous about her new relatives.

'Diana,' Anna said, when the recorded voice asked for her

message, 'we can't come tonight. I think you've forgotten it's Tania's birthday today. I'm sorry. Any other time, but not tonight.'

She wanted to send her best wishes to Jamie but she couldn't go on. She remembered when Jamie was three and he was attacked by a dog; his little head on the hospital pillow, stitched like a baseball. She thought of how he had helped her after Tania's disappearance, how he'd believed. She should be there, she knew that, but today she could not drink champagne and toast someone's future, no matter how much she loved them. And this was one more loss.

She collected the breakfast dishes and slowly stacked them in the dishwasher. I think you've forgotten her, she had wanted to say. Diana was Tania's godmother, she was supposed to look after her if anything happened to Anna and Leo. What if something happened? What if Anna and Leo were not there anymore, who would remember their daughter then?

Anna stood shaking by the sink. She didn't know what to do. She wiped at her face with a tea towel. There was no-one; there was no-one there in the dark, where she was.

Then she thought of the memorial; the slow-turning wheel in the park. It hadn't been there on Tania's last birthday. The day was warm. She could make a Thermos of tea and take her book, she could even take a pen and paper, and if she felt like it she could write to her daughter, she could tell her what life was like without her.

First she would drive to the florist's where Tania had worked. There were others closer, but she wanted to tell Harry about Tania's birthday, and have him help her choose the flowers to take. And later, when Diana called, as she knew she would, she would not speak to her, she would not pick up, not that day and perhaps not the next day either. Not until she was ready.

Diana has smoked her cigarette and still Anna has not answered. Their glasses are nearly empty.

'It's all right,' says Anna at last.

'I don't think it is or you would've talked to me,' says Diana.

Anna looks at Diana's light, wide-spaced eyes.

'I don't want to put you on the rack,' says Anna.

'But I have been,' says Diana, reaching for another cigarette. 'You don't know . . .'

Diana begins to cry. Anna fills their glasses. She feels a little drunk.

'What do you mean?' she says.

'The night of Jamie's drinks – the night of Tania's birthday – something happened to Syd.'

'What happened?'

'He got something stuck in his throat.'

'What sort of thing?'

'One of those, you know, crispy chilli noodle things, from a savoury mix. One minute everyone was drinking and talking and the next Syd was gasping for breath.'

'What happened?'

'We called an ambulance. He was bad. He was really, really bad, Anna. I thought I was going to lose him right here in the lounge room. They kept him calm. Gave him oxygen. But they had to take him to hospital to operate. They couldn't get it out. He was there all night.'

'Was he all right?'

'In the end he was. But his throat's still sore.'

Anna thinks about this. She tries to picture the scene. Diana is an innocent, she realises, as she had once been. A noodle, a night in the hospital; this was not the most terrible thing that could happen.

'Poor Syd,' she says, feeling nothing.

'The worst was,' says Diana, 'when Jamie left the hospital and Syd was asleep, I couldn't call you. I'd made a mess of things and I couldn't call. I went outside to get some air and there was a kid with blood on his face, and I asked if I could have one of his cigarettes and he had a friend in intensive care because they were in an accident and I realised it was the first time in my life that something bad had happened and you weren't there.'

'That's how I felt when you forgot about Tania,' says Anna.

'I know, that's what I was going to say. Outside the hospital I knew how you must have felt but so much worse because Tansie's gone, and I'd got excited and forgotten. Sometimes it's hard knowing what's the best thing to do . . .'

Anna is amazed by Diana's fast-flowing tears. She reaches into her bag for some tissues.

'Don't cry,' she says.

'I need to. I've been so upset about all of this.'

Anna watches Diana press the tissues to her eyes. Her nose is swollen and red.

What had she wanted from Diana? she thinks. A pint of blood, a pound of her flesh? She has her tears. She cannot live her life exacting penance from others for her own grief. There are limits on friendship, there are limits even on love. Everyone is imprisoned within their own skin.

There is a place inside her, a black and barren place. It hadn't been there before but now it would be there always, and she cannot ask anyone to go there with her; it's a place she must go to alone. Perhaps it's a preparation for dying.

None of it matters. Diana is in front of her, not looking her best.

'Perhaps you were just careless,' Anna says, meeting Diana's eye. And then it seems obvious what she will say next. 'Like I was when I broke the wine.'

She reaches out to touch the near-empty bottle.

'Are you enjoying it?' asks Diana.

'It's heaven.'

'Good.'

'Thank you.'

They smile at one another shyly.

'Should we finish it?'

'Why not?' says Anna, lifting the bottle.

They look at the pale drink in their glasses.

'Cheers,' says Diana.

'Cheers,' says Anna.

They drink in silence.

'You know,' says Diana, 'your children are your blood and your husband is your heart, but your girlfriends are the air you breathe.'

Diana had recently finished a creative writing course. Anna has never thought about it that way before, but she knows what Diana means.

'How's Jamie?' she asks.

'Happy,' says Diana. 'He seems years older, somehow.'

'I sent him a card.'

'He said.'

Anna's phone rings in her bag.

'That's me,' she says, reaching.

It's Leo. 'Where are you?' he says.

'At Diana's.'

'What are you doing?'

'Having a little drink.' Anna smiles at Diana.

'You two,' says Leo.

'What's happening?'

'That little girl is here.'

It takes a moment for Anna to understand. 'Pearl? Pearl is there?'

'Yeah. She was sitting on the porch when I got home from work.'

'By herself?'

'All by herself.'

'How did she get there?'

'I don't know.'

'Is she all right?'

'She seems a bit shaky. I gave her some toast and she helped me feed the chooks.'

'Does her mother know where she is?'

'I don't know.'

'Didn't you ask her?'

'No.'

'*Leo!*'

'You'd better come home. Are you right to drive?'

'I've only had one.' She lifts her eyebrows at Diana.

'You girls sort things out?'

'Yes.'

'Told you. Has Di got any lemons left on the tree?'

'I'll ask her. Tell Pearl I'll be there soon.'

Anna returns the phone to her bag.

'Ask me what?' says Diana.

'If there are any lemons left.'

'Stacks,' says Diana. 'Is he still making that stuff?'

'It's coming out of our ears!' Anna drains the last of the wine from her glass. 'I'm sorry, I have to go. The girl I told you about has turned up on the doorstep.'

They push back their chairs.

'The girl from the oval?'

'Yes.'

'You sort of thought this, didn't you?'

'Thought what?'

'That you were connecting more with the girl than with her mother.'

'Did I tell you that?'

'Weeks ago.'

'I've got to be so careful, you know, all this stuff,' says Anna, pulling her keys from her bag. 'The mother's got a new boyfriend and she's all wrapped up in him. And it's awful, I know, but I can't help feeling she's still got her little girl, at least she's got someone.'

'Oh, Annie,' says Diana, moving towards her.

'It's OK, it's bad, I know . . .' Anna waves her hands in the air as if she's drying them, feeling herself on the edge of unstoppable tears.

'It's not bad, it's normal. This victim support stuff is too hard on you.'

'Not always.' She takes a deep, shaky breath. 'I can't start bawling, I've got to drive.'

'Come here,' says Diana, opening her arms.

Anna smells the smoke in Diana's hair and feels the aliveness swarming beneath her soft, warm flesh. For just one moment it is a miracle, this aliveness, and then they slowly draw apart.

'The lemons,' says Diana.

'Oh yes, the lemons.'

Ashes

OUTSIDE HER FRONT DOOR, Anna stops and rummages in her bag for mints.

Pearl and Leo are watching the news on TV. Leo has changed out of his work clothes, because they have a visitor. She kisses his forehead and hands him the lemons, indicating that he should go.

She mutes the television, and as she takes a place next to Pearl on the couch she remembers the day she sat there with the detective, and he believed her, and the end began.

Pearl is wearing the same small skirt she always wears, but Anna is pleased to see that she has something on her legs now, a pair of knee-high vinyl boots over a long pair of striped socks. The boots are much too wide for her skinny calves.

'I like your new boots,' says Anna.

Pearl looks down and turns up her toes.

'Mum got them for me,' she says.

She's pale, thinks Anna. 'It's nice to see you,' she says.

Pearl stares at her knees.

Anna is feeling a little drunk, and she hopes it doesn't show.

'I found you in the telephone book,' says Pearl.

'Well done,' says Anna. 'How did you get here?'

'In a taxi. You know, with those vouchers?'

'Does Lily know you're here?'

Pearl remembers when Riley was alive and they were out walking by themselves and people asked them this question. She shakes her head.

'Do you think we should tell her?' asks Anna.

'I don't want to.'

'Why not?'

'I'm too upset.'

'What are you upset about?'

Pearl curls her hands in her lap, and her eyes fill slowly with tears.

'Lily gave Riley's ashes to Adam.'

Anna feels a slow, sick churning in her stomach.

'When?' she says.

'Today,' says Pearl, her tears falling.

Anna has never seen Pearl cry before, and she thinks of Diana.

'What happened?' she says.

'Adam came over. He never usually comes in the daytime. Lily told me to go to the shops, and when I got back they were in the kitchen and Lily was taking his ashes out of the box. They were in one of those, you know, one of those bags.'

She brings both her hands together in a pinching motion.

'A zip-lock bag?' says Anna.

Pearl nods and wipes at her face with the back of her hand.

'And she gave the bag to Adam?'

'Yes. And he put it in his pocket but it was too big.'

'And then what happened?'

'He said, "Thanks, Lily, I know what this means and I'll try to make you proud".'

Once, thinks Anna, before Tania was murdered, she would have sought to allay a child's fears about the nature of adult fancy and motive and trust. There must be some explanation, she would have said. But she is not an innocent anymore, and neither is Pearl.

'Did Lily tell you why she gave Adam the ashes?'

'No, but I know.'

'Why?'

'Because she wants him to be nice and have sex and love her.'

Anna realises that Pearl has given the perfect answer to a question she had not meant to ask.

She tries again. 'Did Lily tell you why Adam wanted the ashes?'

Fresh tears flow down Pearl's face. Anna reaches into her bag. There is only one tissue left and she's not sure it's clean. She hands it to Pearl anyway.

'She said Adam was going to do something artistic with Riley's ashes.'

'Like what?' Anna is so surprised that her question comes out as a demand, and she takes Pearl's hand in an effort to soften the effect.

'I don't know,' says Pearl. 'Mum said Adam probably would win the competition for the memorial.'

'Did you tell Lily that you were upset?'

'She saw me crying in front of her. She said Adam was trying to help us remember Riley.'

Pearl draws her hand from beneath Anna's and covers her face. For a moment, Anna is reminded of peek-a-boo and babies and laughter, but then Pearl's shoulders begin to shake.

'I don't want Adam to remember Riley,' she cries brokenly, 'I don't want Lily to have a baby with Adam.'

The words are a surprise but Anna understands their logic and she knows she cannot argue against it. How should one be with someone else's child? she asks herself, even as she puts her arm around Pearl and draws her close.

Her crying continues, more bitter, deeper. Anna knows this crying and its backlog of grief and the collapsing that takes place inside. If Pearl were her own daughter, she would curl her like a baby in her arms. She is aware of her slight drunkenness and the smell of alcohol on her breath and skin. She wants to tell Pearl that she will look after her, and she will never let anything happen to her, but she can't because it's not true, it can never be true, and she knows that when an adult reassures a child with words freighted by alcohol, the words are almost always for themselves.

Suddenly a small white dog hurtles into the room, its short legs working like a cartoon under its low body. The dog runs around the coffee table and scrabbles at Pearl's boots.

Pearl shifts her legs uneasily.

'No, Scampi,' says Anna firmly, lifting the dog and placing it in her lap. The dog sits for a moment and then it strains towards Pearl again. Pearl jumps away.

'No! Scampi!' growls Anna, pulling him back.

'I get a bit scared,' says Pearl.

'He won't hurt you,' says Anna. 'He just loves children.'

The dog barks loudly.

'Leo!' Anna calls.

Leo appears in the room, as if he had been just outside the door.

'Can you take Scampi away?' asks Anna.

Leo sips the drink he is holding.

'Come here, you,' he says, scooping the dog under one arm. 'Have a taste, I've made a new batch.'

Anna puts her hand out for the glass, wets her lips and shivers.

'Still too much lemon,' she says, handing it back.

'Are you sure?' asks Leo. 'I thought it was better.'

'You're nearly there,' says Anna.

Leo takes another sip of the drink and frowns. Anna watches him as he turns away, his big hand caressing the dog's belly. Pearl is alone with her mother, thinks Anna. I'm alone with Leo. Sometimes it's too much, too much.

'Scampi was Tania's dog,' says Anna, looking at Pearl. Pearl's tears have dried, and there's scarcely a sign of her crying. Anna recalls this: a child's face being like a magic slate, the effects of even torrid emotion erased in a moment.

'Is Scampi a puppy or an old dog?' asks Pearl.

'He's in-between,' says Anna. 'Tania got him for her sixteenth birthday.'

She is about to say it was Tania's birthday last week, but she's suddenly too tired. The wine has worn off and she has a terrible acid hunger and a heavy head. She thinks of Diana and all the tears that have been shed that day.

'We have to ring your mum,' she says.

Pearl nods. Anna thinks for a moment.

'What if we let Lily know you're here and ask her if you can stay the night? Do you want to do that?'

'Yes,' says Pearl.

The three of us will sit down, thinks Anna, the three of us will eat. In the night, there will be three people breathing.

'I'll get the phone,' says Anna.

Pearl reaches down and pulls up one sock and then the other. She puts the wad of wet tissue on the edge of the coffee table and looks at the family of elephants. There are cream and gold curtains on the windows and gold carpet on the floor. On the TV, people are speaking to each other without any sound, and the heater in the wall isn't on. In a tall cupboard with glass doors there are painted vases and some very small cups, and statues of a Spanish dancer and a boy holding a fish.

Everything is strange and still. What if Anna gave her something for dinner that she didn't like? Everything smells different and cold and plasticy.

She's missed *Frasier*. She wants to sleep in her own bed. She wants to lie on the couch with her mother, a blanket over their legs. It's Thursday, they can watch *CSI*. And in the morning she will know where she is, because everything will be just the same.

'Do you want to speak to her or do you want me to do it?' asks Anna, walking into the room.

Pearl doesn't want to stay now, but she doesn't want to be difficult. Anna seems happy somehow.

'Probably I should go home,' she says quietly.

'But you . . .' Anna says. 'Do you want to go home?'

'Yes,' says Pearl.

Anna studies her for a moment, and Pearl's face feels ugly.

'We'd still better call her,' says Anna. 'I don't have my book, what's your number?'

Pearl watches as Anna holds the phone to her ear and folds her other arm across her stomach as if she has an ache. She worries now about what Lily will say. She thinks of how she fed the chickens with Leo and how frightened she was of their horrible eyes. She wishes she could look closer at the things in the cupboard, especially at the very small cups.

'It's engaged,' says Anna.

Pearl can't think of the right thing to say.

'It's a bit cold,' says Anna. 'Are you cold?'

She crosses the room and pushes a button on the heater. There's a ticking sound, and three brilliant blue squares appear and slowly turn to pink and then orange.

'The room won't take long to heat up,' says Anna.

Pearl wonders if really she should stay.

Anna sits next to Pearl on the couch. 'We'll try Lily again soon,' she says.

Anna sighs. Pearl looks at the telephone, and the wet tissue on the coffee table. Everything is quiet.

Suddenly Anna turns to Pearl. 'This is what I think we should do,' she says. 'We'll get pizza. Leo's hungry and I'm hungry – are you?'

Pearl looks at her and nods.

'After dinner I'll take you home, and when we get there I'll talk to your mother about Riley's ashes.'

Pearl stares at Anna. She doesn't look scared.

'What are you going to say?' asks Pearl.

'I'm going to tell Lily that she's done something silly and we have to get the ashes back.'

Pearl takes in two things at once: Anna's unintentional rhyme, and the fact that someone is going to stick up for her.

Two Stories

SONIA EXPECTS ADAM FOR coffee this morning. She's made a lemon tart. He comes in most days now, they talk about films and television, what's happening in the news, sometimes about his work. Sonia tells him about some of the places she's been.

She hadn't seen him the day before because she was busy with the men from the museum who came to pick up the bed. She had agreed to the bed being restored before the exhibition, but she asked that they preserve the moisture rings staining its wings, because they'd become the butterfly's eyes.

She was faintly embarrassed as the men lifted the bare mattress and placed it against the wall.

After the museum van disappeared down the street she took the vacuum cleaner from the laundry and carried it upstairs. She picked up a Tiger Balm lid from the dusty carpet in the centre of the room, and plugged the vacuum cleaner into the wall.

She had worried about this moment, but it was not so bad. Maybe she even felt a bit lighter? Something tinkled its way up the vacuum cleaner hose. Everything had been the same for so long. She wouldn't lay the mattress on the floor in place of the bed, after all. The mattress could go to the Good Samaritans and she would buy a new one when the bed came back. Until then she would sleep in Karl or Gabriel's room, look at different walls.

She shut off the vacuum with her foot. The silence was good, and she looked around her. Tonight she would phone her sons to find out if they were coming home for the exhibition. They had both said they wanted to, but for Karl, the problem was time, and for Gabe, money.

She could see the three of them together at the exhibition. She saw them lift their glasses. 'To Pieter,' she heard them say. She saw herself walking slowly with Gabriel past the furniture, mentioning the past, looking up now and then to find Karl across the room, talking and laughing, the beautiful spaces opening at the sides of his mouth.

She slipped one foot out of its shoe and drew it across the freshly vacuumed pile.

There's a particular reason Sonia wants to talk to Adam today, it's something that came to her in the night. She spent hours lying awake, thinking about her family. Sometimes the second pill didn't work.

Karl and Gabriel weren't coming home for Pieter's exhibition. Sonia thought of how she'd gone to the other side of the world in order to leave a mother who was cruel, and how her sons had gone because they could. One was so much better than the other, which meant that she and Pieter had done their job.

She thought of when Karl and Gabriel were children: their voices bubbling through the house, their hectic limbs – she had made sure that no-one in her home had felt trapped.

She remembered Fionnuala and her brothers, imprisoned in the bodies of swans. It might help Adam to hear that story, she thought. In one way or another, the children of the memorial were all like the children of Lir, sentenced by adult will to loss. She tried to ease her back on the narrow mattress. The detail was everything: the children adrift for three hundred years and three hundred years more, and three hundred years after that.

She hauled all the details from her mind, ordered them and smoothed them into shape. It was heavy work, and the immensity of the darkness pressed in on her. She might have given in to despair had it not been for the small voice inside her already narrating, already rehearsing the story of the children of Lir, as she would tell it to Adam the next day.

Now they sit on the patio in the vine-dappled light. Sonia cuts the lemon tart and places a slice on a plate for him.

'Are you having some?' Adam asks.

'Not yet,' she replies. 'Cook's curse. I'm not really hungry.' She sips her coffee.

'How's your work going?' she asks.

He nods, chewing. He would like to tell her about his plan to make porcelain from the bones of a child. Of course, he'd have to take her through the idea slowly – there were so many taboos surrounding death in Western culture – to help her understand how, from someone lost, he would make something lasting.

Why scatter ashes over water, for example? Wasn't that a further loss, to give a loved one to the wind?

He would have to go into a bit of science in order to explain to her how he's adjusted the recipe for porcelain, but all that could be kept to a minimum.

To finish, the last detail, would he tell her how serendipity, the Muse's industrious sister, had stepped in?

He washes down his mouthful with coffee. He would like to say all this, but he's wary now of property owners and their fears.

'The work's going well,' he says. 'I think I've made a break-through.'

'Good,' says Sonia.

She lets the silence fall between them as Adam takes another forkful of tart and a bird she has never heard before sounds a long, deep note that reminds her of a ship leaving port.

In their pots on the patio, the frangipani are producing the first leaves on the amputee stumps of winter.

'I remembered a story last night,' she says, setting her cup down. 'It's a story about children. I first heard it at school in Copenhagen.'

Adam looks at her above his fork.

'There was a king,' she begins, 'and he had four children. A daughter and three younger sons . . .'

It seems like she's been speaking for a long time and the children have only just turned into swans. She wants to convey to Adam a sense of the children's helplessness against the enormity of their fate, but as Adam comes to the end of his tart and his eyes linger more and more on his plate, a mild panic overtakes her.

She wishes the story were over; it feels like a race suddenly, her words against his interest, and she can't hold him. To catch up she is dropping details – the children's voices in the swans' throats, the black seas, the year after year after year – and each time she lets one detail go she knows that, paradoxically, it is one less hook to hold him.

It's a story that demands a long time in the telling, almost so that the listener will be as weary as the children were weary. But even as she has the children flying towards the Rock of Seals she knows she can't go much further, putting her voice out there against his jiggling leg and restless gaze. She sacrifices the detail of the ice storm and the children's flesh and feathers stuck to the rock – even though this is what the memorial is about: the hurt, the slow work of healing, the scars – and moves on quickly through the cold and the years and the children's discovery that the world they had known was gone forever.

Suddenly she's at the end, her heart cramped, and she delivers the final image: four naked, withered old bodies; set to die. She sees the movement in Adam's eye, almost imperceptible – the slightest of pupil contractions, perhaps – but she recognises it as the same shrinking that she's seen in her younger son's eye, whenever he was faced with an aged body or sickness or frailty.

Her coffee is cold.

'That's a pretty heavy story,' says Adam.

'I didn't tell it very well,' says Sonia.

'I've been getting into the Grimm stories myself,' says Adam. 'I think I prefer them to the one you just told. They always end in escape or recovery, redemption of some kind.'

'I guess it depends on whether you believe in those things,' says Sonia. She feels she doesn't want to try anymore.

'Why wouldn't you?' asks Adam.

Sonia notes the genuine surprise on his face.

'Well, a lot of the children you're designing the memorial for didn't escape or recover.'

'But they'll be redeemed,' says Adam. 'That's what the memorial is supposed to do.'

Sonia is taken aback.

'Have some more tart,' she says.

As she fills her cup with fresh coffee from the pot, she wonders if his problems with the design of the memorial would be fewer if he didn't expect to do so much. She thinks to suggest this to him, to remind him gently that no artist is God, but just at that moment Adam's phone rings on the table next to him.

'Hello,' he says.

'Is that Adam Logan?'

He doesn't recognise the woman's voice. 'Yes.'

'My name is Anna Zanetti. I'm a friend of Lily's. She gave me your number.'

This is unexpected. The thing he has with Lily is, well, secret – they haven't even been outside her flat together. He can't imagine what a friend of hers would want with him.

'Yes?' he says.

'I'll get straight to the point,' says Anna. 'I was hoping I could speak to you about your art.'

Adam's interest is aroused. 'What specifically about my art?' he asks.

'About the ashes,' says Anna.

What the fuck? thinks Adam. What has Lily been saying?

'What specifically about them?' he says, not wanting to say too much in front of Sonia.

'I'd really prefer to talk about it in person,' says Anna.

There is something in her tone, something serious, and suddenly Adam thinks he understands.

'I'm working at the moment,' he says, careful to sound calm.

'Could I come to where you're working? I won't take up much of your time.'

She has some ashes, thinks Adam. He can hear it, and it makes sense. Surely Lily would know the mothers of the other children killed on the oval that day?

'I could see you now,' he says.

Anna Zanetti asks where he is, and he tells her the address and she replies that she is not far away.

'All right,' says Adam, 'my studio's at the back, but it's probably best if you go to the front door.'

He looks questioningly at Sonia, who nods her head.

'I'll do that,' says Anna. 'Pearl and I will be there in fifteen minutes.'

This is a new puzzle, that Lily's daughter is with her, but he doesn't know how to question her about it. He feels vaguely uneasy as he hangs up, but he tells himself that the woman is most likely to be babysitting.

'Do you mind if these people drop by?' he asks Sonia.

'Of course not,' she replies. 'Who are they?'

Adam takes a moment. 'Just the friend of a woman I've been . . . seeing. And her daughter.'

'The friend's daughter?'

'No, the daughter of the woman.' The woman who gave me the ashes, he nearly says. But he remembers he isn't sharing this with Sonia – not yet, anyway – so he thinks of something else instead.

'The woman's son was one of those children killed at the

oval last summer,' he says. 'Her daughter is the only one who survived.'

Sonia remembers the hot night she first saw the images of the murdered children on TV. She thinks back to Adam's earlier comment about the memorial, and wonders if she judged him too quickly then. She thinks she can see now the purpose behind his gaucherie, his charm. His ambition for the memorial was personal, and deep – she could tell this by his hesitation when he spoke of her; he loved a woman who had lost a child and whose other child had surely known terror. Little wonder that he was in the business of redemption.

'Should I make more coffee?' she asks.

'Good idea,' he says.

When the doorbell rings, Sonia suggests that Adam gets it. While he is gone she stands up from the table and crosses the patio. She picks a grub from the underside of a gardenia leaf. She is curious about the visitors, particularly the child. It's a long time since she's had a child in her house, and this one has lived through something beyond her own imagining. Already she has a feeling for this girl; perhaps it's no more than she would feel for a rare and delicate vase on display in a glass case in an important museum, but it's a feeling.

The door opens and closes behind her.

The woman is younger than Sonia but older than she'd expected. She had imagined someone nearer Adam's age, someone more like him. The woman who is introduced to her now as Anna is dressed in tailored camel trousers and a cream silk shirt. Her thick curly hair is the colour of claret and gathered at the back of her head by a clip that looks like a trap for a small animal. Her lipstick is fuchsia bright, but her eyes are huge, dark and sad.

'And this is Pearl,' says Anna.

Sonia looks down at the girl. She remembers when Karl was like this: thin arms and legs, translucent torso, jade veins snaking beneath his skin.

Sonia extends her hand and the girl seems to know what to do. It's not a handshake, but their fingers meet, and hold for a moment. Sonia is aware that she is scrutinising the child for signs of grief or trouble, and when she finds none she experiences Pearl's ordinariness as a form of rebuke, and is chastened by it. She is simply a skinny girl with soft grey eyes and a shyness, a certain reserve. If she passed her in the aisle of a supermarket she might look at her because her hair is pretty and she likes little girls who wear headbands, like Alice – she likes little girls who look like little girls – but that is all.

She asks Anna if she would like some coffee.

'No, thanks,' says Anna. 'I don't want to take up too much of your time, Adam. Maybe we could talk?'

Adam suggests they go to his studio. He's puzzled by Anna, can't make the connection with Lily or the dead children on the oval. He's aware that Pearl is staring at him and he is beginning to feel uneasy again; whatever is going down, it's the business of adults and it would be better if she weren't there.

It comes to him like a revelation. 'Sonia, Pearl has done a great drawing of *Fallingwater*.'

'Have you?' asks Sonia, with surprise.

'What?' says Pearl, knitting her eyebrows at him.

'That picture of the house you drew. The house is called *Fallingwater*.'

There's something wrong with his tone, thinks Sonia.

'It's a famous house,' she says. 'My husband loved it. I went there with him. I was just telling Adam about it the other day.'

'How did you know?' says Pearl, still staring at him.

'Know what?'

'About my drawings?'

'Lily showed me.'

'When?'

'I don't know, a while ago.'

Pearl looks away. What does she do? They know about her drawings; they know things about the house that she doesn't know. The house in Gus's office had been real enough to think about and draw, but it was like a castle in a story, that kind of real, you believed it but you knew it wasn't true. Now they are telling her otherwise and she wishes they weren't all looking at her as she tries to take this in and find a place for it.

'What's it called again?' she says.

'*Fallingwater*,' says Sonia.

'Where is it?'

'In America. In a place called Pennsylvania.'

Pearl is confused. She thought this was where vampires came from, and she isn't sure if it's a real place or not.

'Who lives there?'

'No-one. But you can visit it, you can go on a tour. It's sort of like a museum. Everything in the house is just the same as when its owners were living there.'

Pearl is quiet for a moment.

'Is it good?' she says.

Sonia smiles at her. 'It's gorgeous. I've got some photos – do you want to see them?'

Pearl looks at Anna. Anna will talk to Adam. The house has a name. *Fallingwater*. It doesn't sound strange anymore, almost as if she had never not known it.

∼

It's only when Adam is opening the studio door that he remembers he has left the ashes on the workbench. Anna sees them the moment she enters the room.

Anna takes the old office chair Adam offers her. He clears another for himself and they face each other with nothing but the bare concrete floor between them.

Anna looks him calmly in the eye. 'I'd like you to return the little boy's ashes,' she says.

Adam ceases his swivelling. What what what? he thinks, feeling it like a slug in the guts. He takes a deep breath.

Adam can see when Anna looks at him that she does not find him agreeable. He's accustomed to a register of attraction on the faces of the women he meets, regardless of their age or status and their own appeal, or lack of it. He feels a surge of helplessness, but it doesn't last for long. Her request is so unauthorised, and therefore so powerless, that he could have been excused for laughing.

'Can you tell me,' he says, 'what your connection to these ashes is and why you feel you have the right to ask me to return them?'

'I'm a friend of Pearl and Lily's,' she says.

Adam decides he will speak slowly. 'Maybe Lily hasn't explained to you why I intend to use the ashes in an artwork . . .'

Anna listens carefully to all the things Lily hasn't explained to her. She watches Adam's eyes and hands as he talks.

'But Pearl is upset,' she says, when Adam is finished.

'But Lily was the boy's mother,' he says, 'and Lily made a decision to give the ashes to me.'

Anna looks down at her hands. She straightens her engagement ring and her wedding ring, and the ring Leo gave her that pledges eternity.

Once she would not have been here. Once she would have been sitting down now, having straightened the house, with a cup of coffee and something nice to eat, perhaps to read the paper or watch half an hour of TV. But that was before her daughter was taken from her. Now she is sitting across from this young man who needs to shave, who wears two T-shirts in colours that don't match. She cannot go back, as much as she longs for it, to a time that doesn't contain this man and this bag of ashes. She can only move forward.

'I understand that this memorial is important to you,' she says, her voice almost a whisper.

Adam sits back in his chair and crosses one leg over the other. Finally, he thinks.

'Yes it is,' he says. 'It's very important.'

'Well,' says Anna, running her fingers down the crease of her trousers, 'I know you don't know anything about me but, you see, the reason I know Lily is that I also had a child who was murdered.'

Adam goes to say something but Anna raises her hand.

'And when you have a child who is murdered you meet all kinds of people you never thought you'd meet. Police, lawyers – people like you, for example. People from the newspapers and the television. And some of these people might be interested in someone like you.'

Adam has been sitting quietly, nodding where appropriate, but now his neck stiffens.

'You see,' Anna continues, 'some of these people – a television person, for example – might like to know that one of the artists who is in the competition to design the Children's Memorial has obtained the ashes of a little boy.'

Adam relaxes. She is ludicrous, he thinks, she is speaking

as though she is *on* television, some bad cop show. He laughs lightly.

'None of those people are going to be interested,' he says. 'None of those television shows care about art.'

Anna knows that it is not just Adam Logan sitting across from her now. It's the man who dumped her daughter at sea, the driver of the car on the oval – all the people who have hurt her and of whose heads it was not possible to touch a single hair. It isn't fair what she's doing, not really, not in the old way that she had once understood fair to be. This young man probably has a mother who loves him, who is proud of him.

'You're right,' she says. 'They're not the least bit interested in art.'

She wants to stand up. She wants to walk over to him and circle his chair and lean down close to his ear.

'But you know what they are interested in? You know this, I know you do. They're interested in the victims of crime. Everyone is, don't you think? And as a spokesperson for Victims of Crime – that's what I am now, Adam, that's what I've become – they would be interested to hear that a little girl who hid from a murderer while her only brother was hunted and killed, well, that little girl is upset. I think they would feel it was their duty to tell the story of the artist and the ashes and the little girl, don't you?'

She is nearly there.

'I'll give you a moment to think about it,' she says.

Pearl asks if she can look at the photos of *Fallingwater* again. The album is open on the table in front of them, and her apple juice is nearly empty. Through the dining room window, Sonia and Pearl can see beyond the pool to the workshop and every now and then one of them will turn their head and wonder what is taking place out there between Anna and Adam.

Sonia's chair is drawn up to the table but Pearl stands in order to see the photos better. Sonia tells her that they weren't allowed to take photos inside *Fallingwater*, but there are lots of photos of the outside of the house and of the forest that surrounds it.

'It was autumn,' says Sonia. 'It was freezing cold.'

There are photos like the one on Gus's wall, with the rocks and water, and the terraces floating in the air, but in Sonia's photos there's smoke coming out of the chimneys and the trees are bare, their branches like lace against the silver sky, red leaves carpeting the ground. Sonia is in some of the photographs, wearing the silver bracelets she's wearing now, and it's hard for Pearl to believe this; that she is beside the beautiful house, and here, beside her.

'I love the person who made that house,' Pearl says quietly.

Sonia looks at her. 'His name was Frank Lloyd Wright,' she says.

'Frank?'

'Lloyd Wright.'

'Frank Lloyd Wright,' repeats Pearl.

She bends further over the pages of the album to examine the detail that had interested Sonia's husband. She sees that even the stones of the chimneys take their pattern from the layers of rock the house is built upon.

Sonia studies Pearl's high forehead and her pale lips pressed together in concentration. She doesn't know if she should say it. Perhaps it's not her place, perhaps it will upset the girl.

'Adam told me your little brother died at the oval,' says Sonia finally, 'with all the others.'

Pearl's eyes are on the photographs again, and she barely nods.

'Something like that happened in Frank Lloyd Wright's life, too,' Sonia says gently.

Pearl looks at her. 'What happened?'

This will be the second story Sonia has told this morning. Again there's detail, and she hopes she remembers it all. She will try not to hurry this time, or lose faith.

'Well, Frank Lloyd Wright built a wonderful place,' she begins. 'It had a house and garden, and a farm with animals, where they grew flowers and everything they wanted to eat. There was a stream and a dam, and a chapel, and courtyards with fountains. There was also a workshop where Frank Lloyd Wright worked on his projects and people came from all over to work with him and study to be an architect.'

'Where was it?' asks Pearl.

'In America,' says Sonia. 'Somewhere called Wisconsin. The name of the place that he built was *Taliesin*.'

'Why?' asks Pearl.

'Why what?'

'Why was it called *Taliesin*?'

'I don't know,' says Sonia, 'but I've got a book, I could look it up.'

'What happened?'

Sonia can smell her sweet apple breath.

'He built this place for a woman he loved, so they could live there together and make a happy, creative life.' How much does she need to know? thinks Sonia. That both had left marriages, that there was scandal and blame? Was it necessary to censor a story for a child who already knew the ways of the world? Or was that even more reason to?

'This woman had two little girls,' she continues.

'Did something happen to the little girls?' asks Pearl.

'Yes,' says Sonia. Now that they've reached this point in the story, it's not easy to tell it.

'One day something happened at *Taliesin*. While Frank Lloyd Wright was away, a servant killed the woman that Frank Lloyd Wright loved. And he killed her two daughters, and another child who was the son of the gardener, and three other young men who were apprentices and workmen there. And then the servant started a fire and the whole house was burnt to the ground.'

Pearl stands very still, gazing at a point past Sonia's shoulder.

'That's seven people,' she says, at last.

'Yes,' says Sonia.

'How did he kill them?'

Sonia had not foreseen this question, but it seems too late to lie.

'He killed them with an axe.'

'Oh,' says Pearl, and turns back to the photos of *Fallingwater*.

Sonia is not sure if she's done the right thing. She studies Pearl closely as her eyes move over the pages. Pieter had told her the story of Frank Lloyd Wright and the events at *Taliesin*, a long time ago. It was a story of loss, like the children of Lir, but unlike that story, it held hope. Or that was how Pieter told it. *Taliesin* was rebuilt and Frank Lloyd Wright lived there again with a new love. A child was born, and in the architect's very long life there was more creation; more building and beauty.

'Did he make this before?' asks Pearl, pointing to *Falling-water*.

'Before what?' says Sonia.

'Before all the people were killed?'

'No,' says Sonia. '*Fallingwater* was just one of the many things that he designed after.'

'How long after?'

'I don't know. But I could look it up in the book. Do you want me to?'

Pearl looks at her and nods. She sits down on the chair and waits for Sonia. She's forgotten about Anna and Adam and the ashes. Something had happened to the man who made *Fallingwater*. She wonders if all along the house has told her this. She leans forward and studies the photographs again. The rocks, the water, the floating.

'The people died at *Taliesin* in 1914,' says Sonia, returning to the room. She is holding a book open with her thumb.

Pearl can do the sum. 'That's a long time ago,' she says.

'Yes,' says Sonia, pulling up another chair. Pearl watches her turn to the back of the book.

'And *Fallingwater* was built in 1936,' Sonia says.

'It's an old house,' says Pearl, with surprise.

'Just a bit older than me,' laughs Sonia.

'I thought it was new.'

'Did you? Why?'

'Because it looks new.'

'Maybe that's what's so special about it,' says Sonia.

In her head, Pearl takes fourteen away from thirty-six.

'I'll see if I can find out what *Taliesin* means,' says Sonia.

The house came twenty-two years later. If she adds twenty-two to her own age she gets thirty. But she doesn't know anything about thirty, it's in the future, and the future is a secret.

'*Taliesin* is a Welsh word,' says Sonia. 'It means shining brow.'

'Like eyebrow?' asks Pearl.

'No, more like forehead, or the top of a hill.'

'Maybe it was built on a hill.'

'Maybe.'

There's a knock on the window. Pearl and Sonia look up and Anna is standing outside. It's a long window and Pearl can see that one of Anna's feet is in the garden, standing on a plant. She looks at Sonia but Sonia doesn't seem to care, she's getting up from the table, inviting Anna to go to the back door, to come inside.

Anna's eyes find Pearl's. Anna lifts one of her hands and points excitedly to the red handbag under her arm.

Riley's ashes are back.

The Season Shifts

PEARL TRIES TO REMEMBER what Anna has told her: 'Lily can't stay mad with you forever.' But as the nights follow the days there's no end to her mother's silence. If Pearl sits down next to her on the couch, Lily draws her legs in tight, like the sea anemone they once had at school.

Adam doesn't come over anymore and Lily says it's Pearl's and Anna's fault. 'Are you happy now?' she asks Pearl. Lily has told Anna not to visit, but Anna and Pearl talk on the telephone and Lily says nothing. Riley's ashes are in the shoebox again, this time under Pearl's bed. She is not happy that the ashes are back, that's not what she feels, it just feels right, but when she tries to explain this to her mother, Lily says, 'And you always have to be right, don't you?'

Nothing has changed in Pearl's room since Riley's been

gone. His toys lie around, and all his clothes are still mixed up with hers.

She kneels on the bedroom floor and one by one takes Riley's things from the drawers. There's a pile for his socks and one for his undies, another for T-shirts and bottoms. She folds his old rocket pyjamas. She takes her own clothes from the bottom drawer and places them in one of the drawers above, and then she pulls out the empty bottom drawer, tugging first on one handle and then on the other.

Pearl carries the drawer into the hallway and past the lounge room, where Lily is watching television. She feels her mother give an angry twitch. She has to go sideways through the doors. She puts the drawer down on the kitchen table while she opens the front door, and then goes sideways to the outside.

It's not easy to lift the drawer over the railing but she can do it if she stands on her toes. She tips the drawer upside down and crumbs and fluff float away on the air, while stickers and bits of crayon drop to the carpark below. She shouldn't really be doing this, she knows that, but there's no-one to stop her, and the drawer has to be perfectly clean.

The telephone rings in the lounge room as she walks back down the hall.

The drawer is hard to get in. She has to fit one end, and then the other, and then wriggle it the rest of the way. Lily is talking on the phone. Riley's underwear goes into the drawer first, and then his pyjamas.

Pearl hears her mother's footsteps and guesses that Lily is going to her bedroom. It's not so bad when Lily is lying down, when her door is closed. But her mother doesn't walk past, she stops and leans against the doorframe.

'Whatcha doing?' she says.

Everything inside Pearl rushes towards her.

'Making a drawer for Riley's things,' she says, folding his blue shark T-shirt.

'You're a good girl,' says Lily.

Pearl feels the warmth in her cheeks. She looks up at her smiling mother but then a dark suspicion creeps in.

'Who was on the phone?' she asks.

'Those people who gave us the TV,' says Lily. 'Remember?'

'From the TV program?'

'Yeah. Them.'

'What did they want?'

'They just rang to say hello. To see how we were.'

'What did you say?'

'I said we were good.'

'What did they say?'

'They said good.'

Pearl picks up Riley's little baseball cap.

'Do you want to put his toys in there too?' asks Lily. 'Will they fit?'

Just one drawer, thinks Pearl. She hopes that if Riley can see her now, he will know that it is only his things that she is packing away.

'They'll fit,' she says.

When Anna rings to talk to Pearl that night, Lily is in the bath. As Anna tells Pearl about her day shopping with Diana, Pearl can hear water pouring from the taps and the bath squeaking, and there's no anger in these sounds anymore.

When Anna finishes her story she asks Pearl how her day has been. Pearl tells her about the change in Lily's mood, and that they had Chicken Treat for tea.

It was a long way to Chicken Treat, and normally Lily didn't like walking. The sky was a deep blue and the air smelled of cars and flowers. They walked quietly through the streets of flats and houses, listening to dogs and babies, and the clattering in kitchens. They had a competition to see who could count the most televisions; sometimes it was only a flickering light against a wall or a whitish glow behind blinds, but everything was included. Lily was quicker than Pearl and every time she got another one she smiled to herself. When they turned into the main road, the lights stretching into the distance were blurry and bright in the growing dark. A car sounded its horn and a boy hung out the back window and yelled something at Lily. Pearl looked at Lily as they passed beneath a streetlight. 'It's good to be out,' Lily said.

'Did something happen to make Lily feel better?' asks Anna.

'I don't know,' says Pearl. 'Some people from the TV rang up.'

'What people?'

'I don't know.'

'What did they want?'

'Lily said they wanted to know how we were.'

There's silence on the other end of the line, and Pearl hears Lily calling.

'That was nice of them,' says Anna finally.

'Lily's saying do I want to hop in the bath with her,' says Pearl.

'Go, blossom,' says Anna, 'I'll talk to you tomorrow.'

Anna puts the phone down on the bedside table. Through the open window she can hear Leo tinkering about in the garage, whistling a tune that makes her think of Frank Sinatra. She had thought she would never hear it again, this strong, sweet whistling; Leo lighthearted. She closes her eyes for a moment to listen.

She slips off her shoes. She will have a bath too, she wants to be close to her husband tonight. As she undresses, she thinks of Pearl and Lily. The TV people will be calling them again, she's sure of that. And somehow she is responsible for it. Not responsible in the way a stone-thrower is responsible for a broken window; as responsible as a dreamer, perhaps, as one whose dream becomes the future.

She had no intention of going anywhere with a story of an artist and a little boy's ashes; she knew no people, she was a spokesperson for nothing. But Tania's death had taught her about people's cowardice, and about her own ability to bully and bluff, and it had not been difficult to make Adam Logan believe her threats.

She had known, however. Even as she pretended to Adam Logan about television contacts and victims' stories, she'd known there was a possibility that she was conjuring something in Pearl and Lily's lives.

Anna slips off her bra and pants and rubs her hands lightly over her skin. Her bare feet move quickly across the carpet.

One day the season shifts and you no longer feel cold when you take off your clothes. The windows stay open. You hadn't noticed, you were thinking of something else, but all this Anna notices now: everything is a little kinder.

Devotion

ADAM WRAPS HIS TOWEL around his neck and moves to the exercise bike. On the TV screens above him, a god in canary-yellow pyjamas tears into the wind and unleashes his might. It's cricket time again. Adam wishes he could afford a better gym; this cavernous, echoing old warehouse with its hangover blue lighting and sweat and chemical smells reminds him of an abattoir, or prison.

It's mid-morning, the hour when the lone wolves prowl the gym floor, their arms stiff with muscle and rope-like veins, their eyes taut and edgy as a seagull's. Adam watches these men at a distance, from the treadmill or rowing machine or through the protective grimace of his own weightlifting. He feels a greasy, slithery pleasure in watching them; he imagines it's like the pleasure once known to the audiences of freak

Deborah Robertson

shows: the freedom to turn a diamond-hard gaze upon another human being different in the extreme to oneself, and to feel the animal response within one's own body, unencumbered by modern sentiment or guilt. But he has to be careful of these men also, their vigilance, and their radar, finely tuned to threat, insult or sexual suggestion; there's always the possibility of bristling psychic war, the chance of true violence.

Adam checks his pulse rate and pumps his legs harder. These men don't interest him today, because today he's been keeping his eye on a woman. He has seen her a few times before, penetrating the arena of hard-core weightlifters. She is not like the bunnies with augmented breasts and headlight-yellow hair that sometimes accompany these men: she's as thin as a whippet and her complexion is slum-child grey. No colourful Lycra clads her body, nothing trim or tight: just a checked flannel shirt and baggy black trackpants, grimy sweat-bands wrapping both stick wrists. The men clear a wide space around her.

Adam is free to study her without reproach, not just because she's female, but because her own gaze is always turned inward. When her narrow body lifts its astonishing weights, she wears the look of a person at prayer.

He pushes through a lactic acid burn and watches as she moves to a new apparatus. She's lifting weights with her neck. Why any girl would want to lift the equivalent of half a wheel-barrow full of bricks with her neck, he doesn't know. She's arranged on all fours and her head moves slowly, rhythmically, up and down; as though she's administering a blow-job to some invisible dick, some godhead of her own imagining.

Adam drinks from his water bottle and wipes the sweat from his neck. He thinks of how he might create a life-size version of her, for a white gallery space: a fleshless woman on her hands and knees, a beast of the world's burden, a look of ecstasy upon her face. He'd make her so real that people would draw close to see if she were breathing. He would make her devotion beautiful, not pornographic, or insane, as it is now. He would name her Theresa, after the saint. There would be feminist interpretations of the work, art history interpretations, religious interpretations. People would talk.

He leans forward on the bike and pushes his pulse rate. He would, would, would, would, would, would . . .

'Here we go again,' a voice inside him says, 'grand plans, fantasies of fame.'

He abruptly terminates his pedalling, and yanks his feet from the stirrups. What's he doing? he thinks, his heart pounding in his chest; where the fuck is his head?

In the shower, he can't help but think of Lily as he soaps his chest and stomach. He hadn't known what to do after the business with the ashes. He knows Lily must think he just slunk away from her; scolded, low and weak, like a dog. He had thought that he'd learnt something from Marlo, but he still doesn't know how to look a woman in the eye and tell her she isn't wanted – for all their beseechings, do they really want that? It's easier for everyone if he's that dog. He misses Lily; who knows for how long he might have gone on in her warm, nocturnal world, so blessedly at the end of the earth – in a way, so brave? But the ashes had changed everything. They both knew now just how much she was prepared to give.

He takes care not to soap the itchy patch of skin that has appeared beneath his lower ribs. He had Googled 'ringworm', and then other non-specific dermatitis, but he still doesn't know what it is, and he can't afford to go to the doctor. He has barely enough money in the bank to last until the end of the month. Now that it's warming up, his friend Saxon will have some housepainting jobs for him, but the deadline for the memorial is looming, and he can't stop now. He is trying to put the memorial before everything, but the previous night his hunger had broken him. He leapt up from the table where he was working, scoured the flat for money, and drove fast to Hungry Jack's. He felt pinched and stupid, leaning out of the window of his winged chariot to order a child's meal.

After he pulled out of Hungry Jack's he drove one-handed down the road, his other hand furiously feeding himself chips. At a red light he had stopped and looked down to unwrap his burger when a body suddenly lunged across his windscreen. He'd seen these kids before, a group of them worked the inter-sections in this area. Funkily dressed, plucky, cool-as, and no more than fifteen or sixteen.

The boy flicked the water from his squeegee onto the road, and reached across Adam's windscreen again. Adam saw a perfect white stone on a leather thong fall from the neck of the boy's shirt, and he suddenly felt ashamed. He had only twenty cents to give him. There was no use checking, he knew; it was in the ashtray, it was all the change he had from his meal. He wanted to bang on the windscreen and tell the kid to stop, tell him that he couldn't pay him for his youth and beauty and bravado, but it was too late because he had already finished, and was hanging by the open window, hunting Adam's eye.

'I'm sorry, mate, this is all I've got,' he said, handing over the twenty cents.

If the kid had said nothing, if he'd simply flipped the coin and pocketed it and turned away with a look – *yeah, sure, you wanker* – then it would not have been so bad. But the boy studied Adam for a moment, taking in the sad little burger cooling in his lap, and then he dipped his head graciously, because he believed him.

Adam turns on the cold water to bring him to his senses. He has to put all these worries aside. He has to get out of the shower, go straight to the studio, he has to keep working. He needs this memorial. And, he has to believe, this memorial needs him.

Adam's Valiant is parked on an area of broken concrete and weeds at the back of the gym. He has unlocked the car, thrown his backpack in the boot, and is behind the wheel, reaching for his seatbelt, when the young woman he was watching earlier comes round the side of the building. Her hair is wet also, but she's wearing the same clothes; clothes too hot now for the sun that's beating down.

She bends towards a bike that leans against the wall between a row of rubbish bins and a pile of cardboard boxes. He decides he will wait for her to leave first through the narrow exit; he can even watch her as she leaves. In the meantime, he will try to get the car radio to work.

When Adam looks up again, she's not on her bike. Instead she is doubled over, and then, to his alarm, she is vomiting. She's heaving like a ship on rough seas, a mess of dark yellow gruel pooling at her feet.

He can't leave now. He can't drive past and have her know that he has seen her, he will have to sit it out. But still she spasms and shakes. She drops to her knees, and he recalls her exercise inside the gym and his Theresa in her white gallery space. His car keys are in the ignition. Every now and then Triple J crackles alive on the radio.

Here comes trouble, he thinks, as one of the lone wolves rounds the corner. His gym bag looks like Barbie's handbag at the end of his bulging arm, and his puffy legs move him like a toddler in nappies. Here's trouble, he thinks, because that is what he always thinks, in some part of himself, when he sees these men, and because he has witnessed their aversion to this girl's de-sexed discipline.

He can see only trouble.

But the man moves swiftly when the girl comes into sight; no hesitation, no pause. Adam notes it with surprise. The man throws his bag to the ground and crouches beside her, places a hand on her back. There's vomit everywhere but the man reaches with his free hand for his towel.

Adam leans back in his seat. The man's hand cups the girl's forehead as she retches again, and a small brown beetle journeys slowly across the car's windscreen.

The man is holding, Adam is watching. He feels it deep in his belly, and as a sudden clarity in the air, but this time it is not a certainty about art that comes to him. He has looked too much, he realises, he has made others too strange. When he is the one trapped behind glass.

There is nothing for it but to turn off the damned radio, and start the car, and travel past them as if oblivious. Oblivious; he had always thought this was how everyone best kept their dignity.

As the car coughs and rattles past them, he's aware that the man has helped the girl to her feet, that she is drinking, that it is over.

Telling *Taliesin*

PEARL WATCHES GUS'S FACE as he opens the door of his office. She expects him to be surprised to see Lily, waiting there on the chairs with her, but he acts as if nothing is different.

'Come in,' he says.

Gus's room is warm with sunlight. The blind is tangled at the top of the window. Lily sits where Pearl usually sits, so Pearl takes another chair. Her view of the room is different, but she can still see *Fallingwater*.

Gus asks Pearl and Lily how they are. Good, they both say. Gus has had a haircut, his curls seem tighter on his head and it makes Pearl like him a little bit less. He's wearing a bright orange shirt. Lily crosses one leg over the other and rests her hands on the bag in her lap. Her foot in its silver heel turns clockwise circles in the air. Of course, Pearl could tell Gus what this is all about, why Lily is here. But it was Lily who insisted on coming and she has already decided it's Lily who should talk.

'So,' says Gus, 'it's been a long time, Lily. Is there anything in particular that brings you here?'

'I just wanted to know how Pearl's getting on,' says Lily.

Pearl feels Gus's attention turn to her but his eyes don't leave Lily's face.

'Have you asked Pearl that question?' he says.

'She says she doesn't know.'

That isn't really true, thinks Pearl. She hadn't ever answered Lily in words, she had just shrugged and looked away.

'Perhaps she doesn't know,' says Gus, looking at Pearl now. 'Perhaps that's really how she feels and we should listen to that.'

'But how do you think she is?'

Pearl can tell by Gus's face that he doesn't want to answer. She wonders if this is because he thinks she is doing badly.

Gus shifts in his chair and tugs at the knees of his trousers. 'I don't know that I . . .' he says, but then he looks at Lily's foot going around and he starts a new sentence. 'I think Pearl is doing the best that can be expected under the circumstances but I hope I'll be able to help her even more.'

This is not how Gus usually talks. He's not giving Lily the answer Pearl knows she wants. Lily sighs, and moves her bag around in her lap as if it's a hot pizza.

'Well, I think she's really good,' says Lily. 'She doesn't cry anymore and she does all her drawings and stuff. And she's going to go back to school.'

'That's great,' says Gus, nodding his head.

Pearl can feel Lily thinking about how to get past what Gus has just said.

'If she does all those things it means she's really good, doesn't it?'

'Why does this matter so much to you, Lily?' asks Gus quietly.

Pearl looks at him closely, and waits. She wonders how Lily will say it.

'The TV people think she's doing really well and they want to tell people about it.'

She just said it, thinks Pearl, plain and fast.

'Right,' says Gus.

And then there's silence.

'How do they know she's doing really well?' he asks.

'I told them.'

'Why do they want to tell people?'

'Because, you know, how Pearl was the only one who got away. And it's good she's doing so well. They say it'll be inspiring for people.'

'Who are the TV people?'

Lily tells him the name of the TV program.

'That's very popular,' says Gus.

'Yes. It'll be inspiring for a lot of people.'

'Do you mind if I ask you if they're offering money?'

'I don't mind,' says Lily, her foot changing direction. 'They are.'

'Seven thousand dollars,' says Pearl.

Lily and Gus both look at her.

'How do you feel about this, Pearl?' asks Gus.

'She won't do it,' Lily says quickly.

'Do you want to do it?' asks Gus.

Pearl shakes her head.

'Have you got a reason?'

'Because I don't know what to say.'

Gus rocks his chair back and forth. They wait for him to speak.

'We've talked a lot about how Pearl is,' he says, 'but how are you, Lily?'

Lily looks surprised. 'I'm good as well,' she says.

Gus waits. Pearl knows what he's doing because he does this with her. He waits because he thinks there are more words to come.

'I wasn't too good before,' says Lily finally. 'My boyfriend left and I missed my little boy.' Her voice trembles but Gus lets the quiet go on.

Lily pulls a tissue out of her bag. 'I feel better now, though,' she says, 'since the TV people rang up.'

'Why do you think that is?' asks Gus.

Lily looks at Gus as if she doesn't like him. 'Because someone cares. You always feel better if someone cares, don't you?'

'Yes,' says Gus. 'Yes, you do.'

'It's helped take my mind off things,' says Lily quietly.

All of a sudden it seems there is nothing more to say, and nothing to wait for, either.

'Can I see Gus like normal now?' asks Pearl. She scans her mother's face for signs of hurt.

Gus glances at his watch.

'You mean on your own?' says Lily.

'Yes,' says Pearl.

Lily looks at Gus.

'I think that's a good idea,' he says.

Lily gathers up her bag and puts both heels on the floor.

'I'll do some shopping,' she says.

Lily is taller than Gus when they both stand up, but only because of her shoes. She draws her hair out from under the strap of her bag.

'Half an hour?' says Gus.

'I don't have a watch,' says Lily.

'Can you ask someone?'

Pearl feels as if she and Gus are sending Lily out to play, and her chest tightens.

'Mum, your bow's undone,' she says, reaching towards Lily's peach dress.

Lily brushes Pearl's hand away. 'I can do it myself,' she says, stepping towards the door.

Pearl moves to her usual place as Gus takes his chair, and slowly the room comes back to normal. She remembers when the light through the window was so bright she couldn't see him properly, and if the blind isn't fixed it will soon be like that again. The fish on the computer screen swim slowly back and forth. Out of the corner of her eye she can see *Fallingwater*. She knows everything in this room, and now that she is used to Gus's haircut, she feels the same as always.

'Do you want to talk about the TV thing?' asks Gus.

'Not really,' she says.

Gus nods.

She has to speak before he does; she can't stand to wait one more moment.

'I know about *Fallingwater*,' she says. She feels her arm lift and her fingers stretch towards the photograph on the wall, as if they want to touch it.

Gus looks quickly behind him and turns back to her, smiling. For the first time, Pearl sees a piece of gold at the side of his mouth.

'How did you know it was called *Fallingwater*?' he asks.

'Someone told me,' says Pearl.

'Who?'

'Her name is Sonia. She went there.'

'She went there?' says Gus. 'Wow.'

'That's what I thought,' says Pearl.

She feels shy suddenly, as though everything has happened too fast. She looks down at the coffee table. When she hadn't wanted to look at Gus or Lily, she had studied the cover of a book there. The first word of the book's title is Darkness, and the first letter of the second word is V, but the rest of the title is hidden by other books on top. She thought about words she knew that started with V, but nothing made any sense.

The silence in the room is different, because now it includes *Fallingwater*. Pearl finds herself lifting her foot and pointing the toe of her boot towards the books on the coffee table. Her toe is going to nudge the other books aside, she can see that. It's as though her foot thinks it's all right to move around in Gus's room and touch his books in this way, even if she's not sure it is.

Darkness . . . ? *Darkness Visible*. She hadn't thought of that, but she thinks she understands.

'Why do you have *Fallingwater* on your wall?' asks Pearl.

'Because I love it!' says Gus, springing to his feet.

There is stuff all over the noticeboard, but as Gus unpins bits of paper from around the photograph of the house, Pearl sees that all this time she has been looking at the top half of a calendar. The squares for the days are blank. Gus removes the drawing pins from the top of the calendar and carries it across the room. He opens it on the table in front of her.

'Have a look,' he says.

Pearl leans forward in her chair. The photograph that she knows so well is the first photograph, for January, and as she slowly turns the pages she sees that, unlike Sonia's husband, the person who took these photographs had been allowed to take his camera inside. There are rooms with chairs and tables and rugs. There's light streaming in the windows and patterns of light on the floor. Everywhere she sees the same shapes that comprise the outside of the house – right angles with long, stretching horizontal lines – and at the end of each line is a vase of flowers to look at, or a painting on the wall, and then it's June and a fire burns on the stones beside a red bed, a lamp lights a desk.

It's too much all at once. She stops at October, the month they are in.

'Where did it come from?' she asks, folding her arms on her knees.

'My wife gave it to me for Christmas,' he says. 'She gives me a calendar every year.'

'But you didn't write on it.'

'No, I forget. I just like looking at it.'

'But you didn't even change the pictures.'

'I like looking at the whole house.'

Me too, she thinks.

'Why do you love it?' she asks.

Gus folds his hands behind his head.

'Probably for the same reason you do,' he says.

Gus isn't expecting her to speak, he seems to be thinking too. But then he leans quickly over the table and turns the calendar back to the beginning, back to the first picture of the house.

'And I've always thought that *Fallingwater* was like our own minds,' he says, pointing to his head. 'And that interests me.'

Pearl looks down at the photo. 'How?' she asks.

'Remember when we talked about the conscious and the unconscious mind?' he says.

'How my dreams come from my unconscious?'

'Yeah. And other things. Memories. The way our bodies move.'

He points to the lower half of the photograph. 'See how underneath the house there are all these different levels of rock? And how the water flows over the rocks?'

She nods. Of course I see, she thinks.

'To me that's like the unconscious mind. Sort of wild and natural but still formed in its own way, by its own rules. Sort of timeless and heedless. But then, the house has been built *on top* of the rocks.'

It's not really possible to point to the exact spot where the rocks become the house, so Gus just circles his finger over a general area. 'And the built house is like the conscious mind,' he says. 'Hard-won, learnt, layered, dynamic, yearning.'

He leans back in his chair and gives a little laugh, as if he's embarrassed. 'Do you know what I mean?'

Pearl studies the different sections of the house and how they fit together; the parts that look solid and safe and the others that float bravely above the rocks and water.

'Kind of,' she says.

'You couldn't just have the house without the other part, it wouldn't be the same, it wouldn't mean the same thing. And that's what the mind is like – the unconscious and the conscious together.'

'It makes me want to try hard,' says Pearl.

'What does?'

'*Fallingwater*.'

Gus looks at her for a moment and then he looks down at the calendar. 'I think I know what you mean,' he says.

Pearl wonders when they will talk about the thing that happened to the architect of *Fallingwater*. Maybe Gus doesn't want to mention it because it's like what happened to her, and usually he won't talk about that unless she does first.

'Did you know,' she begins slowly, 'that Frank Roy Dwight made *Fallingwater* twenty-two years after what happened at *Taliesin*?'

'Frank Lloyd Wright,' says Gus.

'I get mixed up,' she says, shaking her head.

'What happened at *Taliesin*?'

'You know – the thing.'

Gus shakes his head. 'I don't really know much about Frank Lloyd Wright,' he says. 'I know he designed *Fallingwater* and lots of other wonderful buildings.'

Pearl can hardly believe it. When Sonia told her about the tragedy in Frank Lloyd Wright's life, she thought she was learning something that everyone else already knew, like when she found out what a Catholic was. She feels a moment of excitement that she will be the one to tell Gus; if he loves *Fallingwater* and thinks it's like the mind, she's sure he will think this is an important thing to know.

But this isn't how it usually is in Gus's office, and she feels nervous now. She remembers how Lily cried when she saw the newspaper photos of the children's hats and the smashed-up kite on the Eric Cahill Oval. 'They have no respect for the dead,' Lily said.

Pearl doesn't want just to blurt out that an axe killed the people at *Taliesin* and a fire burnt everything down, because then Gus might remember these things the most. She knows, and Gus will know too, that when she speaks about the murders at *Taliesin* she will also be speaking about Riley, and the other children, and Trish and Bree, and she wants to do this as Lily would want, with respect for the dead.

She will start where Sonia started, when everything was good, so that when the thing happens Gus will be able to feel the shock, it will show him what Frank felt; how everything is normal and then it isn't.

She settles her headband with her fingertips. 'Well,' she begins, 'there was this place . . .'

It's hard at first, remembering to breathe and getting used to her own voice filling up the quiet room, but then the story starts to come out strong. She pulls her hands from beneath her and lets them move as they seem to want. Sometimes she strays from the facts as she has heard them – it seems not enough to say that there were beautiful gardens at *Taliesin*, she tells Gus about white and gold roses, and red ones that were so dark they were almost black – but she doesn't think this matters because it feels true enough.

Gus watches her. There is none of his usual fidgeting; his chubby fingers rest on the arms of his chair. As Pearl draws closer to the events at *Taliesin* she realises she knows nothing about the people who are about to be killed. She doesn't know their names or their ages or the kind of people they were. She sees the story gaping open in front of her and she knows she cannot mend it by imagining, as she had done with the garden, because she cannot imagine, and it would not be true. When the time comes to tell Gus she can only say what she knows: seven were dead and three of them were children.

Gus's eyelids twitch. She reaches for something but the story is suddenly empty. The dead are gone and *Taliesin* is ashes and there is just Frank Lloyd Wright, alone. There are twenty-two years to go before *Fallingwater*, and who and where and what he is in those years she cannot say.

She looks at Gus. She knows he is thinking about her story but about the day at the oval also. She wonders if there will ever be a time when she does not see what happened to her living in other people's eyes. How far in the future would she have to go? Twenty-two years – as far away as that?

'Did Sonia tell you this?' asks Gus.

Pearl nods.

Gus moves his head slowly from side to side. 'Incredible,' he says.

'I thought he would've made *Fallingwater* before the thing happened,' says Pearl, 'but Sonia looked in a book and said he made it after.'

'How many years did you say?'

'Twenty-two.'

Pearl can see him weighing the number, feeling its length.

'Why did you think *Fallingwater* came first?' asks Gus.

Pearl is surprised by his question. 'Because it's beautiful,' she says.

'But why would it come first?'

'I thought the good thing would come before the bad thing, not the other way round.'

'Maybe he created something as beautiful as that because of the tragedy,' says Gus. '*After great pain, a formal feeling comes.*'

Pearl stares hard at him.

'It's a line from a poem,' says Gus.

'What poem?'

'An Emily Dickinson poem.'

There's more, Pearl thinks, even more. There are these words to think about. And there is someone called Emily – what had happened to Emily?

For one long, silent moment she feels as free as the bird sitting in the tree outside the window; looking in, and looking around too.

Gus checks his watch. 'Your mother should be back,' he says. 'Shall we leave it there for today?'

'Yes,' says Pearl.

'We didn't talk about the TV thing,' says Gus.

'No,' says Pearl. 'Lily might forget about it.'

'Do you think so?'

'I don't know.'

They are both on their feet. Pearl pulls her skirt around the right way. Gus bends over the coffee table and picks up the calendar but instead of taking it back to the noticeboard he closes its pages and begins rolling it up.

'I want you to have the calendar,' he says. 'I'll just find an elastic band.'

As Gus rummages on his desk, Pearl searches for the right thing to say about something she can hardly believe.

When the calendar is secure, Gus pings the band once and hands it to her.

'Thank you,' says Pearl.

'Thank *you*,' says Gus, 'for telling me that story.'

They shake hands at the door.

Lily is not waiting for her outside, and there is no-one behind the reception desk.

A sign on the lifts tells her that they are out of order and she guesses that her mother didn't want to walk up. She pauses at the top of the stairs and puts her eye to the end of the rolled-up calendar, but there is only the shiny dark.

She has gone down one flight of stairs and is turning to go down another when she sees two women coming towards her. Between them they're carrying a stroller, lifting it high over the stairs, puffing a lot. As she gets closer she sees that there's a little boy in the stroller. He's old enough to walk up, she knows that; Riley hadn't been much bigger when they first started going out. He is wearing Bob the Builder socks and Velcro-strapped shoes. The two women look at her, and roll their eyes and laugh. Pearl looks into the face of the little boy, and he stares back with bright blue eyes and a pressed-together mouth. *I'm the King*, she knows he is thinking, and their eyes remain locked until they have passed each other.

Lily isn't downstairs. Pearl pushes open the glass doors and stands outside on the pavement. She's in other people's way, so she moves close to the building. She doesn't lean; she knows it's not good to lean. Cars travel back and forth as she searches for the peach of Lily's dress. She wonders if the people who pass by are curious about the important-looking cylinder she holds in her hands.

Lily is on the median strip, waving, waiting for a break in the traffic. People are looking at her, she looks happy. Her silver shoes flash as she hurries across the road.

'What you got there?' she says, holding out her hand to Pearl.

'Something Gus gave me,' says Pearl. 'I'll show you at home.'

'We'll go home in a while. There's something I want to show you.'

'What?'

'A dress.'

'What kind of dress?'

'A dress for TV,' she says.

Pearl still hasn't taken her hand.

'C'mon,' says Lily, 'please?'

Pearl moves the calendar to her other hand and reaches for her mother's dancing fingers.

The Retrospective

A SKY-BLUE BANNER bearing Pieter's name billows silkily over the entrance to the museum.

She should have eaten something, thinks Sonia, as her stomach churns. Her narrow skirt and new heels constrain her movement up the steep steps.

Inside, she lifts a glass of champagne from a passing tray and takes in her surroundings. The space around her is not like a gallery with art on the walls and patrons patrolling its margins, it's more like a furniture showroom – more like Ikea, she thinks – a series of micro-habitats created around items of her husband's furniture. The large crowd is wandering and talking, drinking. She feels lost.

There will be old friends and clients here, people she hasn't seen that much since he died. She searches faces but they are all strangers to her. She doesn't understand the new fashion; the women all look like they've fled their dressmakers halfway through a fitting – their clothes have raw, unhemmed edges and loose threads, puckered seams, gatherings and drapings, tacking. So much that is messy and unplanned takes place inside the body, why do they want to look that way on the outside too?

The men seem lovelier to her, in their sober suits and understated shirts, their buttoned and pressed simplicity. She'd like to move close to them to smell their soap and cologne. Perhaps this is what she misses the most: a man just out of the shower.

She feels someone's warm hand on her arm and turns to see Natasha. The curator looks different. She has a new short haircut, like a boy, and she's wearing a pale pink strapless dress and fine pearl earrings. The gloss on her lips shines like glass.

What would it be like to have a daughter? thinks Sonia. What would you feel about her bare neck and shoulders?

'I'm so nervous,' says Natasha.

'So am I,' Sonia replies.

They both press a hand to their ribcages.

'Have you had a look around?' asks Natasha.

Sonia drains the last of her champagne and shakes her head. 'I've just got here,' she says.

'Did you come alone?'

'Yes,' says Sonia.

They both reach for a champagne and look around them in silence.

'I wanted to show the furniture living,' says Natasha, frowning, gesturing with her empty hand. 'Everything here, like your bed, is still in everyday use in people's homes or in public buildings. There's something joyful and generous in all your husband's work and I wanted to show how those feelings impart themselves to those who live with it.'

Sonia sips her champagne and listens to this earnestness.

'How do you live, Natasha?' she asks suddenly. 'I mean, do you live alone?'

Natasha looks startled. 'Yes, I live alone,' she says. 'Why? Was I talking too much?'

Sonia laughs. 'No, of course not. I was just interested.'

'I have a one-bedroom flat,' says Natasha. 'It's a bit poky but I'm slowly doing it up.'

'I'm sure it's lovely.'

'I fantasise about having a Pieter Marstrand piece,' Natasha says.

Sonia wonders about the blush that steals over Natasha's face and neck. It is the blush of confession but what, exactly, is the nature of the confession? That she wants something she thinks she can never have? Sonia remembers herself at Natasha's age, and what she'd wanted. She had been a lucky woman; it would be a crime to forget it.

'What's your favourite piece?' asks Sonia.

'The three-tiered coffee table,' says Natasha. 'Do you remember it? Glass and Queensland ash, 1970?'

'I remember it. Pieter got the idea from a Lego he and Karl built. Is it in the exhibition?'

'No. I desperately wanted it, there's nothing else like it from that period. But it went to auction recently and the new owners wouldn't let it go.'

'Who are they?'

'Some young couple. They said it would leave a hole in their interior design.'

Sonia thinks about Rupe and Gertie Schippers, the original owners. Rupe had lost a leg fighting in New Guinea, and while Pieter was working on the table, Gertie handcuffed herself to a politician in protest at the Vietnam War. They'd had no children and it was a lingering sadness, and now, she supposes, they are dead. People live with all manner of holes in their lives, she thinks.

'I'm going to have a look around,' says Sonia.

'I'll catch up with you later,' says Natasha. She leans towards Sonia and touches her lips to Sonia's cheek. The kiss is slightly sticky.

What would it have been like, to have had a little girl?

She wishes Karl and Gabriel were here, she'd like to take someone's arm. Ahead of her lies an encounter with memories of her life with Pieter, and she wonders if she's ready.

The exhibition is arranged in long, loose avenues. Already she can see that the work is displayed chronologically, four decades nudging into a new century.

She thinks Natasha has made a good choice for the beginning: the handsome desk is one of the first pieces Pieter made in Australia. The client was a Danish businessman whose name they had been given by friends in Copenhagen. He'd been paid well and his name passed on.

She reaches for another glass of champagne, and moves slowly down the line of furniture. Here is marriage, here is a new country. They were, she remembers, adjusting deeply to both. Pieter was discovering Australian timbers. From the little workshop at the back of the ironmonger's on Kanya Road, they set out in the old blue Volkswagen to drive all over the city to lumberyards and small specialist suppliers.

Deborah Robertson

The simple round table she sees now doesn't tell the whole story. 'Small table', the display card reads. 'Blackheart Sassafras, 1963.' It's a table for two – for a marriage proposal, palm- reading, tea and sympathy. A table for the touching of hands. The wood is deep brown and cream. There's an ice cream Sonia sometimes buys that reminds her of this wood – a mouthful of vanilla bursts into a river of chocolate in a way that is almost indecent. This ice cream didn't exist when they first saw blackheart sassafras, such an ice cream couldn't even have been imagined, but standing in Ted's small office with sawdust at their feet and the fragrance of wood all around, the wood's voluptuousness made them laugh out loud. The display card says nothing of Ted and what Pieter learnt from him, the money he gave them to help buy their house, the boating accident that had taken his life.

'Myrtle Cabinet, 1963.' He lost a thumbnail on this. It came away clean as a fish's scale.

There are memories for her here but Sonia begins to wonder about Natasha's decision to include so much of Pieter's early work. The pieces show his love for the new woods and his skills were getting better all the time, but it was the work of a young man working earnestly for respect, to make a living for them both, to make good the decision to leave everything a long way behind. Buried within each piece is a knot of concentration; it was too late for him to turn back but he wasn't yet able to go forward. The work is strong and virtuous, and unsurprising.

She's come to the end of the first line of furniture and her glass is empty. Soberness is creeping back in, dragging with it a grey feeling. She holds the glass to her chest and looks around.

There are lots of people in the next aisle but no drinksperson to be seen. A small crowd is gathered in front of the first exhibit, and she moves behind them and waits for an opportunity to move to the front.

She's been expecting it, but still. 'The Butterfly Bed, 1965, Red River Gum.'

There are thick creamy sheets on the bed and across the sheets, as though dropped from the shoulders of an expensive woman, a throw of brunette fur. She would have preferred the bed not to be dressed at all, to be simply the thing it always was, simply a bed, not the way of life these heaped pillows and lush fabrics are suggesting. But she understands what's at work here, has seen the name of the linen company on the list of sponsors.

The bed's wings are spread at different angles, demonstrating its many possibilities for shape-shifting, and under the light it glows dark red. The restoration has brought out detail that she hasn't noticed in years.

'It's sexy,' says a woman behind her.

'I think it's creepy,' says another.

Sonia stands very still and looks at the bed as if for the first time. He'd been labouring at fine, respectable furniture, and then he had made this. It was not a bed to please a client or to press his craftsman's credentials upon the world; it was their bed, in which he had imagined their marriage, the life they would make together. It was audacious and hopeful, but it was also private, and its spread wings seem now too revealing, as if it's her own young self spread there. Deep inside her she remembers the intimacies of that bed. She wishes there were a railing to hang on to, like there is at the zoo, so that you can keep equilibrium, so that you won't be lost when you meet and hold the eye of the living thing on the other side of the bars, a creature utterly not you, but so like you too.

Sonia clutches her glass and casts her eye further down the line of exhibits. She can see bentwood and tubular steel and slabs of glass in abstract, organic shapes; an aisle of furniture so different from the one she has just walked down that it seems the same person could not be its creator. The bed had been a turning point, a moment of release. Of course, it hadn't been possible, in the swirl of life, to see it then.

She wonders if she will ever sleep in this bed again. She longs to slide the wings away and lie down in its familiar, contracted energy. It would be delivered home to her, she'd been promised this. The new mattress would arrive. But something has changed; it's the way she felt after her sons left home. She saw the dust of the world on their shoulders then, and knew that nothing would be the same again.

In the distance, Sonia glimpses a woman carrying a tray of drinks. If she could just fill her glass, lift her mood. She turns away from the bed and starts down the aisle.

'Sonia?' a man's voice calls. 'Sonia Marstrand?'

Sonia turns reluctantly in the direction of the voice and sees that it's a stranger who has called her and is smiling widely, gratified to have his speculation confirmed. Out of the corner of her eye she sees hands lifting glasses from the tray. The person who has called her is a man of perhaps her own age, and he is standing in front of an exhibit with his hands behind his back, like a salesman at an expo. He has silver hair gelled into an upright disarray and he wears a tailored leather jacket and black T-shirt.

'I'm sorry, do I know you?' she says, taking a step towards him.

'It's Reg,' says the man. 'Reg Bell.'

He offers his hand, which is soft and dry. Sonia looks around her for clues. She can see now that the piece of furniture he's guarding is the walnut table Pieter made shortly before he completed their bed. She checks the display card: 'The Bell Table.'

'Reggie,' she says, unable to smile, 'yes, I remember you.'

She had not seen this man or his gracious parents since that hot evening at their home – was it really more than forty years ago? Pieter had planned some shelves for Godfrey and Yvonne's study, shelves that would go all the way to the ceiling, with a sliding ladder, but then the accident happened. Yvonne fell down the stairs. She fell a long way. One of her arms was broken and there was something internal, and a headache that wouldn't go away. The work in the study had been postponed until Yvonne was stronger, but Pieter had never finished the job. At first he'd called Godfrey and Yvonne often, but as time went by he worried that they would think his concern was not for Yvonne but for the work and, regretfully, he let the relationship lapse.

Everyone said it was fortunate that Yvonne wasn't alone when she fell. That Reggie was there.

'I'm so happy to have been able to contribute my table to the exhibition,' Reg says.

'It's very nice that you did,' says Sonia flatly.

There was so much of her life that she'd forgotten, but not the white table napkin that Reggie had flung at his father over this dinner table. Pieter always said she remembered only the bad things.

'Your husband has left a marvellous legacy,' says Reg.

'Yes,' replies Sonia.

She remembers what he looked like then, although his face now is lined and loose, like hers. His lips are stained a dark red, but there's no glass in his hand. She doesn't know why she has not simply excused herself and moved away. Pieter had ceased communications, but here she is, taking them up again. The display card tells her the table is loaned, courtesy of Reginald Bell.

'Your parents,' asks Sonia, 'have they died?'

'No, no,' says Reg. 'They're in nursing homes. They're both very old now, of course.'

'Are they well?' she asks. And has your mother's head stopped hurting?

'As well as can be expected,' he says. 'But I'm still in the house – you remember the house?'

'I do. I remember your mother showed me around the house.'

'Yes. I felt someone should keep the house going. They were great supporters of the arts, you know.'

'I know. Do you live there alone?'

'No, no, I have my friend with me. You should meet her. She's just gone . . .' He turns and looks anxiously down the aisle. 'Look! Here she is now.'

Sonia follows his eye. Walking towards them, balancing two glasses of red wine, is a short, slender woman with spiky, eggplant-coloured hair, who is wearing a tight grey dress that looks as if it's on inside out. Her aggressively artistic earrings tilt and balance like mobiles on the rise and fall of her step. She eyes Sonia warily as she hands Reg his drink.

'Sonia, this is Jilly,' he says. 'Jilly, Sonia was Pieter Marstrand's wife.'

Sonia bristles at his use of the past tense. Death has not unmarried them. It seems to her that Reg is practically glowing, practically radioactive, with the pleasure of introducing, to a woman of his own age, his younger lover. Jilly looks as if she's been around the block a few times and has now, perhaps, decided to take the final lap slowly; but younger she undeniably is.

'I would've known Sonia anywhere,' he says, shimmering at her.

Sonia catches a look in Jilly's eye. He's getting more than one thrill out of this introduction, she realises. He is also displaying to his younger lover his relationship to the artist they are gathered here to celebrate.

'I still remember the first time I met Pieter and Sonia,' he says, dreamily.

'I think we've only met once?' says Sonia.

'Surely not? No, no, that can't be true. I remember, Sonia, you were wearing black.'

'Like you are now!' says Jilly, superfluously.

'You would've loved my parents' marvellous dinner parties, Jilly,' Reg continues. 'They were high times, weren't they, Sonia?'

She watches the wine empty from their glasses. Her own glass is now just something to hold on to. A blood vessel spasms painfully in the side of her head. He's getting away with something, she thinks, and she would like to stop him. It feels no more personal to her than a bystander's pursuit of a bag-snatcher, but she will not move on. She is seriously sober, and teetering towards serious pain.

'My parents recognised Pieter's talent immediately,' says Reg, looking at Jilly as a salesman looks at a customer. 'And I imagine their patronage was important to him at that time, wasn't it, Sonia?'

His voice has taken on an edge. Like the edge he had placed them on, all those years ago. He wants something from her now, she realises, he wants to close his pitch.

'Pieter was very fond of Godfrey and Yvonne. Their support meant a lot to him.' She looks directly at Jilly as she speaks. 'He'd been going to do a big job for them – sort of a library – but Yvonne fell down the stairs.'

She feels something in Reg sharply retract.

'Fell down the stairs?' says Jilly.

Sonia feels sorry for her, but it doesn't matter.

'Yes,' says Reg quickly. 'Mother fell down the staircase at home.'

'The big one?'

'Yes,' says Reg.

'And what happened?'

'She was quite badly injured, wasn't she, Reg?' says Sonia.

'Well, yes, she was. But she recovered.'

'Did she?' asks Sonia. 'We always wondered.'

'Wondered what?' asks Reg.

She can hardly believe that he's asked this question. But it had not been asked out of stupidity, she's sure of that. He needs to know what she knows.

We wondered if you pushed Yvonne down the stairs, she wants to reply to his perfect cue. It was not strictly true, of course, it was only she who had wondered. Nothing in Pieter's life had taught him to recognise the tyranny she'd felt at work in Yvonne and Godfrey's home. He couldn't smell weakness, and its cruel logic. Pieter had thought he stopped making calls so as not to be misunderstood, but it was Godfrey and Yvonne who retreated, as she knew they would; Godfrey and Yvonne who had thrown a cover around the shame in their lives.

The blood pounds in her head. She craves to say it: the real answer to his question, everything she really feels. She can almost taste the pleasure of the words. But these thoughts are a fantasy of being someone other than who she really is. She cannot stand in front of a table her husband has made and split the night open. Were there really people who challenged others in this way? Or only drunks who cried later to take it all back, cried for forgiveness?

'We always wondered if she recovered,' says Sonia. There, she thinks regretfully, the stopper is back in the bottle.

'Yes, she did,' says Reg.

Sonia feels his relief.

'But she was always accident-prone, wasn't she?' says Jilly suddenly. 'In the end it was the reason she had to go into the home, wasn't it, Reg?'

Sonia looks at him. She's interested in his answer, she wants him to know that. It isn't hard, she doesn't have to say anything.

'There were a lot of factors, Jilly,' he says.

'What sort of factors?' asks Sonia.

'She had lots of problems caused by her —'

'Injuries?' says Sonia. He had hesitated for just a moment, and she had supplied the word. Still innocent; unless, of course, you are not.

'Well, yes,' he says, his eyes avoiding hers, 'problems caused by her injuries.'

'I completely understand,' says Sonia. 'I had a mother like you.'

The words go out. They go to Jilly, and to Reg, and she feels each of them struggle in their own way to take them in. Sonia makes a sound. It is not a laugh. It is not making light.

She places her hand on Reg's leather forearm. 'I meant a mother like yours,' she says, smiling kindly at him. 'Of course.'

Jilly smiles too, believing her. There's no need to look at Reg.

There's nothing inside her now but pain. She needs to go. She puts her glass down on something, and says goodbye.

Light scintillates at the edges of her vision as she weaves her way towards the stairs leading to the exit.

'I'm leaving,' she says, as Natasha leans out of a circle of people.

'Is something wrong?'

'I've got a headache. Probably all the build-up, the champagne.'

'What a shame. How are you getting home?'

'Taxi.'

'Do you want me to call one for you?'

'Would you? Yes, please. I'll wait outside on the street.'

'Do you want me to wait with you?'

'No, thanks. I'll be fine.'

'You sure?'

'I'm sure.'

'I don't mind.'

'No, you stay here, really. Thanks, Natasha.'

I can't be with anyone now, she thinks.

In the darkness of the kitchen, Sonia fills the kettle. The strong painkillers are at the back of the cupboard. She swallows two, with her sleeping tablets, and eats a banana.

When her tea is ready she takes a seat at the bench.

A light rain is falling outside. She rests her head in her hands, waiting for the tea to cool, knowing that inside her the pills are slowly unfolding.

She had thought that, in order to leave her mother, it was enough for her to marry and move far away, learn a different language and raise children of her own. Perhaps Reg had hurt his mother, and perhaps not. Either she was right, and she'd been right because of what she had experienced with her own mother, or she was wrong, and she'd been wrong for the same reason. Pieter always said she remembered only the bad things, but he never asked why.

She sips her tea. She wishes she could go upstairs and lie down in her own bed, but she needs to be stern with herself now. She must not court pointless longing. She must not stray into self-pity; self-pity was the quicksand that had dragged her mother down. She has a warm, safe place to sleep, and the bed will come back.

She rinses her cup under the tap and turns it upside down on the draining rack. In her stockinged feet she makes her way upstairs, feeling the boundary between herself and the outside world slowly melting, the drugs starting to work.

Her reflection in the bathroom mirror is pale and shocked. She thinks of Reg and Jilly and the preparations they are making, together, for bed. She cleans her teeth and splashes cold water over her face and neck, sighs into the towel.

She strips the clothes from her body and bundles them into the laundry basket. Her nightgown hangs on the back of the door.

She wishes someone were there, but she doesn't know who. There is no-one in the world of the living or dead she can imagine with her at this moment. Perhaps this is how you learn to be alone, she thinks, how the nerve of need is numbed. You simply stop imagining, you forget the taste of others, which once you so loved.

She reaches to close the window and sees that Adam has left the lights on in the workshop again. She would like to leave it but it doesn't feel safe, the backyard lit like this.

Outside, the air is cool and sweet, leaves tremble and glisten in the rain. Her thin nightie brushes her bare legs, and the ground wets her feet.

Tomorrow she will do some work in the garden; it's time. She'll forget about tonight. And when she is ready she will go back to the exhibition, there are better memories still to meet.

She goes lightly down the patio steps and heads into the darkness at the end of the pool, sorting through the bunch of keys in her hand to find the one to the workshop.

She knows what's happened even as she begins to fall. Her foot has caught something – the rake, the scoop, she's not sure. She hears the hum of the pool and smells its chemicals. She doesn't know where her body is or what it's doing as the air turns upside down.

It's dark, she's falling.

She needs a mother now. Not her own mother, full of rage and persecution; not a real mother needing a mother of her own, but a bright, strong, warm mass who will surround and lift and carry her, and breathe the words she needs to hear, the words she can't find inside herself, now, as she falls: *everything will be all right, Sonia, everything will be all right.*

This Hush

PEARL AND LILY SHARED a vanilla slice at the shops, and now they don't want any dinner. If they get hungry later they can have cheese on toast.

They don't feel like watching TV. It's still light outside and the kitchen door is open to catch the warm breeze. All the shopping has been put away. Pearl begins a drawing at the table, and Lily sits down opposite with her new magazine.

'Why do people like her?' Lily asks, pointing to the skinny film star on the magazine's cover.

'I don't know,' says Pearl, looking up. She is trying to draw the lava lamp from memory, but it's hard.

'I think she's up herself,' says Lily, flipping the page.

The lava lamp is shaped like a small rocket. Inside the lamp there's a red liquid, like strong cordial, and in this liquid float bright green shapes. The lamp sits on the chest of drawers in Pearl's bedroom, beneath the calendar of *Fallingwater*.

She first saw the lamp at a shopping centre that she went to with Anna. She had nachos there, and Anna had a noodle soup. The lamp glowed in the window of a joke-and-gift shop; the green drifting slowly in the ruby red, forming soft shapes and breaking apart and lazily forming new ones.

'Haven't you seen one of those before?' asked Anna, as Pearl peered closer.

'Never,' replied Pearl. 'How does it work?'

'I don't really know,' said Anna.

'What's it for?' asked Pearl.

'It's a kind of lamp,' said Anna, 'but really it's just for looking at.'

Pearl watched as a globule of green gently separated into two large teardrops.

'It would be good in the dark,' she said. 'You know, in the night.'

Anna looked down at her. They both knew about the dark in the night.

'I could buy it for you,' Anna said.

Pearl's heart lifted and dropped; it was complicated.

'Or I can ask Lily if I could buy it for you,' Anna added. 'If she says yes we can come back and get it.'

She knows, thought Pearl.

Lily and Anna were becoming friends again after what had happened with Riley's ashes, but Lily had told Pearl to remember that she was Pearl's mother, not Anna, and that Anna already had her own daughter, although unfortunately she had died. Lily would like it if Anna asked her permission to buy the lamp, although she would probably say to Pearl later that if Pearl did the story for the TV, they could afford those sorts of things themselves.

'But what if the lamp goes?' said Pearl.

'It won't,' said Anna.

'But it might,' said Pearl. She knew she was being difficult, she felt how she had hunched her shoulders and stuck out her neck. But Anna should know that you can't say it won't, because it could; anything could happen.

'You're right, we wouldn't want it to go,' said Anna, searching in her bag for her phone. 'I'll call her now.'

Lily turns the pages of her magazine. Pearl has decided to draw the green before filling in the red. Downstairs in the carpark they can hear boys playing a game.

'They're using bad language,' says Pearl, her head low over her drawing.

Lily snorts. 'Say fuck,' she says.

Pearl shakes her head.

'Please?' says Lily. 'Pretty please?'

'No,' says Pearl, and clamps her lips shut.

'If you don't say it, I'll kick you.'

Pearl grips her pencil and steadies the page. She shakes her head again.

'Right!'

Lily's shoe taps her shin, and she lifts her foot and kicks back.

'Ow!' laughs Lily.

'It wasn't hard,' says Pearl.

'It was – it was this hard!'

Pearl drops her pencil and grips the side of the table with both hands, flailing her feet wildly under the table. Lily is still using only one foot but she's landing more blows. Pearl slumps low in her chair, giggling.

'Give up?'

'No!'

'I'm getting ready for the big one,' warns Lily, leaning back.

'FUCK!' yells Pearl, dropping both feet to the ground and scraping back her chair. The word feels huge and sharp in her mouth.

'Thank you,' says Lily, pulling a schoolteacher's face. She turns another page of the magazine.

Pearl straightens her chair and her page. She feels dizzy. She pushes back her headband and picks up her pencil.

'You're horrible,' she says, trying not to smile.

Lily lifts her eyebrows and tosses the magazine onto the table.

'Boring,' she says. 'Want some Coke?'

'No, I'm still full,' says Pearl.

Lily goes to the fridge and takes out the bottle. It fizzes loudly when it opens. She pours herself a glass and sits down again. The boys' game has finished now and the sky outside is purple–blue.

'Is it *Cold Case* tonight?' Lily asks.

'Tomorrow,' says Pearl.

'I wish we had a DVD player.'

'Anna's got one,' says Pearl.

'If you did the TV thing we could have a DVD player,' says Lily.

Pearl doesn't answer, she's trying a different green. Lily drinks her Coke. There are kitchen sounds from next door.

'Can I have a piece of paper, Pearlie?' Lily asks quietly.

'What are you going to do with it?' asks Pearl, surprised.

'I'm going to wipe my bum on it. What do you think I'm going to do?'

Pearl turns to the back of her sketchbook and slowly tears out a fresh sheet of paper.

'Ta,' says Lily.

Pearl concentrates on her drawing. When she wakes in the night now, the lava lamp is glowing. The green shapes drift silently in the dark, casting a weak light across the part of the calendar where she has begun writing in the empty spaces.

In her drawing she wants to capture the sense of the lamp's shapes moving. Nothing ever stops inside the lamp, nothing ever stays the same. Everything inside the lamp is always about to change. She is aware of Lily's hand reaching occasionally for another pencil, but she doesn't know what her mother is doing on the other side of the table, only that a deep silence has settled over the kitchen.

She makes one of the shapes very thin in the middle, as if at the point of separating.

It's her appointments she likes to write in the empty spaces on the calendar: Anna's visits, the times of TV shows, the days that she goes to see Gus.

She thinks about *Fallingwater* as she colours in the green. She wonders if the person who made the calendar knows the story of what happened to Frank Lloyd Wright. It's strange, to feel this way about someone she hasn't even met, but she thinks if they don't know, then they are not as lucky as her, and even though they took all those photographs, they don't know as much about the house.

She and Gus don't talk about *Taliesin* often, but the people who died there are always in the room with them now. She knows that soon she will ask Gus something she's been thinking about: can a story be like a memorial too? Because there's another story the world tells – the story about the man and why he came to the oval that day, the reason Riley and the others died. She has thought hard about the difference between this story, and the one that only she knows – she thinks about it at night, gazing in the dark at the lava lamp – and she believes she understands the difference now: the real story is sadder. And so there is the next question she must ask Gus. Aren't memorials supposed to be sad?

She glances across the table. Lily is shielding her drawing with her arm, her hair hanging down over the page. She has never seen her mother concentrating like this before, but it is only when Lily lifts her eyes that Pearl realises she is the subject of her drawing.

She looks down and keeps her pencil moving. If she goes over the green a second time the colour is nearly right. She can feel Lily's eyes moving up and down from her page.

She colours close to the line. The smell of fried sausages drifts through the open door, as their hands travel over the pages. It reminds her of something, this hush. It feels like it did a long time ago when Riley was a baby and Lily put him in his cot and he slept. After all his noise and mess, there were just the two of them, liking the peace and quiet but longing, also, for him to wake up again.

'You've got a sweet little face, you know, Pearlie,' says Lily.

Pearl looks across at her. Lily's eyes are on the page, and Pearl realises that Lily is talking to the face she is drawing.

'I'm getting hungry,' says Pearl.

'You said you were full,' says Lily.

'Now I'm not.'

'Have some Coke.'

Pearl gets up from the table and goes over to the fridge. As she is reaching for the Coke, Lily says, 'If we got some money from the TV people, maybe we could move.'

Pearl turns to look at her. She is colouring something mauve, probably Pearl's headband.

'Move from here?'

'Yeah.'

She can't see her mother's face.

'Where would we go?'

'Anna said her friend Diana's got a villa to rent.'

'What's a villa?'

'You know, like a home unit, a little house.'

'On the ground?'

'Yeah, with a backyard and clothesline and stuff.'

Pearl stands there, letting all the cold out of the fridge. She can see some of Lily's drawing now because she is no longer bothering to hide it. She sees that the drawing looks nothing like her. It makes her look like she's wearing lipstick and Lily should have used a lighter colour for her hair.

But it doesn't matter, Pearl realises with surprise, it doesn't matter at all. Because Lily's is a different kind of drawing, and the drawing is really good.

The Brothers

GABRIEL SCANS THE FLIGHT information and sees that his brother's plane has already landed. It's good that he's the one waiting, that he's had time to get over his own jet-lag, and be alone in the house for a while. If he has to live side by side with Karl for the next week, he wants to start out feeling strong. They have to get through Sonia's funeral together, everything has to be settled. He doesn't want to be walked on.

He makes his way to the arrivals gate, thinking of Brian Eno's *Music for Airports* and how he can hear no music now. The only sounds that play to him are the hiss of a coffee machine and the wheeling of baggage. He doesn't understand why Karl has decided to bring one of his daughters with him – Poppy or Lottie, he's forgotten which one – but he suspects it's his brother's way of asserting his moral authority: his famous maturity and accomplishment.

He is looking around, planning to choose a seat from which to observe people's greetings, when the doors open and Karl is suddenly there. It occurs to him that this prompt delivery has probably got something to do with his brother flying business class. He moves slowly towards the barrier, watching Karl's eyes search the crowd, temperamentally unsuited to the waving and exclaiming that is breaking out around him.

Karl has become even more like their father. Gabriel sees Pieter's long, sober face, and his lanky elegance. He wishes immediately that it was his father he was meeting again, but as he draws closer he sees Karl's blurred features and exhaustion, and understands that his brother has been crying.

He moves more quickly through the crowd. He's aware of a child sitting on the luggage trolley that Karl pushes, but it's his brother's face that compels him, and when he is close enough, he calls out his name.

There is no Sonia or Pieter between them now; no referee or arbitrator or judge.

Their chests meet in a stiff embrace.

Gabriel turns away from his mess of feelings to take in his niece.

'This is Lottie,' says Karl, gesturing towards his daughter in the manner of an aide-de-camp introducing his miniature general.

Gabriel looks down at a child with fine black hair in ladybird bunches on either side of her head. She has round, bright, chocolate eyes and high half-moon eyebrows and a deep red bud of a mouth. Bracelets of baby fat wrap her wrists. She is wearing a velvety purple tracksuit, glittering sneakers and a small backpack, and the sense of a woman's hand, a woman he doesn't know, hovers over her.

The child says his name and as he looks into her face he understands that she has been waiting to meet him, to place this piece in the puzzle of family. For Gabriel she has been a mere shadowy fact, a manifestation somehow of his abiding difference from Karl. And yet now, as he leans towards her, he experiences a strange tugging in his veins. He kisses her warm, soft cheek, and straightens and looks at her again, and the feeling is still there; emphatic, unmoving, caring nothing for his embarrassment or surprise: a love of blood, love for his brother's child.

'How old are you, Lottie?' he asks, aware that he should probably know.

'Four,' she says, holding up three fingers of one hand.

'Four going on forty,' says Karl. 'She kept me together on the flight.'

Gabriel looks closely at his brother. Karl is wearing new rimless glasses; they seem hardly more than a trick of the light. Another precision instrument, he thinks. Any new development in opticals, communications, automobile engineering, and Karl must have it. And he will want to point out to you the achievements of its design, the whole brave new world of it.

His brother's eyes are actually puffy, womanly. Where had he been crying? In the toilets? In his seat? There was more space in business class, more privacy.

His own flight hadn't been hard. He'd read a JG Ballard novel, listened to music, watched two films, and taken every bit of food and drink he could get. The knowledge that his mother was dead seemed to express itself in a certain ambience

– everything around him was plain and dull and slow – rather than in any clear feeling within.

'You look tired,' he says to Karl.

'We both are,' replies Karl. 'You didn't sleep much did you, Lots?'

Lottie shakes her head. To Gabriel, she looks freshly minted.

'Do you want me to carry you?' he asks.

She looks at her father.

'That's a good idea,' Karl says. 'Hop off the trolley now and we'll give Gabe his present.'

She puts her arms up and Gabriel lifts her, like feathers in his arms. He glimpses the Bang & Olufsen box beneath the duty-free bags and feels a rush that straight away he tries to quell. It might not be for him, he thinks. Why would it be for him?

But Karl shifts the luggage on the trolley and pulls at the box and it is for him. He hears himself laugh foolishly.

'I've sort of got my hands full,' he says, looking at Lottie. He can see now the extravagance of her eyelashes, and the mauve satin of her eyelids.

'You might not want to unpack it, anyway,' says Karl. 'It might be better to take it back to London like this.'

'What is it?' asks Gabriel. The box is so damned discreet.

'I'll show you in the catalogue later,' says Karl.

Gabriel wants to get him in a headlock and show him his fist. Tell me now, you'd better tell me now.

'Thanks a lot,' he says.

'That's OK,' says Karl. 'Lottie helped me choose it.'

'Did you, Lottie?' he says, splaying his hand over her purple belly.

Lottie moves her head up and down.

'Papa told me what you like,' she says.

'I told her what you *are* like,' corrects Karl. 'And she went from there.'

What am I like? thinks Gabriel. Does Karl know?

'Let's get out of this place,' he says.

'Where's the car?'

'Thataway.'

Karl straightens the bags and suitcases on the trolley and Gabriel shifts Lottie to his other side, and they turn and head towards the glass doors.

'I'm straight for the shower,' says Karl.

Gabriel looks at his brother's cream linen suit and spotless T-shirt.

'Are you grotty, Lottie?' he asks.

'Nooo!' she answers, squashing up her neck and pressing her palms together as if killing a bug.

'Did you tell Gabe you can speak German?' says Karl. 'Onkel Gabe?'

'Onkel Gabe,' says Lottie.

'And Flemish, Lots. How do you say "uncle" in Flemish?'

'Don't know.'

'Yes, you do.'

'No.'

She is squirming in Gabriel's arms. The glass doors open in front of them.

'Ah! Smell Australia!' says Karl, stopping and inhaling exaggeratedly. 'Can you smell Australia, Lottie?'

She breathes in imitation of her father and nods.

Gabriel looks down the long line of taxis.

'You can't smell much here,' he says, 'but the trees are great at the house.'

'I'm going to swim,' says Lottie.

The brothers' eyes meet.

'She knows there's a swimming pool,' says Karl.

'It's still pretty cold,' Gabriel tells her, and tilts his head. 'The car's this way.'

He walks ahead with Lottie as Karl negotiates the trolley.

'Are you right with her?' asks Karl.

'Yeah, sure.'

Lottie arches her back and crooks one arm behind her head like a screen goddess. She's yawning, Gabriel realises.

'Did you get the booster seat?' Karl calls from behind.

'Shit, I forgot,' answers Gabriel, turning to him. 'Sorry.'

Karl says nothing.

'Does it matter much?'

Karl looks at him steadily. 'The seatbelt will cut into her neck,' he says. 'And it's nice for her to be able to see out the window. It's a new place and everything.'

'Can she sit on your knee?'

Lottie's backpack slips off the pile of luggage.

'That wouldn't be at all safe, Gabriel,' Karl says flatly.

There it is. Scarcely ten minutes since they clapped eyes on each other, and there is that tone.

Gabriel turns his back and continues walking. Karl's child feels like a sack of potatoes. He doesn't know how he's going to get through it. The week, the funeral. That fucking tone. Why is he so stupidly helpless against it? It's as if he's hurtled backwards through time, leaving everything he's known – London, music, lovers, friends – to find himself right back where he began; back being Karl's brother.

Lottie sighs and rubs at one eye with the heel of her palm. But, Lottie, he thinks. What *will* she be able to see from the backseat of the car? The sky, the tops of buildings, the backs of their heads? It doesn't seem enough.

Gabriel turns to Karl and takes a long stride towards him.

'How about we put her on a suitcase?' he says. 'This small one would work. There's a blanket in the car. We could cover it, make it comfy?'

'Sounds good,' says Karl.

'Is that OK with you, Lottie?' asks Gabriel. 'I'll get your booster seat later but for now you can sit up nice and high on the suitcase?'

Her little mouth trembles. Karl reaches for her.

'It's OK, darling,' he says, 'we're nearly there.'

It's late afternoon and Karl and Lottie are sleeping. Gabriel sits on the patio steps smoking a small black cigar, having given up cigarettes. He's sure that's what killed his father. He looks at the swimming pool and workshop, the garden in flower. Adam Logan had called him in London to tell him Sonia was dead. This person he had never heard of, telling him how he had found her, half in and half out of the water, how she had hit her head.

He asked Adam Logan to give his brother and him some privacy this week, and told him that they would make a decision about the workshop soon. He wonders if he is intending to punish Adam somehow; this messenger.

A slow wind stirs the trees in the champagne light. This place isn't his home anymore, but there's something here he has to reckon with. He'd known it last time, when he returned for Pieter's funeral, and here it is again, this time springtime, this time dusk.

It's the light he has to reckon with, Australian light. In the northern hemisphere, light falls only on the outside of him. Light doesn't reach into his bones there; it doesn't quicken, it doesn't teach. Once this hadn't mattered to him because he had antiquity to interest him, and antiquity had its own effects. But now he's here again, and the light is becoming pink. It will only be this way for a short while, he knows this from childhood – the last, stretched minutes of play before it was time to go in – and he wishes Lottie would wake and is at the same time surprised by such a wish. But he wants to show her the apricot sky and have her listen to the currawongs in the flame tree.

While they've been sleeping he has scooped the pool free of insects and leaves. The water has to be tested before she can swim, he remembers something about a meningitis germ that could get into her brain. He has called a pool man to come round in the morning, and the funeral people will come after that.

As he dragged the net slowly across the surface of the pool he tried to imagine his mother's fall, her meeting with the water and her end, but the moments stayed closed to him. And maybe that was as it should be, he thought. That was private, that was right.

In the car on the way home from the airport, Karl had turned to him and said: 'Can you take care of the music for the funeral?'

Gabriel stared ahead into the traffic. They had argued over the choice of music for their father's funeral. He wanted John Coltrane but Karl wanted Miles Davis and although they knew they were splitting hairs, neither of them would give up. Sonia wept and told them they could have one playing as everyone went into the chapel, and the other as they went out. But away from her hearing they continued to argue about the choice of tracks and the order in which they would be played until, exhausted, angry and sad, feeling cheated beyond words, they were forced to compromise.

Compromise, sharing, taking turns: the can of soft drink, the last ice cream, the lick of the bowl; the seat next to the window, the seat in front; the television, the comics, the stereo; who bats and who bowls; who plays drums, who guitar; who goes first in the game, last into the shower; who gets the meat, who gets the fat, who gets the bone. Blighted desires and sour outcomes, their lives riddled by blood-in-the-mouth, steam-in-the-head, crazy-making injustices.

Sonia didn't understand.

Finally, there were native flowers on the coffin and Bach going in and Bach going out. The jazz was saved for the wake, where it was played loudly, and beer and spirits were served.

Gabriel's eyes hadn't moved from the road.

'Do you want me to take care of the music?' he asked.

'If it's OK with you,' Karl said.

'It's cool with me.'

'Great.'

The traffic thinned. There was silence.

'Do you think Lottie would like to help with the flowers?' asked Gabriel.

'She'd love it.'

'Is that cool with you?'

'It's fine with me.'

'Great.'

'Great.'

Gabriel hears a noise in the kitchen. He throws the end of his cigar into the garden, takes one last look at the sky and goes inside.

Karl is standing in black boxers and black socks in front of the open refrigerator.

'I'm looking for juice for Lottie,' he says.

Neither of them wanted to sleep in their old bedrooms. Gabriel had already made a bed for himself on the couch. They guessed that the bed missing from their parents' room had gone to the exhibition and so, with Lottie lending a hand, they lifted their old mattresses and carried them across the landing and laid them down next to each other on the unfaded square of carpet where the big bed had once been.

'How many times did you knock your shins on those fucking wings?' asked Gabriel.

'Or squash your fingers sliding them in?' said Karl.

'That's why we weren't supposed to touch them.'

'Yeah, but who could resist?'

'We should go.'

'To the exhibition?'

'Yes.'

'We should've come back.'

'It only feels like that now.'

'Doesn't matter. It might never have happened.'

'You can't think like that,' said Gabriel.

'I can think any way I like.'

'I mean, it doesn't help to think like that.'

'What does help, then?'

Karl and Gabriel looked at each other across the floor of their parents' bedroom.

'Nothing, I guess,' said Gabriel.

They stood for a moment in silence, until Lottie entered the room, dragging two pillows behind her.

'Here's the Lobster!' said Karl, turning and smiling.

Lottie helps, thinks Gabriel. Against all expectations, Lottie helps.

Karl leans into the fridge and pulls out one dish after another, each sealed tightly in plastic.

'Look,' he says, placing them on the bench. 'Mum's left-overs.'

Gabriel moves closer.

The end of a piece of fish, congealed carrots. A serving of dessert.

'Oh, shit, rhubarb pie,' he says.

'I know,' says Karl quietly.

This is the last time he will ever see her rhubarb pie, thinks Gabriel. Suddenly it's unbelievable to him. He's dimly aware that beyond this wall of disbelief may be a place of pain unlike anything he's ever known before.

'You should eat it,' says Karl.

'I can't,' he says.

Lottie pads into the room. Her hair is out of its bunches and she's wearing pink knickers and a matching pink singlet.

'Lottie,' says Gabriel, gazing at her across the kitchen floor. She's like television or an open fire, he thinks. 'You've been hiding your pinks under your purples.'

'I'm not hiding,' she says, as her father scoops her into his arms.

'Gabe is going to have some pie,' says Karl, grinning at him.

Karl's face is calm now, rested. His pale chest is long and boyish, like their father's. Gabriel has a fleeting memory of being held against that chest.

'What pie?' Lottie says, running her palm back and forth over her father's head.

'This pie,' says Karl, bringing her closer.

'What is it?' she says.

'Rhubarb,' says Karl.

'I don't know rhubarb.'

'Really?' says Gabriel.

'Really,' Karl nods.

'There might be some rhubarb in the garden,' says Gabriel. 'Want to have a look?'

She squirms to get down.

'Is it cold outside?' asks Karl.

'Nah,' says Gabriel.

'Nah,' says Lottie.

Gabriel shepherds her through the house, trying to imagine how strange this place – as familiar to him as his own hand – must seem to her.

It's dark outside. Lottie runs on tiptoe across the patio and down the steps, and crouches by the side of the pool.

'This way,' he says.

They see by moonlight. He anticipates leading his niece along the neat rows of vegetables, naming them, showing her how to choose the best ones and pick them gently or pull them from the ground. He can't remember it but Sonia must have shown him once – how else could he have learned?

He senses even as he follows the fence down the yard that something is wrong, and as he draws close to the vegetable garden he can see that there's no order there, nothing plentiful. He sees that the patch is ruined, and he slows his steps towards it.

When he'd thought of his mother at all, he had imagined her, alone now, but living much as she always had, secure in the family home, and in memories. But as he takes in the neglect that lies in front of him he wonders if somehow her fall had already begun. There's a sense of her, in the weed-choked earth, the struggling plants; a sense of some part of her that he'd known nothing about. A part of her that had nothing to do with her being his mother.

Something crawls over his hand, and he brushes it away anxiously and looks around for Lottie. She's standing a little way off, gazing at him, her palms resting on her bent knees. In her pale luminosity, she's an earthly counterpart to the moon.

Who is she? he thinks. And what part of Sonia exists in her blood?

'No rhubarb, I'm afraid, Lottie,' he says. He's made an effort to keep the worst of the regret out of his voice. So, he thinks, this is what you do for a child.

Karl opens the duty-free cognac. Lottie lies sleeping between them on the couch. They breathe the liquor's fumes, drink, and rest their glasses in their palms. Every now and then, Karl's hand moves to Lottie's feet to brush away a grain or two of sand.

They had driven to the beach. They put the booster seat in the back of the car and took the roads Pieter took, even though it was dark. You should always take the scenic route, Pieter said. They ate fish and chips on the grass and taught Lottie how to feed the gulls so they didn't come too close. The sand was cool in the moonlight. Smell the sea, Karl said, ad infinitum.

Gabriel swirls the drink in his glass. 'Did you ever think maybe we were the victims of a happy marriage?' he says.

Once he would not have said something like this to his brother, something about where they came from and who they'd become, even if it were spoken, as this is, half in jest.

He wonders if it's their parents' absence, or Lottie between them, that makes the difference.

Karl laughs. 'I've never thought of myself as a victim of anything,' he says.

They both drink. Lottie's breathing is the only sound.

'I sometimes wonder, though,' says Karl.

'Wonder what?'

'I saw something once.'

'What sort of thing?'

'I saw Sonia . . . affectionate. With another man.'

The brothers are not looking at each other.

'Yeah?' Gabriel says.

'They were having a party,' says Karl, gesturing loosely around him. 'I was only small. I could never sleep when they had parties. I came downstairs and made my way to the kitchen, and when I got to the doorway I saw her and a man. They didn't see me. She was taking a tray of sausage rolls out of the oven – I guess that's what I'd come downstairs for, the sausage rolls – and the man came up behind her and ran his hand slowly over her hip and up the side of her body, and touched her breast.'

Gabriel squirms at the thought of his mother's breast. It's not possible for him to imagine her as a young woman, younger than he is now.

'Probably some sleazebag,' he says.

'She was happy,' says Karl. 'She was radiant and happy.'

'Probably pissed,' says Gabriel.

'I thought it meant she was going to leave us.'

'You what?'

'You heard me.'

'But it was nothing.'

'I was a kid. I'd never seen anyone else touch her. She wasn't warm in that way, only with Dad. I was always waiting for her to leave us.'

She has, thinks Gabriel.

'I'd watch her for signs and listen for it in her voice. For years I interpreted everything she did in the light of what I saw that night.'

Lottie snores lightly. Karl strokes her toes. Gabriel recalls his brother's face at the airport and he thinks again of the vegetable patch. Perhaps for Karl, their mother had always been more fully human. He thinks he understands the burden of this.

In the end there's no music at the funeral. Gabriel realised that while there was always music in the house, the choice had never been Sonia's. She preferred the radio; it was people she liked to listen to.

They decided on a white coffin, because it was the one that least reminded them of their father's work. Lottie chose sunflowers and sunflowers seemed right.

Gabriel thought they should have female funeral directors but Karl claimed that Sonia hadn't liked other women.

'I don't think that's true,' said Gabriel.

'I think it is. Did she have women friends?' asked Karl.

'Some.'

'Think about it. They were always really Dad's friends, often people who'd been clients. She was friendly but she didn't have friends.'

Once Gabriel would have argued, once it would have been important to win. But he understood now that Karl had been watching her when he hadn't, and perhaps he had earned the right.

They went with men, and they asked for pallbearers because someone had to be with Lottie and it was not the way they wanted it, that one convey the coffin without the other.

The funeral is conducted to the sounds of birdsong and a distant lawnmower. The doors of the chapel are flung open and the warm air smells of grass. Gabriel looks away from the coffin – it seems suddenly like the coffin of a bride, or a virgin – and studies the honeyed light streaming through the long windows.

The brothers sit in the front row with Lottie. She is quiet now, but it hadn't been that way earlier. She didn't want to wear the white dress that her mother had packed for the funeral.

'But you have to dress up for a funeral,' said Karl, exasperated.

'It is dress-ups,' Lottie cried, tears streaming down her face.

Gabriel stood at a distance, watching in silence, recalling the argument that had taken place on the day of their father's funeral when Karl insisted that he wear a jacket over his shirt. He watched his small niece wield power over his weakened brother, and he felt slyly avenged.

She sits between them now in her glittery sneakers and pink tutu and Lady Penelope T-shirt, her dark hair gathered high on her head, like a spout from a whale.

A man they have hired reads a poem they have chosen from a book of consoling verse. There are three rows of strangers and one or two faces they know. They picked some names that seemed familiar from Sonia's address book, and made some calls.

Karl stands to speak. Gabriel looks at the gold light patterning the carpet and feels only a dull emptiness. Lottie swings her legs back and forth. Sonia is not there, or anywhere near. Karl's voice is tender but he's not really listening. You could cut that light into pieces, and serve it with tea. He can't imagine her lying in the clothes they chose, inside the coffin that seems wrong for her now. Is this a very serious mistake, the wrong coffin? Air moves through the chapel and a woman's perfume reaches him, jasmine-sweet, jasmine-sad.

He remembers sitting on his mother's knee, playing with her bracelets. He could separate one bracelet from the rest and turn it around her wrist or he could bring all the bracelets together and slide them up and down. He had seen Sonia's bracelets on the shelf in the bathroom. Just one more sign, like the rhubarb pie and the clothes in the laundry basket, the message on the answering machine and the mail arriving each day. The bracelets should go to Karl's girls.

In a blue room after the funeral service, someone places a cup of tea in his hands. People approach him, and move away again. Out of the corner of his eye he can see Karl receiving the same people with a tight smile. Someone wearing a pinstripe suit introduces himself as Adam Logan. He offers some words about Sonia, but Gabriel cannot forgive him for being there when he wasn't, and soon Adam turns away.

Gabriel looks around for Lottie and finds her on a bench by the wall, a biscuit in each hand.

He sits down beside her, uncomfortable in his tie and stiff shoes.

'Let's go for a swim when we get home,' he says.

Lottie fits one of the biscuits into her mouth. She nods her head vigorously.

Gabriel looks slowly around him and notices a young woman with short hair standing alone in the small crowd.

Unlike Lottie, she is wearing a white dress, like a good girl. A girl speaking up for life.

The young woman turns and catches his eye, and although he looks away he soon realises that she is walking towards him.

'Excuse me,' she says, stopping. 'Are you Gabriel Marstrand?'

'Yes,' he replies.

'I'm Natasha Creely,' she says. 'I knew your mother. I curated your father's show.'

She's standing, and he is still sitting. He doesn't quite know what to do about that.

'Are you the Tash who left a message on Sonia's answering machine?' he asks.

There was only one message. He played it to Karl.

'Hello, Sonia,' the light female voice said. 'It's Tash. I'm just calling to see how your headache is today. Better, I hope. Maybe you're out enjoying the sunshine. I hope so. I hope you enjoyed the exhibition – well, what you were able to, with your headache and everything. I hope it made you proud.'

They both laughed grimly about all the hope the message contained, but it was important to them. They used it to explain the drugs found in their mother's body, and perhaps it went a little way towards explaining her fall.

'Yes, I left a message,' says Natasha, 'but I didn't hear back from Sonia and then Adam told me.'

'You know Adam?' He's not sure if it's his feelings towards Adam that have caused him to ask this, or something else.

'I'm the one who introduced Adam to Sonia.'

'Right.'

It isn't quite the answer he was looking for, but she's making no sign of leaving.

'Sorry,' says Gabriel, 'would you like to sit down?'

'Thanks,' she says.

Natasha takes the edge of the bench as Lottie clambers onto his knee, smearing his shirt with crumbs and biscuit cream. She stares at Natasha with raw, open curiosity.

'This is Lottie,' he says.

'Hello,' says Natasha. 'I like your outfit.'

Gabriel notices the simple watch with the black strap on her thin arm and the tiny holes in her earlobes. She had chosen not to wear earrings, and this interests him.

'Did you bring both your daughters?' she asks.

She's smiling at him. It takes a second or two for Gabriel to understand, and then a premonition comes to him of a moment, just a few breaths away.

'I'm not the one with the children,' he says. 'Lottie's my niece. Her father's over there.'

'Oh,' she says.

The moment is felt as a dilation of the atmosphere around them, a dilation of possibilities. It shimmers and is gone.

'She looks more like you,' she says.

Gabriel looks down at Lottie. Her big dark eyes are still fixed on Natasha.

'That's weird,' he says.

She has seen me, he thinks, she has taken me in.

The top comes off the cognac again. They have hardly spoken since the funeral.

'Will it wake Lottie if I put some music on?' Gabriel asks.

Karl shakes his head. 'Let's listen to Dad's old vinyl,' he says.

Gabriel takes some time to decide. It seems important, what he plays for his brother now. Pieter's record collection is full of music that might poignantly underscore the strangeness and difficulty of the day they have just lived through. But he goes for Led Zeppelin. The stylus lowers and he listens with a sharp, aching joy to the static and the beat of silence before the guitar slices in.

Karl looks up from where he is standing by the coffee table, pouring their drinks. 'Good choice,' he laughs.

They sit and drink their cognac, and listen.

'Have you ever been to Copenhagen?' asks Karl, after a while.

'No,' says Gabriel. 'Have you?'

'No.'

'Do you want to?'

'Not really. I don't know. One day, maybe. What about you?'

'Yeah. Same here.'

'We should probably go to the exhibition in the morning,' says Karl, reaching for the bottle.

'I'll have some of that,' says Gabriel. 'I was hoping to sleep in tomorrow.'

'There's not much time.'

'Lottie wore me out in the pool this afternoon.'

Karl smiles.

'She's full-on,' says Gabriel.

'Not compared to her sister, she's not,' says Karl. 'Poppy's like Dad, always got to be doing something.'

'Like you, you mean,' says Gabriel.

Karl drinks from his glass and looks at his brother.

'I don't know if you've noticed,' he says, 'but Lottie has a few problems.'

'What kind of problems?'

'Well, her speech for one. She's way behind in her language skills.'

'I just thought she took after Mum. The strong, silent type.'

Karl shakes his head. 'And she doesn't relate well to kids of her own age.'

Gabriel wants to defend her; did children have to be precision instruments too?

'Maybe she's like Mum was in that respect also – you know, the whole friends thing.'

'Maybe, I don't know.' Karl takes off his glasses and rubs hard at his eyes.

Gabriel looks at his brother and feels his own tiredness again. Someone should put their arms around both of them, he thinks.

'I couldn't sense Mum at the funeral,' he says quietly.

'I know what you mean.'

The record finishes. They listen to the needle lift and return.

'We've got decisions to make,' says Karl.

'Not now.'

'No,' says Karl, leaning towards him with the bottle. 'Not tonight.'

The brothers are tired and hungover when they get to the exhibition. After a while, there's no-one else there, and the silence makes them lower their voices. You can touch, they tell Lottie, feeling entitled, but be gentle.

They buy copies of the exhibition catalogue; they walk around the exhibition twice.

They were boys and Pieter was their father, outside in the workshop, making things. It wasn't art; it was just their lives.

When Lottie grows bored she slides over the floorboards

in her ballet slippers. She can slide further if one of them holds her hand.

In front of the Butterfly Bed, Karl says to her: 'When Gabe and I were little we used to jump up and down on this and get into trouble.'

Lottie's eyebrows knit. 'Was it in your house?' she asks.

'It was in the room where you and I are sleeping now,' says Karl.

Gabriel looks at the bed. Red river gum. Does it really grow by a river? What river? He studies the bed's wings and tries to imagine who his father was at the moment this idea came to him.

Natasha told him that the bed would be returned at the end of the exhibition. There had never been any family heirlooms, any clue to the past, and he'd always thought of this as a freedom. But now, as he opens the handsome catalogue again, he questions whether it's a freedom he has used well.

Lottie drags on Karl's arm.

'She's getting restless,' says Karl.

'I'm thinking of staying,' Gabriel says casually, turning the pages.

'You want to look round a bit more?' asks Karl.

'No,' says Gabriel. 'I mean, in Australia, in the house. How would you feel if I moved back?'

'What about London?'

'I think London's over.'

'I've always felt that way about London myself,' laughs Karl.

Gabriel waits.

'I like the idea of you being in the house,' says Karl finally.

'Cool,' says Gabriel.

'Much less trouble.'

'Yeah.'

He turns the page and there is a photograph he has never seen before. Pieter is standing outside the workshop. There's no pool and only the beginnings of a garden. His father's face is lifted, squinting, smiling into the light. It steadies him, to drop to his knees and show Lottie.

Adam is working at the kitchen table when the phone rings. He thinks he should let the machine get it, but it's too late, his hand has already reached for the distraction. He's been here for days now; eating nothing but bread and cheese, going without sleep, not speaking, alone.

The deadline for the Children's Memorial has passed but he's negotiated an extension until the next morning. Art school had taught him that. He has a long night ahead of him, with no time to spare. But it's not like his hand knows.

'Hello?'

'This is Gabe Marstrand,' the caller says.

My stupid fault, thinks Adam, and moves some papers around.

'Hello, Gabriel,' he says.

'We've made a decision about the workshop,' says Gabe.

Adam doesn't reply. He's still smarting from his encounter with Sonia's son at her funeral. He had found their mother dead, and she'd been kind to him, there were things he felt he should say. But it was obvious Gabriel didn't want to listen.

'I'm staying on in the house,' says Gabriel, 'and I'm going to need that space for music, for a studio.'

Sweet, thinks Adam. Fart around in that big house all by yourself, swim in the pool, play your gee-tar out the back.

'I understand,' he says.

'We don't have to talk about money, so we were hoping you could be out by the end of next week.'

Adam feels outnumbered, opposed.

We? he thinks. What's this 'we'? The Marx Brothers? The Grimm Brothers? The brothers fucking Karamazov? Where had 'we' been in their mother's last days?

'Sure,' he says.

'Cool,' says Gabriel. 'So I'll see you when you leave me the key.'

He is always returning keys.

'Yeah, I'll see you then,' he says, and hangs up the phone.

Adam leans back in his chair. The kitchen is in darkness but for the lamplight over the table and the occasional strobing of a helicopter on the lookout for crime.

Everything's all right, he says to himself, breathe deep, just let it go.

He stares at his work in front of him. Pages and pages of designs, and still none of them right. He tries to imagine what might exist for him beyond the memorial, beyond the morning, but he can see nothing.

What had he really planned to say to Gabriel at the funeral? That Sonia seemed peaceful in death? It wasn't true, but would he have said it anyway?

He knew she was dead the moment he saw her, half in and half out of the pool, the garden hose looped around her foot. He'd seen Katy, he knew. But he reached into the water and felt for a pulse anyway. Then he phoned the police and ambulance and took a chair from the studio and placed it by the pool. He would wait with her; who knew for how long she had waited alone?

It was a warm day. He wondered if a body could still burn,

because her legs were bare. He waited, and worried about it.

He wouldn't look at her, he would spare her this. He remembered the first time he saw her. She had opened the door to her home, and invited him in. She was wearing black, but it wasn't the black of a widow, even though he knew she was one. She smiled at him. Her eyes always lifted at the corners when she smiled.

He waited, and still no-one came. The sun beat down on both of them. Sonia wasn't restful, sprawled across land and water; there was nothing lovely. After a while, he got up from his chair and found where he had dropped his keys and went out to his car.

His gym bag was in the boot. He opened it and unzipped the bag and pulled out his towel. It was a towel with a floral pattern that his mother had been throwing out. It was thread-bare in parts, sometimes around the other men it embarrassed him. He sniffed; it didn't smell unclean.

He shook the towel out in the sunlight. And then he went back through the gate and crossed over to the pool and knelt down. He had lifted Katy's body like this. One body was young, and the other not. There was no way of looking at that thought, and understanding the place that he found himself in.

He leaned into the water and gathered Sonia's heavy body in his arms and slowly hauled her out. There was dark bruising on her head. He laid her at the side of the pool, and untangled her hair from her face. As courteously as he could, he tugged her nightgown into place.

She would once have been a beautiful woman, he had thought that day she first smiled at him. But he hadn't known then, hadn't seen, that her beauty hadn't really been over.

Nothing about her had been over until this final moment, this last hard reality; his mother's towel with the faded roses leaving his hands, coming down, covering her.

I'm sorry, he whispered, knowing it was what everyone said, but meaning it, in his own way.

Adam gets up from the table and crosses the sticky floor and fills a glass of water at the sink. He needs to breathe deep, and let it all go. He pours himself another glass of water and stares out at the blackness, feeling the ocean not far away.

One day while they were drinking coffee, Sonia told him a story, one that she herself had been told: Frank Lloyd Wright had drawn the plans for *Fallingwater* in thirty minutes.

The architect's clients had been waiting, Sonia said. The land had been chosen and they were eager for their new country home. They had been patient, they understood art's slow method. But still the day came when the clients phoned. 'Frank,' the Kaufmanns said, 'we have men wanting work, we can't wait any longer, we all have our lives.'

It's now or never, they said, you're on the line.

'Thirty minutes!' he remembers Sonia laughing. 'The time it took me to make this hazelnut slice!'

He's hungry again, and tired, but the memorial is calling. He will drink one more glass of water, cross the floor, and sit down.

Fallingwater, created in thirty minutes. Was this story true? Or was it just a fairytale, of the kind that he himself liked? Escape, redemption, a chance at the end. Are his thirty minutes waiting for him?

He has all night to find out. He turns and moves towards the table.

It's now or never, Adam; you're on the line.

Gabriel puts down the phone.

'That's done,' he says.

'What did he say?' asks Karl, closing the door of the cupboard, a record in his hand.

'Not much,' says Gabriel, disliking his small taste of power. 'What could he say?'

'Thanks for the rent-free use of your father's workshop for all these months?'

'We don't know what her life was like,' says Gabriel. 'What are you putting on?'

Karl shows him the album cover.

'I hate that. Messed-up girls' music.'

'I know, but what do you want? Sorted-out girls' music? Soon you'll have all the time in the world to listen to what you want.'

'When's your flight?' asks Gabriel.

'Late tomorrow night.'

'I'll drive you.'

'Thanks.'

'Where's Lottie?'

'In the bath.'

'Is that OK?'

'What do you mean?'

'Is it safe?'

'Yeah, I'll go up in a minute. She isn't a baby.'

'Isn't she?'

Before Karl can answer, the phone rings. Gabriel gestures to Karl to turn the music down.

'Hello,' he says.

Karl watches him. Gabriel turns his head away.

He speaks quietly. He bends over the coffee table and writes something on the edge of a newspaper with one of Lottie's coloured pencils, and looks at the vase of daffodils sent by someone neither of them knows.

'Who was that?' asks Karl, as Gabriel puts down the phone.

'Tash.'

'Who?'

'Natasha. The curator. You know.'

'What did she want?'

'She asked me to dinner, at her place.'

'Nice invitation,' says Karl.

'Yeah,' says Gabriel.

'When?'

'Next week.'

'Aren't you going back to London to pack up?'

'I can get someone to do it for me,' says Gabriel. 'To tell you the truth, my life in London wasn't very – complicated.'

'Do you want it to be?' asks Karl.

'What?'

'Complicated.'

Gabriel looks at his brother and tries not to return his smile.

'I'm not answering that,' he says.

Lights burn in every room of the house, and clothes churn in the washing machine and dryer. Karl and Lottie are leaving.

The mattresses have been stripped and carried back to their bedrooms. Gabriel wanders from room to room, anticipating the silence, the time when he will be alone with his decision. He will doubt it, he knows, perhaps he is doubting already. But the bed will come back. There's dinner with Tash. This is all he knows of the future, but it's enough.

Already he can feel Karl turning towards home. They've hardly spoken about Karl's wife, except when mention was made of Lottie's mother, but he can almost hear her now, calling.

The night has turned cool. He finds a black jumper of Sonia's that fits him. In the lounge room, Lottie is standing close to the TV, wearing the bathers she refuses to take off.

He sits down on the couch.

He doesn't know what's on the television, he can't tell with Lottie jigging up and down in front of it. She has a way of standing on her toes and bending at the knee and bouncing quietly to some private, springy joy. She pauses only to fling herself backwards occasionally over the coffee table, her eyes seeking and holding his, laughter spilling from her throat.

Karl comes into the room carrying a small plate.

'Here's your sandwich, Lobster,' he says.

Lottie reluctantly turns her head from the television and looks at him. 'I don't want it,' she says.

'Yes you do,' says Karl wearily, setting the plate on the table, 'you said you did. It's cheese and tomato. You know, those lovely tomatoes you picked out with Gabe? The big red ones?'

He can sing a song about that sandwich, thinks Gabriel, but she isn't going to eat it.

'I want jam,' she says.

'You want a jam sandwich?'

'No!' she says fiercely, glaring at him. 'On toast!'

She doesn't have a language problem, thinks Gabriel. Sometimes her limited use of words seems like nothing less than a subtle form of contempt.

'OK,' says Karl, raising one hand in surrender. 'Jam on toast.'

Lottie incorporates a horsy skip into her movements now.

She and Gabriel conduct a long discussion, punctuated by flopping and giggling, about the number of ants in her pants.

She'll be gone soon. She is so ridiculously perfect in her red bathers, her hair clumped and damp at the ends, her small shoulderblades, the buttons of her spine. He wants to seize her and hold her tight, so that he can take in, for remembering, the warmth of her girl-engine, the energy of her bouncing, prancing baby-horse. But it's not the moment, when Karl is out of the room and she is happy inside her own small freedom.

Lottie has moved a little and now he can see the television screen. There's a man speaking from behind a desk. The sound is low, and he can't really hear what's being said. Lottie is not watching the screen so much as hanging within its field, like a moth around a light. Gabriel looks at his watch and thinks of ringing London. Now that he has made his decision, he wants things to happen quickly.

When he looks back at the TV screen, the man is gone. He has been replaced by images of ambulances and police cars, and what looks like a sports oval. The date on the bottom of the screen tells him that this is not an event of the day, but something that took place closer to a year ago. The static, smiling faces of children appear, one after another, and Gabriel knows these are the faces of the dead. He wonders how he knows this. Because this is a convention of television, and he has learnt to understand a slow series of photographs in this way? Or is it something else, something stranger, harder to understand? As if a fine dark veil, scarcely visible to the eye, falls over all worldly images of the dead the moment they leave the earth.

Karl returns with Lottie's order. He has also cut some carrot and apple into amusing shapes.

'Here, Lots,' says Karl, holding the plate out to her.

Lottie stands quite still, her eyes on the screen.

'Lottie,' he says, 'here's your toast and jam.'

She doesn't move. Gabriel can see the curve of her cheek, the plume of her dark lashes above her unblinking eye.

'Lottie?' says Karl.

'What's she doing?' asks Gabriel.

'I don't know,' says Karl.

'I mean – does she do this?'

'I've never seen it before.'

'Is she sleepwalking?'

'She wasn't asleep, was she?'

'No.'

'Well, then, she's not sleepwalking, is she?' says Karl. 'What the hell is she watching?'

'I don't know,' says Gabriel. He doesn't say, 'Something about dead children.' He doesn't say it because he feels that it's somehow his fault that Lottie has left them. He'd known what was on the TV screen; should he have stopped her from knowing too?

'Where's the remote?' asks Karl sharply. 'Have you got the remote?'

Gabriel reaches for the remote beside him.

'Turn it up,' says Karl.

Cautiously, Gabriel increases the volume.

On the screen, a girl is speaking. The camera is close, as still as Lottie. The girl on the screen is older than Lottie, but she's small. She has twiggy legs and jeans tucked into boots, a headband holding her long, fine hair.

'I was colouring in,' the girl says, 'and all the children were playing.'

'Do you understand what this is about?' asks Karl.

'No idea,' says Gabriel, guiltily.

'I saw what happened,' the girl says. 'Everyone was talking and laughing about the man's hair.'

'Lottie?' says Karl.

'The man didn't come to the oval because he had a shaved head,' the girl says. 'That's not what's true. He didn't come to kill all the children –'

'Shut it off!' says Karl.

Gabriel mutes the sound.

'No, the whole thing! Turn the whole effing thing off!'

Gabriel does as he's told. The screen blanks. There is silence.

Lottie's eyelids fall luxuriantly, and open again. She turns slowly and looks up at Karl.

'Poppy?' she says, her lips trembling.

'Poppy?' repeats Karl, frowning. And then he crouches beside her. 'Darling, that wasn't Poppy. That was another girl.'

Tears stream from Lottie's eyes. 'Poppy,' she says softly.

'We'll see Poppy very soon,' says Karl, stroking her back. 'We're going on the aeroplane and then we'll see Mama and Poppy.'

This is his family now, thinks Gabriel.

Karl edges the plate within Lottie's vision. She heaves a deep, shuddering sigh and reaches for a triangle of toast.

'Did she look like Poppy?' Gabriel asks.

Karl gets to his feet and checks that Lottie is not looking before shaking his head. Gabriel feels a sudden, steely love for him; for this checking.

Karl walks over to the couch and sits down. 'But I suppose she had the same air of authority that Poppy does,' he says quietly, turning to Gabriel. 'The same "I have something to say and you will listen".'

'Well, there you go,' says Gabriel, 'she recognised the command of the older sibling.'

The brothers grin, and shoulder and shove each other.

Epilogue

The Children's Memorial

THE RAIN POURS DOWN, dissolving the horizon. The bobcat driver climbs from the cabin of his vehicle and confers with his supervisor. Yes, they will leave the work for today. It's nearly summer, things won't take long to dry.

The bobcat stands alone on the muddy ground high on the cliff. Below it, the sea is grey and steady. There's always tomorrow.

Blue parts the clouds. The sun appears and the earth steams. Coming slowly down the hill, the car pulls to a stop at the side of the road and two women look out at the cliffs and the sea.

'Maybe this is a good place to walk,' says Serena, in the passenger seat.

'Do you think we'll need an umbrella?' asks Rose.

'We're not going far, are we? Just to stretch our legs?'

'Let's risk it.'

Rose glances in the rear-vision mirror at her daughter sitting behind her.

'Are you coming with us, Ava?' she asks.

The girl lifts her head from the book she is reading. 'No,' she says.

'It'll be good for you,' says her mother.

Serena leans into the space between the two front seats. CDs and a box of tissues slide to the floor.

'Go on, come with us,' she says.

'I've got a stomach ache,' says Ava.

'Leave her,' says Rose.

'What's your book about?' asks Serena.

Ava takes the postcard from her lap and marks the page she's reading. The postcard is a photo of a kitten from her friend in Japan.

'Well, it's about this girl called Pan but really she's Pandora,' Ava says, 'and her parents die in this terrorist bomb, see, and they were trying to get back together but they got killed and she goes to live with this funny aunt and one day she's playing on her aunt's computer but she isn't supposed to and she finds this round thing on the screen and it's called The Wonderzone and she clicks the mouse and gets all dizzy and when she wakes up she's in this . . .'

Serena's eyes begin to cloud over, but she doesn't turn away. Rose lifts her handbag from the floor at Serena's feet and searches through it for a roll of mints. She puts a mint in her mouth and then she finds her ChapStick and runs it over her lips and presses them together. She checks for messages on her mobile phone.

'. . . and that's as far as I've got,' says Ava.

Serena and Rose incline their heads and laugh, but only for a moment.

'We're not going far,' says Rose, 'just along the cliffs. Have you got your phone?'

Ava feels in the pocket of her parka and nods.

The women get out of the car and close the doors gently. Ava opens her book and finds the line she was reading. It's warm inside her puffy parka and the fur collar is soft on her cheek. She reaches inside her pocket for the Fantales the man at the video store gave her. As she unwraps one, she looks up. Already Serena and her mother seem far away. They are walking across the grass towards the edge of the cliffs. She watches as her mother puts her arm around Serena's waist and Serena leans her head on her mother's shoulder and they part and walk on. She knows Serena is sad about her boyfriend today. 'She feels as if no-one loves her,' Rose had said.

Ava doesn't know how much time has passed when she looks up again. A small pile of Fantale wrappers lies in her lap. She looks for the women and sees they are on their way back and that their walk must nearly be over. She watches Serena point to a bobcat sitting on a patch of land that juts out over the sea. Next to it is a large sign and orange triangles flying on a string.

She wants to be with them now. She places the postcard between the pages of her book and pushes the Fantale wrappers into her pocket.

Rose stops and lifts her arm as she sees her daughter coming across the grass towards them. Her arm hangs in the air until Ava's shoulders slide into place beneath it.

'Tummy better?' Rose asks.

'Yes,' Ava says.

Serena has reached the bobcat and is standing in front of the sign.

'This is where that children's memorial is going to be,' she calls out.

They look at the muddy earth and the immense view, and they read the sign.

'That's what the memorial will look like,' says Rose, pointing to a drawing.

'Look – the architect who won the competition to design it is a woman,' says Serena.

'That's good,' says Rose.

'But not if it's a kind of token female thing, you know, because it's got to do with children.'

'No, not for that reason,' says Rose.

They all study the drawing.

'It just looks like a huge, big seesaw,' says Ava.

They read that a mechanism will slowly oscillate the bronze plank upon its copper pivot through the minutes of every hour, through every hour of every day.

'I guess it's about imagining there are kids playing on it,' says Serena, 'and hearing their laughter.'

'And about the ups and downs of life,' says Rose.

'It's simple,' says Serena.

'Yeah,' says Rose, 'but sort of strong.'

'It looks like one of those memorials you can take your own grief to,' says Serena.

The women fall silent. Ava looks at them.

'But what if you don't have any grief?' she says.

Serena makes a high, surprised sound and then she presses her fingers to her mouth and turns to look at the sea.

Ava's mother lifts Ava's hair away from the collar of her parka and draws it into a ponytail.

'Nearly time for a trim,' she says.

There are questions her daughter asks for which there are really no answers.

Acknowledgements

I AM INDEBTED TO the Eleanor Dark Foundation for a
Varuna Writers' Fellowship, and to the Literature Board of
the Australia Council for a residency at the Tyrone Guthrie
Centre, Ireland.

The detail of the sideboard mentioned in the chapter 'The
Taste of Others' was inspired by a work by Shulim Krimper,
at the Ballarat Fine Art Gallery, Victoria, Australia.

I am grateful to Peter Straus, Brenda Walker and Tim
Winton for their guidance and support, and for the day at
Fallingwater, thanks to Helen O'Leary and Paul Chidester and
their daughter, Eva, who likes sad books best.